AFTER THE RESCUE

"Rafe," Jessie groaned. Something had passed between them just then, something hot and hungry, something so intimate that it shook her to the core of her being. She still didn't know who she was, but she knew what she felt: desire.

Capturing her fingers in his hand, Rafe placed a ～ k kiss on her palm. "You were going to tell me about the nightmare," he said. "You mentioned hearing rushing sounds . . ." It was the same dream, he guessed, that she'd had several times since he'd rescued her from the icy river.

She winced. "Horses," she whispered. "And the sound of roaring water." She arched her back, trying to stretch tense muscles. "I'm afraid to go to sleep," she said. "Rafe?" Her voice sounded strangled as she reached out a hand to him.

Rafe captured her hand and drew her nearer. He knew he should leave her, yet he could not. To see her lying there, so close, knowing she desired him as he desired her, was too much to resist.

"I want to kiss you, Jessie," he whispered.

Her body tightened in a wildly responsive way and her head tilted back; her lips parted on a trembling breath, as she invited his possession . . .

BOOK YOUR PLACE ON OUR WEBSITE AND MAKE THE READING CONNECTION!

We've created a customized website just for our very special readers, where you can get the inside scoop on everything that's going on with Zebra, Pinnacle and Kensington books.

When you come online, you'll have the exciting opportunity to:

- View covers of upcoming books
- Read sample chapters
- Learn about our future publishing schedule (listed by publication month *and author*)
- Find out when your favorite authors will be visiting a city near you
- Search for and order backlist books from our online catalog
- Check out author bios and background information
- Send e-mail to your favorite authors
- Meet the Kensington staff online
- Join us in weekly chats with authors, readers and other guests
- Get writing guidelines
- AND MUCH MORE!

Visit our website at
http://www.zebrabooks.com

A PLACE IN MY HEART

Betty Brooks

Zebra Books
Kensington Publishing Corp.

http://www.zebrabooks.com

ZEBRA BOOKS are published by

Kensington Publishing Corp.
850 Third Avenue
New York, NY 10022

First Printing: April, 1999
10   9   8   7   6   5   4   3   2   1

Printed in the United States of America

Chapter One

Texas Hill Country
1880

The water was icy, almost numbing, to the woman who fought so desperately to stay afloat in the flood-swollen river. Mindlessly, she flailed out, using every ounce of her waning strength to fight against the current that sucked greedily at her, seeming intent on tearing the breath from her body.

Oh, God, she cried silently. *Help me!* But God didn't appear to be listening. She was sinking again, the water closing over her head, swirling her beneath its surface and turning her over and over again. She couldn't hold her breath much longer. Even now her lungs were burning, crying desperately for air that meant the difference between life and death. But she was so tired.

Why continue to fight against the inevitable? an inner voice whispered. *It's a useless battle anyway. You'll never survive the flood. Make it easy on yourself. Just stop struggling. Let yourself go.*

No! She would not! Every fiber of her being rebelled against the idea of allowing herself to drown without fighting for her life.

From somewhere deep inside, she found the strength to renew the fight. It was only a tiny spark, but it was enough to send her surging upward. Her head cleared water and she coughed urgently, spewing muddy water from her mouth, then sucking greedily at the life-giving air, intent on filling her lungs while there was time. She had barely done so when the current caught her again and sucked her into its murky depths.

She kicked out frantically, reaching upward desperately, and felt a sudden, sharp pain against her knuckles as they struck something solid. Something rough. A log?

Instantly, her fingers curled, grasping at the rough bark and she pulled herself upward. Her head cleared water and she blinked rapidly to clear the muddy water from her vision. Green. Her savior was an uprooted tree. Even as the thought occurred, the current intervened. Like a living entity bent on her destruction, it swirled the tree around, wrenching it from her grasp.

Feeling herself sinking again, she kicked out with leaden feet and her reaching fingers brushed against one slender branch, but the limb was too small and the weight of her sodden clothing too great. The limb went under, allowing her to sink beneath the water again.

Desperately, her hands sought more substance, creeping upward toward the thicker trunk that would surely hold her weight. Her head broke the surface again and she saw the thickness of the trunk swirling nearer. Closing in fast. Too fast, she realized. But the thought occurred too late. Her head collided with rough bark.

Pain lanced through her temple and was instantly followed by a blur of red dots that clouded her vision until the red gave way to darkness.

As the shadows swirled around her, she reached desperately for her only hope . . . the insubstantial mass of green leaves that could never bear her weight.

The early morning breeze blew tendrils of dark hair across Rafe Sutherland's lower jaw as he studied the muddy Colorado River with intent gray eyes. The river was in full flood. If it didn't crest soon the lower fields would have to be replanted. A movement beside him shifted his gaze toward his son.

"Never seen the river so high before, Pa." Danny's expression was a mixture of unease and excitement. The twelve-year-old boy knew enough about farming to be aware of the consequences of a flooded crop, yet he was still young enough to enjoy the sight of a rolling river. "How much higher do you think she's gonna rise?" He never took his eyes off the flood-swollen river lest he miss something.

"Don't know, Danny," Rafe replied somberly. "Let's hope the river's already reached its crest."

As Rafe watched, a sapling willow growing along the riverbank quivered, its roots obviously undermined by the water lapping greedily at the soil. A moment later the willow toppled from the bank and slid slowly into the river, joining the rest of the debris already floating there.

The sapling was quickly caught by the current and swirled outward where it bumped against a log that floated more than a hundred yards away. Then, with another swirl, it began the long journey downstream that would eventually lead to the Gulf of Mexico.

"Time's a-wasting, Danny boy," Rafe said, clasping his son on the shoulder and turning him away from the river.

"We've got a heap of work that needs doing before night-fall."

"There's always a heap of work that needs doing around here." Danny cast one last look at the flood. "Not that I'm complainin'," he added hastily. He was proud of his ability to help his father. "It's just that—"

He broke off suddenly, his body becoming rigid, tense. "Pa! Look! I think there's somebody out there!"

"Some*body*?" Rafe questioned, his gaze ricocheting from his son's face to the muddy water. "On the river?"

"Yes! See him? On that tree!" Danny pointed toward the middle of the river. "The big tree, Pa! The one with all the new leaves on it. See there! The tree's shifting around now. You can just see a little bit of blue among the branches."

Rafe pinpointed the tree that had swirled around. Sure enough, there was a hint of blue among the green foliage. But it was quickly gone, covered by a blur of green and brown as the tree continued to swirl. It made a complete circle before he pinpointed the object again. "You're right, son," he said grimly. "There is somebody out there."

"What are we gonna do, Pa?" Danny's voice was shrill with anxiety. "We can't just leave him out there."

"No." Rafe shaded his eyes against the glare of the morning sun and tried to judge the strength of the current. "The water's running too swift and that tree is too far away. Nobody could swim that distance through the flood."

"What about the boat?" Danny looked toward the dilapidated pier where the rowboat rested amidst a tangle of weeds. "Maybe we could row out there and—"

"No. The boat's out. It sprung a leak the last time we used it."

"I forgot."

Rafe's expression was grim as he watched the tree float swiftly downstream. His thoughts whirled as rapidly as the old oak caught in the current. He realized he had to do something. But what? What in God's name could he do?

What he couldn't do, he decided, was stand there dithering while the man was swept out of his reach downstream.

Downstream. That thought sent his gaze skittering to the bend in the river farther down.

"We might be able to help at the riverbend," he mused aloud.

"Yeah, Pa." Danny's expression lightened. "The current runs closer to the bank there. That ol' tree shouldn't be no more'n a few yards away when it reaches the bend." His brow furrowed and he pushed a hank of dark hair out of his eyes. "But . . . you ain't gonna try to swim out to that feller, are you, Pa? The flood might of changed the course of the river. You know how the sand shifts around on the bottom. Especially when it's in flood."

"Don't worry, Danny." Rafe gripped his son's shoulder and squeezed it gently for encouragement. "I'm not about to do anything foolish. But we have to be quick. Run, boy, fetch some rope from the barn." As Danny sprinted away, Rafe remembered the frayed rope coiled just inside the barn. "Danny! Make sure you bring the new rope!"

"Okay!" The word was faint since the boy's stride never faltered.

As Danny ran across the field toward the barn, Rafe raced downriver, his long legs covering the distance at a ground-eating pace. He neared the bend and sent his gaze darting across the murky water, searching for the tree that carried its hapless victim.

There! he thought with exultation. But, dammit, the oak was closer than he'd imagined it would be. Would there be time to wait for the rope?

He twisted, looking anxiously toward the barn in the distance. There was no sign of Danny. No sign of any movement at all. His gaze skittered to the river again. The tree was almost at its closest point.

Dammit! He couldn't wait for Danny. Not with the current carrying the tree along so fast. The river was too powerful. All too soon, the tree and its helpless cargo would be far beyond his reach. If he was going to help, then he must act now.

His muscles tensed as he watched the tree swirl closer. Closer. His eyes measured the distance. If he leaned out as far as he could, he could almost reach one of the lower branches. Almost, but not quite.

"Come on," he muttered. "Bring it just a little closer." He leaned toward the river, stretching his long arm to the fullest. No. Not quite enough reach. He straightened once to ease the strain, then leaned out again as the tree swirled nearer. The current seemed to be teasing him, as though daring him to snatch its prey from what would almost certainly be a watery grave.

Rafe swore softly as his fingers brushed the leaves before the limb swirled out of reach again.

Dammit! It was useless. The man was as good as dead.

Even as that thought occurred, he knew he couldn't accept defeat.

He acted without thought, kicking off his boots, then filling his lungs with air before diving into the muddy river.

The icy water slid around his body smoothly, chilling his flesh and reaching into his bones. Although he felt its numbing effect, he tried to close his mind to it, concentrating his efforts on reaching the safety of the tree.

Rafe felt his head clear water and blinked rapidly as he reached for a tree branch. But it was not there. His clutching fingers closed on water as the limb swirled out of reach.

The current seemed to be alive as it pulled at Rafe, trying to force him beneath its surface again, but he was strong from endless hours of hard labor and his strokes were swift and sure, carrying him forward, closer to his destination.

As he pushed closer to the tree, the river seemed determined to foil him, first bringing the oak closer, then swirling it quickly away.

Rafe knew he was tiring fast. The current was so strong. It continued to suck at him, draining the strength from his limbs until they began to feel like lead weights. The water closed over his head again and he came up gasping, sucking for the air that would stop his lungs from burning. He wondered, fleetingly, if he was fighting a losing battle. But the thought had barely occurred when his fingers closed around rough bark.

Breathing harshly from exertion, Rafe threw one long leg over the tree trunk and gripped tightly while he swung himself upright. When he was secured firmly, he turned his attention to the victim whose head was turned away, the face hidden from view. The fingers that were locked in a death grip were pale, totally absent of color, and the copper-colored hair was long, streaming in wet tendrils around slender shoulders.

Rafe leaned closer and saw pale, delicate features. Long, auburn lashes curled against soft cheeks.

Suddenly, realization struck Rafe. The victim was a female. And if he was any judge of age, she was barely more than a girl.

"Lady," he said, his voice hoarse, "are you hurt?" *Stupid,* he chided himself silently. Of course she was hurt. She was unconscious, perhaps even dead. And she surely wasn't going to answer his question.

He gripped her upper arm and shook her slightly. "Lady! Can you hear me?"

There was no sign of movement, not even breathing. Had he reached her too late? That thought was almost unbearable.

He touched her hair, the color of a newly minted penny, and was surprised to find it smooth, silky, beneath his fingers.

Pushing aside the wet locks, his gaze found the ragged gash that extended from her hairline to her left eyebrow. As he watched, blood seeped slowly from the wound. Rafe knew a momentary relief. She was alive. Blood would not flow from a dead woman. Her skin was icy cold, though, and when he found the pulse at her throat, it was thready, barely discernible beneath his thumb. Even if she regained consciousness, she wouldn't have the strength to help in her own rescue.

He looked anxiously toward the shore. No sign of Danny. His gaze quickly scanned the area around the barn. There was no sign of movement there.

Dammit! He needed the rope.

"Hurry up, boy," Rafe muttered. "Hurry up before it's too late."

With his son nowhere in sight, Rafe knew he could delay no longer. The current would soon move the tree to mid-river again. His gaze swept the area, searching for other means of survival.

There! His gaze pinned the three large rocks that rose above the water between the tree and the riverbank. Although they usually rose a good twenty feet above the surface, at the moment a mere five feet showed.

But five feet of solid rock could mean the difference between life and death.

Coming to a quick decision, Rafe looped his left arm beneath the woman's breasts and bunched his muscles for the leap. But, even as he did so, the current intervened, swirling the tree around, carrying it and its two passengers farther away from safety.

Rafe cursed himself roundly for delaying too long. But even as the words left his mouth, the tree swung around again. As if pushed by a giant hand, it made a complete circle, then headed straight for the three rocks.

"That's it," Rafe muttered, readying himself to make the leap. "Just a little closer. Just a—" He broke off as the tree swirled outward again.

Cursing fate's frivolous hand, he tightened his grip on the woman, filled his lungs with air, and leaped outward. As the water closed over his head, Rafe kicked upward, forcing his body toward the surface again. But the weight of the woman, frail though she was, pulled at him, making progress almost impossible.

Were they both doomed?

Dammit, no! he cried inwardly. He couldn't die, couldn't leave his children alone, completely dependent on charity.

Desperation lent him strength and he kicked harder, pushing himself and the woman through the water. His lungs began to burn, silently screaming for air, but he ignored the pain, struggling frantically to reach safety.

Then, suddenly, his free hand struck something hard. Debris? he wondered. No! The object was solid, unmovable. The rocks.

Hope flared deep within as his fingers scrabbled desperately across the hard, slick surface. He felt a niche, a shallow crack wide enough to slide inside. He latched onto it and gripped hard.

With his hold secured, Rafe pulled himself up until his head cleared water. Then, with one desperate heave, he pushed the woman onto the rocks.

"Pa!"

Danny's voice mingled with the muted roar of the river, but Rafe could hear the fear and blinked rapidly to clear the muddy water from his eyes. In the distance he saw his son, racing along the riverbank, one arm upraised to hold the long coil of rope where it rested across his shoulder.

"Hold on, Pa! I'm coming!"

Suddenly a wave crested, swamping Rafe. Startled, he sucked in a sharp breath, inhaling water as he did. He coughed then, spewing it from his mouth just as another wave struck him, tugging at his sodden clothing. He groped desperately at the slick rocky surface, trying to anchor himself to it. But before he could do so, another wave surged forth and Rafe had only a glimpse of his son before he went under.

Danny stood on the riverbank, frozen with shock as he watched his father being swept away.

Weak and desperately needing air, Rafe was tempted to give in. But only for a moment. He couldn't allow himself to drown. Not with his son watching.

Drawing on some inner strength, Rafe fought his way to the surface again, his fingers clawing at the muddy rocks. He found the crack again and clutched frantically, his fingers digging into the gap and using it to propel himself upward. With his last spurt of strength he pulled himself onto the rock and lay beside the woman, his chest heaving rapidly as he fought for breath.

"Are you all right, Pa?" Danny shouted across the roaring flood.

From somewhere deep inside, Rafe found the strength to lift his arm and wave at his son, but he was too exhausted to make an effort toward speech.

"The rope!" Danny hollered. "I got the rope, Pa! I'm throwing it over now."

Although Rafe needed time to regain his energy, he couldn't find his voice to relate that need to his son. He raised his head and saw the boy twirling the rope above his head, spinning it outward in a wide loop that dropped into the water a good two feet from the rocks.

Danny quickly pulled the rope in, made his loop, and tossed it toward his father again.

Rafe's muscles bunched as he pushed himself upright,

reaching out toward the rope. His fingers snagged the stiff fiber and moments later he secured it around his chest. Only then did he realize the futility of his efforts.

Danny was only a boy. He weighed no more than a hundred pounds and would never be able to pull the combined weight of two people.

Tasting the bitterness of defeat, Rafe silently cursed himself. Danny was yelling again, words that made no sense.

"She's coming, Pa! We'll get you off there."

What did he mean? Rafe wondered.

Suddenly he glimpsed movement in his peripheral vision. His head jerked and his gaze narrowed on the pony and the rider on its back. Sun glinting off white-blond hair revealed the rider's identity. Karin.

Rafe gave a sigh of relief. "Good boy, Danny," he muttered. His son had obviously anticipated their needs and enlisted the aid of his sister.

It was only a matter of minutes before Danny's end of the rope was secured to the pony's saddle. Then, readying himself for the pull, Rafe circled the woman's body with his arm again, wedging her firmly against him as he waited for the rope to tighten.

At Danny's urging, the Shetland pony turned away from the river, and with each step the stiff fiber circling Rafe's chest tightened.

Uttering a silent prayer, Rafe filled his lungs with air and slid into the water. Although the current tugged at him, the steady pull of the rope was unrelenting, and finally he felt solid ground beneath his feet.

Moments later he lay on the riverbank, coughing water from his lungs and sucking greedily at the fresh air.

As he recovered, he remembered the woman who lay beside him and rolled over to study her white face.

He was too late. She was dead.

Chapter Two

"She looks dead, don't she?" Danny's voice was hushed as he knelt on the wet grass beside them. "Is she dead, Pa?"

Rafe spared a brief glance for Danny, whose expression revealed his deep concern. Then his gaze moved on to Karin, who stood stiffly erect, her hands clenched together in a white-knuckled squeeze. "I'm afraid so, son."

He had never told them less than the truth, not even when their mother was dying, and Rafe wouldn't start lying to them now. Not even to take the anguished looks from their faces.

"Can't you do something, Pa?" Karin's lips quivered and her blue eyes appeared larger than usual as she took in the woman's pale skin. "Make her breathe, somehow."

"I don't know how, Karin."

"Maybe if you ... remember how Lucy Walker near drowned last year? She stopped breathing an' her pa pounded on her back until the water come right outta her lungs."

"She's right, Pa," Danny said quickly. "I seen Lucy in town the other day and she looked just fine to me. Even said howdy when we passed on the street. Some folks say she ain't quite right in the head since her pa started her breathing again, but I reckon she'd rather be called addlepated than be rotting in a cold grave."

Karin's distressed cry had Rafe sharply reprimanding his son. "That's enough, Danny."

Rafe had heard the story about Lucy Walker and had wondered many times if her father had actually brought her back to life.

Although he felt any effort on his part would prove useless, he knew he had to do something. Maybe he could get some of the water out of the woman's lungs.

Suiting thought to action, he flipped her onto her stomach and positioned her cheek against the new spring grass. Then, lifting her arms slightly, he pressed his palms against her back and pushed hard.

He hoped the stories about the Walker girl were true, hoped there was a chance the frail woman might live. She was too young to die, younger even than his Gerta had been when she'd died shortly after giving birth to Sissy. Just thinking about that time brought the pain of his loss to the surface, as though it had happened last week instead of almost three years ago. He forced his thoughts away from those terrible days, concentrating instead on the woman he was trying so desperately to help, even though he felt certain his efforts would prove useless. But somewhere, deep inside, there remained a spark of hope. It was a fact that Lucy Walker's heart had stopped beating for several minutes, yet she was alive. Forgetful, maybe, but wouldn't anyone, given the choice, choose to be a mite forgetful rather than stone-cold dead?

His thoughts were interrupted by a sudden gurgle from the woman's throat. The sound was followed by a trickle of water leaking from her mouth.

"It's working, Pa!" Karin dropped to her knees beside them. "She's not dead. See? Water's coming outta her mouth. She's spitting it out."

"She ain't neither, Karin." Danny's voice was harsh. "It's Pa that's squeezing the water out. He's pushing it out with his hands. Ain'tcha, Pa?" His voice sounded angry, high-pitched, but Rafe knew the anger was directed at fate rather than his sister. "She's dead, Karin. Anybody can see that. She's dead as a doornail."

"Stop saying that!" Karin's expression was stricken. "She's not dead!"

"Well, she ain't breathing, is she?" Danny's unnaturally bright eyes told Rafe the boy was barely holding onto his emotions. "And if you don't breathe, then you're bound to be dead."

"That's enough, Danny," Rafe said quietly. "You're upsetting Karin." *Never mind yourself,* he added silently. He knew, though, that Danny was right. Despite his best efforts, the woman was still, appearing utterly lifeless. But she had been breathing when he pulled her out of the water. He was almost positive of that.

Realizing he couldn't give up on her yet, he continued the rhythm, pressing against her back, pushing more water from her body. He was certain his efforts were useless but he wanted to be sure—in his own mind—that he'd done everything possible.

Had he, though? he wondered.

"It's not working anymore, Pa," Karin whispered shakily.

Rafe flicked a quick look at his daughter, saw the tears streaming down her face, and wished she was anywhere but here, watching death claim another life.

"You gotta do something else, Pa," Karin whimpered. "She's gotta have air."

Grimly, Rafe flipped the woman over onto her back.

Although her skin had a waxen look, her lips were tinged with blue.

Rafe cursed silently. He could not allow the woman to slip away so easily. He was not ready to give up yet. She needed air. Well, he'd damn well give her some. Even if he had to blow it into her lungs.

He pinched her nostrils together, inhaled a deep breath, and blew into her mouth. Once, thrice, three times he blew. He paused momentarily to view the results. Nothing. No change whatsoever. He pushed against her chest several times, then blew air into her mouth again. Once, twice, and then once again.

As his palms went to her chest again, she moved and sucked in a quick breath. A violent cough shook her; then water spewed from her mouth.

"Well, I'll be damned." Rafe sat back on his heels and stared at her in stunned amazement.

A soft groan, then another, and muddy water gushed forth.

As Rafe watched, her eyelids flickered, then stilled.

"You done it, Pa," Danny said almost reverently. "You done it. You made her come alive again."

Suddenly, Karin flung herself at her father, wrapped her thin arms around his neck, and buried her head against his chest. Sobs shook her thin frame as she cried out her relief.

Patting his daughter soothingly, Rafe watched the woman for some sign of movement, but there was none. Only the slight rise and fall of her chest beneath the blue riding habit.

"She's going to be fine now, Karin," he told his daughter.

Karin raised her head and looked at him with brimming eyes. Her face had regained some of its color. "You made her live again."

"You're the one that wouldn't let me give up. If you hadn't kept me working on her we'd be sending for the undertaker instead of the doctor."

Karin drew a shaky breath and gave him a wavery smile. "I'm glad she's not dead." She looked at the woman's sodden clothing and long tresses, heavy with water. "We gotta get her home and outta them wet clothes, Pa, lest she come down with the croup."

"You're right. She's not out of the woods yet."

Danny looked at the Shetland pony. "Chigger could carry her home."

Rafe shook his head. "She'd have to ride belly down or be held in place and Chigger's not old enough to carry double yet. Makes more sense for me to carry her and you to ride the pony. She'll need Doc." Bending over, he scooped the woman into his arms and found her weight easy to bear. Such a little thing, he thought. And so easy for the river to capture.

With the woman held firmly in his arms, he began the long walk to the house. Karin followed quickly at his heels, her shorter legs causing her to take three steps to his one.

Danny followed behind them. "Should I go for Doc now, Pa?"

"Yeah. And hurry him along, boy. Tell Doc Smith what happened out here and tell him I said to come real quick-like."

"Okay. But I ain't so sure it'll do much good." A worried frown creased Danny's forehead, drawing his dark brows together. "Ol' Doc Smith's rhumatiz was acting up some-thing awful yesterday, Pa. If you'd been to church services, you'd of seen how Bill Sweeney had to help Doc climb up in his buggy. Reckon he might still be ailing."

"If Doc Smith can't come then bring Granny Wyatt."

Danny's forehead wrinkled. "Granny Wyatt is near eighty years old, Pa. Why don't I bring the new doc? I was talking to him after church an' he said he's got lots of time to spare since none of the folks 'round here put much faith in newcomers. He'd be right pleased to come."

"Go to him, then," Rafe said, striding briskly toward the house he'd built from cedar logs almost fifteen years ago. "Don't even bother Doc Smith or Granny Wyatt. Go straight to Doc Lassiter. It's past time folks gave him a chance."

Doctor Jacob Lassiter had moved to Castle Rock straight out of medical school. But he was too young, folks said, to know anything about medicine. They preferred the old ways of Doc Smith, who'd been practicing medicine for more than forty years. Never mind that his methods were outdated. Never mind that the young doctor was filled with all the latest knowledge in the medical field. Folks around these parts didn't trust newfangled ways, preferring the old tried and true.

"You bet!" Danny was thrilled to have found a patient for the young doctor. He vaulted onto the Shetland pony and reined it toward the road leading to town. "Eee-yahhh!" He slapped the pony with the reins and Chigger whinnied, then wheeled around and raced across the pasture.

Rafe turned his attention to the woman in his arms. She was so pale. And, although her breasts rose and fell with each breath, he wondered if she would ever fully recover.

His thoughts were interrupted by his daughter's voice.

"Do you think she'll be all right now, Pa?" Karin's breath came in short, jerky gasps as she trotted along beside him.

"I imagine so." He refused to give voice to his own worry. "She'll more'n likely wake up soon. Probably have a bad headache since she has a nasty cut on her forehead.

Probably need stitches there. If she's got any other problems the doc oughtta find 'em soon enough.''

Karin's face became pinched again, and Rafe realized
she was worrying anew. He cursed himself silently for making her do so. Although she was only thirteen, she'd been
trying to fill her mother's role for the past three years.
She took care of the house and Sissy and—Sissy! He'd
completely forgotten his youngest child.

He forced his tense body to relax. "I guess Sissy is still
abed." He made the words a statement rather than a question.

Throwing a quick glance at her father, Karin nodded.
"I checked on her before I left the house, Pa. She was
sound asleep."

Rafe's lips pulled into a quick smile. "You're a good
little mother, Karin. Don't know what this family would
do without you." As he'd hoped, his words of praise erased
his daughter's pinched look and her cheeks began to glow
with rosy color.

Moments later they reached the house and Rafe circled
the settee in the parlor, entered the hallway, pushed open
the door to his bedroom, and hurried to the four-poster
bed.

"Wait a minute, Pa. She's wet clean through. If you lay
her down like that she's gonna get the bedclothes wet."

"We'll worry about that later," Rafe said. "Just pull back
the covers so I can put her down."

After the woman was stretched out on the bed, Rafe
removed her shoes and tossed them aside. "We need to
strip these clothes off and get her in something dry."

Karin looked flustered. "My clothes won't fit her, but
there's some of Ma's things in the trunk . . ."

"We'll have to use one of her flannel nightgowns."
Noticing his daughter's hesitation, he added, "Just for

now. We can put it back later, after this lady's own clothes are washed and dried.''

Karin brought the garment while he fumbled with the buttons on the riding habit. It had been more than three years since he'd dealt with feminine garments and his efforts brought back memories of his dead wife.

They'd thought they had a lifetime to enjoy each other. But fate had intervened and taken her from him.

He had done everything he could for Gerta, but it had not been enough. And Doc Smith had done his best. But there had been something wrong inside, something that happened with the birthing, and Gerta had bled to death before their eyes.

But Rafe had fought death this time. And he had won. Before him lay proof of that.

To save both his daughter and himself from embarrassment, Rafe found a chore that would take her out of the room.

"Build up the fire in the kitchen," he said. "This lady needs some heated rocks to warm her feet."

When he was alone with the woman again, he stripped her sodden garments away. And, despite his best efforts at control, his lower body tightened and swelled when he exposed her high, firm breasts.

Silently chastising himself for being so aware of her femininity, Rafe pulled a corner of the quilt across her body and worked her linen drawers down her legs. Then, with the quilt tucked firmly around her, he began toweling her hair dry.

"Poppa!" a shrill voice cried. Rafe turned to see his youngest child running toward him. Her hair was a mass of tousled blond curls and her eyes were alight with joy. "I woke up, Poppa!" she said, holding her arms out eagerly, wanting to be lifted into his arms.

"You're flushed." He brushed his hand against her cheek again. "But you don't seem to have a fever."

"That's good." She smiled weakly and twisted her hands together nervously. "It's past time I got out of my sickbed. I've been a burden to your family long enough."

"You haven't been a burden."

"It's kind of you to say that, even if it's not true. Here I am taking your bed when you and your wife must need it."

A sudden silence filled the room, a tension so thick she could feel it. What had she said to cause it?

"My wife is dead." His voice was flat.

She covered a cry with her fist. "Oh, God. I'm sorry," she whispered. "I had no idea."

"Of course you didn't."

Jessie's gaze flickered between Rafe and the girl who was obviously his daughter. "You must be Karin."

The girl nodded and her long, flaxen hair swept forward, covering the swell of one small breast completely.

"I'm making eggs," Karin said softly. "Do you want some?"

"That sounds good, Karin. But I can't allow you to wait on me. I'm sure if I can get on my feet I'll recover faster." Jessie pushed herself upright, slung the covers aside, and swung her legs off the bed. The action caused a bout of dizziness but she gave no indication of her feelings.

Although he'd been caught off guard, Rafe reacted immediately, lifting her legs and turning her so they were stretched out on the bed again. "Stay where you are," he ordered. "You're in no condition to be up and around yet." He pulled the quilt up to her waist and tucked the edges in around her.

"But I can't allow the lot of you to wait on me," Jessie protested.

His expression was stern. "I can't let you out of the bed, Jessie. Not until Doc Lassiter gives his okay."

"I need to get up," she whispered, feeling a blush stain her cheeks. "For a few minutes, anyway."

"Pa . . ." Karin tugged at her father's sleeve. "Maybe she needs the slop jar."

Rafe lifted a dark, inquiring brow at Jessie and her fiery cheeks told him his daughter was right.

"I'd rather not use the um . . . slop jar."

"Okay." He nodded abruptly. "But the facilities are outside. I'll have to carry you there."

"Oh, but surely—"

"Your choice," he said bluntly. "Use the slop jar or I carry you outside."

"I-I . . . um . . ." She looked away from him, unable to meet his eyes, and when she spoke again, her voice was barely discernible. "Outside."

He scooped her up into his arms; then, motioning for Karin to follow them, he carried Jessie down a path to the outhouse. Using his foot to open the door with the half-moon carved near the top to allow for ventilation, he deposited her inside, then waited a short distance away until he was needed again.

Although embarrassed to be causing so much trouble, Jessie called out to Rafe, who returned her to her bed.

Later, while Jessie was enjoying a breakfast of ham and eggs and biscuits, Danny entered the bedroom to be introduced. He smiled shyly and offered his hand. Motherless he might be, but his manners were not lacking in any way.

Breakfast was over and Jessie was enjoying a second cup of coffee with Rafe when a toddler with golden curls entered the room, a tattered rag doll draped over her arm. She wiped sleepy eyes and looked around the room; when she spied Rafe in the rocking chair, she went immediately to him and curled up in his lap.

"Morning, dumplin'," Rafe said, leaning over to give the baby a quick kiss on the cheek. "You're up mighty early this morning."

"I woked up," she explained, her chubby arms curling around his neck.

"You certainly did." He cuddled her close. "You're just in time for some breakfast."

"I wants oatmeal," she said, straightening in his arms. "Not eggs. Oatmeal."

Karin had followed the toddler into the room. Her lips curled in a sweet smile as she held out her arms. "Come with me, Sissy," she coaxed. "I'll fix your oatmeal."

"Okay." Sissy slid off her father's lap and hurried to her older sister. Then, hand in hand, they left the room.

"She's a lovely child, Rafe," Jessie said softly. "I know you must be proud of her."

"Very proud."

Jessie sipped at her coffee, her gaze thoughtful as she studied Rafe. "It must be hard raising the children on your own. How old is Sissy?"

"Almost three."

"So young to be without a mother. She must miss her terribly."

"She can't miss what she never had."

Although Jessie was curious about his wife, she held her silence. It would be rude to ask questions, possibly even hurtful, for she had no way of knowing how long it had been since Rafe lost his wife, nor even the way that she'd died.

Uttering a deep sigh, as though shrugging away unwanted memories, Rafe drained his coffee cup, then rose to his feet. "Guess I'd better get some chores done," he said abruptly. "I've let things slide the last few days."

Because of me, Jessie thought. "I'm sorry, Rafe."

"Not your fault."

"Yes, it is. You let your chores go because you were looking after me."

"Not all the time. It rained hard several days before we found you. That's why the river was in flood."

He left her alone then and she heard him speaking to his children in another room. Shortly afterwards, his footsteps sounded on the porch and she knew he was leaving to begin his chores.

It was quiet after Rafe left the house. Karin came into Jessie's room to inquire if there was anything Jessie needed; then, upon being told there was nothing, she left to begin her own chores. Jessie could hear the girl moving around the house as she did the daily cleaning, and found the sounds soothing to her mind. Before an hour passed she was sound asleep.

Time passed, and Jessie drifted in and out of sleep until the sound of an opening door woke her. A moment later a tall, slim, redheaded man entered the room. His black medical bag clearly identified his profession.

"Good morning." The doctor crossed the room swiftly, pulled the rocker next to the bed, and seated himself. "I'm Jacob Lassiter," he said brusquely.

"I'm very pleased to meet you."

He wasted no time with his examination. He pulled her right eyelid up and peered into her eye for a long moment. Then, releasing the eyelid, he examined the other eye. "Appears normal enough," he muttered. "Bright and clear. Not the least bit clouded."

After listening to her heart and counting her pulsebeat, he checked the wound on her head. "Looks like you're healing nicely." The chair squeaked as he leaned back and studied her quietly. "Rafe said you were having some trouble with your memory."

"Some?" She laughed, and the sound was harsh, even to her own ears. "I remember nothing, Doctor. Nothing at all. Not even my own name."

"I wouldn't worry overmuch about it."

"I think you're wrong there," she said quietly. "I think anyone would worry about it."

"You listen to Doc Lassiter, young lady. He knows what he's about, right enough."

The voice, cracked with age, startled Jessie and she looked toward the door and saw an old woman standing just inside the room. She was stooped with age, her snow-white hair drawn tightly into a bun at the back of her head, making the wrinkles in her face look so deep they could have passed for wagon ruts.

Realizing she was staring, Jessie flushed. "I'm sorry. I didn't see you standing there."

The old woman laughed abruptly; then, gripping her cane tightly with her right hand, she hobbled closer. "Reckon you're wondering who I am," she croaked. "Name's Becky Wyatt. Folks don't use it much, though. Not the Becky, anyways. They just call me Granny. Or if they done have a granny, they calls me Old Granny Wyatt." She stopped beside the bed, reached out a gnarled hand, and fingered a dark, coppery curl that fell across Jessie's breast. "You got hair like silk, girl. Mighty fine hair. And I oughta know 'cause mine was just that same color when I was young. But time has a way about it that ages most things. And now my hair is more like cotton. Tangles up something awful when it's let down."

The old woman took the rocker the doctor had vacated the moment she entered the room. After seating herself, she gave a relieved sigh. "These old bones are mighty tired these days. Can't hold me up very long at a time." She looked over at Jessie. "Now, what was we talking about?"

"Your hair," Jessie replied. "It's very beautiful. The

color of new snow." Her lips curled into a smile. "My grandmother used to . . ." She broke off and stared at the doctor with dismay. "I-it's gone." Moisture flooded her eyes. "For a moment, I almost remembered something."

"Don't worry about it," Dr. Lassiter said sympathetically. "It only proves that your memory will come back. Given time, your mind will heal like your body. Then you'll remember."

Jessie remembered his words later and tried her best to force the memory to come, but it did no good. Her memories remained elusive, hidden.

Late that afternoon Jessie was awakened by the clip-clop of horses' hooves accompanied by the sound of wagon wheels. She shoved back her tangled hair, combing it with her fingers to tidy it, and waited for whoever had arrived to announce themselves.

Footsteps sounded on the porch and a feminine voice rang out.

"Anybody home?"

The voice was unfamiliar to Jessie. She waited for Karin to reply, but when she didn't, Jessie realized the girl must have momentarily left the house.

"Hello?" the woman called again.

Jessie wondered if she should call out, but before she could do so, the visitor entered the house. There was the sound of approaching footsteps; then, a moment later, a woman appeared in the doorway.

"Hello, there. I see you are finally on the mend." The woman was of medium height and slim build. She had dark brown hair that was braided and wrapped around her head like a coronet.

Jessie flushed, feeling as though she'd been reprimanded for lingering in the bed too long. "Yes. I am on the mend, thank you."

"Good." The woman seated herself in the rocker. "I

know you must feel terrible, imposing on this poor family the way you are." She handed Jessie a basket. "I brought some apples. Thought they might help you regain your strength faster. Karin has so much to deal with already without an invalid to care for."

Jessie's flush deepened. Although the woman sugar-coated her words, her animosity was obvious.

"Are you related to the Sutherlands?"

"Not yet. But I intend to be eventually." The woman smiled sweetly. "Rafe and I have an understanding."

"Oh." Jessie felt as though she'd been kicked in the stomach by a mule.

She didn't know why that should be so, though. Rafe was everything a woman could want in a man and it was only natural that he'd be spoken for.

Footsteps on the porch caught her attention and she felt relief flow through her. Karin must be returning.

Moments later the girl appeared in the doorway with Sissy at her side. She looked at the visitor and stopped abruptly. "Miss Jones." Her voice was hesitant, and the smile she gave belied her words of welcome. "Uh . . . how nice of you to call."

Miss Jones slid her eyes over Karin's faded blue gingham dress, then lifted to her tangled hair. "Your hair is a mess, Karin. It's too bad you have no mother to help you with it. Just a minute. I think I have a ribbon in my reticule to tie it back with."

Karin shook her head. "No. Don't bother, Miss Jones. I'll brush it soon as you're gone."

Miss Jones arched a dark brow. "It sounds as though you're trying to hurry me away, dear. And I'm sure that wasn't your intention, now was it?"

"Uh . . . no," Karin said, flushing a rosy pink. "I just meant that I won't take time now . . . while you're visiting and all."

"Well, if you're sure. But I really don't mind fixing your hair, dear. I know your dear mother would want me to do whatever I could. You're far too young for all the responsibility that's been heaped on your young shoulders. And God alone knows how you manage to keep this family fed, let alone clean. I've told you time and again that I'd be willing to help with whatever's needed around here and . . ."

"I know," Karin interrupted. "And I do appreciate it, Miss Jones."

"Then why haven't you asked for help?" She frowned heavily at the young girl.

The woman's voice was grating on Jessie's ears and she caught her lower lip between her teeth to keep from telling the Jones woman to shut up. After all, the woman claimed to have a close association with the family.

Karin straightened her young shoulders and met the woman's look with determination. "As I said, Miss Jones, if and when I need your help, then I will most certainly ask for it. Now . . ." She turned away, motioning for the other woman to follow her. "Could I offer you some refreshment before you leave? Granny Wyatt stopped by this morning with an apple pie."

"No." Miss Jones looked at Jessie as though she would like to say something else, then shrugged her shoulders and followed Karin from the room. "Thank you for the offer, Karin, but tea is waiting for me at home." The heels of her shoes clicked against the wooden floor as she made her way across the kitchen to the door, then outside where the buggy waited.

Their voices were merely murmurs, indistinguishable to Jessie's ears, but soon she heard the sound of jingling reins and a loud "giddyup" and knew the woman was leaving.

Almost immediately, Karin entered the room and slumped down in the rocking chair. She rubbed her hand across her eyes and leaned her head back against the chair. "I don't think that woman is ever going to give up." She looked ruefully at Jessie. "Did she wake you?"

Jessie grinned. "You might say that. Who is she, anyway?"

"The teacher at Castle Rock. Her name is Corabelle Jones. And she wants to marry Pa."

Jessie choked back a laugh. "I take it you don't look favorably on the match."

"No! Neither does Danny. And if Sissy was old enough to know what was going on, then she wouldn't like it, either."

Jessie folded the edge of the coverlet, keeping her eyes away from Karin so the girl couldn't read her feelings. "And what does your father think about Miss Corabelle Jones?"

"He can't stand her, but the old biddy doesn't seem to have any sense. She thinks if she keeps reminding Pa we don't have a mother—as if we could forget something like that—he'll give in and marry her." She curled her legs in the chair and tucked them under her skirt. "I just wish she'd stop coming here. She did for a while, but—"

"But now she uses me for an excuse," Jessie finished the words for her.

"Yes." Karin blushed hotly. "But it's not your fault. If you weren't here she would find another reason. She usually uses the fact that we need to be schooled."

"You're not in school?"

"No. Not since Ma died. Pa needed somebody to take care of Sissy. And there's so many things that he can't do alone. Things that take two backs and four hands. Ma used to help him, but after she died . . ." Her voice trailed away and she looked out the window, but not before Jessie saw the tears in her eyes.

"You miss her, don't you?"

"Yeah." Karin's voice was muffled. "We all do. I used

to hear Pa crying late at night when he thought everybody was asleep.'' She looked quickly at Jessie. "He'd hate for anybody to know that, though. So I shouldn't have told you. He's a strong man. None stronger than him. But losing Ma was awful hard on him. He loved her so much, you see.''

Jessie did see. And knowing Rafe had mourned his loss with tears didn't make her think any less of him. In fact, it made him seem more human to her, more loving.

Although Jessie wanted to know more about him, she knew they shouldn't be talking about his feelings for his dead wife. She decided a change of subject was in order.

"You know what, Karin? I feel much better now. What do you say to me dressing and helping you with the evening meal?''

"I don't know, Jessie. Pa said you was to stay in bed.'' Karin gave her a long, steady look. "He's likely to be upset if we don't listen to him.''

"Yes, I imagine he might.'' Jessie thought about her options. She didn't want to disobey Rafe, yet she wanted to feel as though she were helping. "Tell you what, Karin. Suppose I help you, then come back to bed before your father returns.''

Karin twisted a long, flaxen curl. "Wouldn't that sorta be like lying to Pa?''

"No. Because I wouldn't be staying up.'' Jessie motioned the girl closer. "I might need your help to get up, but once I'm on my feet—if I can make it that far—then, who knows?''

The girl was agreeable enough. She helped support Jessie as they went into the kitchen. Soon they were both seated at the table. Jessie peeled and sliced potatoes while Karin mixed cornbread. The aroma from the red beans boiling on the stove was familiar, yet Jessie had no memory of cooking herself.

She sighed heavily. How long must she wait for her memory to return?

"Does your head ache, Jessie?" Karin asked suddenly.

"Yes." Jessie rubbed at her temples. "How did you know?"

"Your face is pale again." She frowned at Jessie. "Maybe you should go back to bed."

"Maybe you're right," Jessie agreed.

Moments later she stretched out on the bed and closed her eyes against the pain that continued to stab at her temples. She was getting stronger each day, and soon would be able to take on some of the household chores.

But first she must convince Rafe of that fact.

Chapter Five

With each new day, Jessie felt stronger. On the fourth day, she was pronounced well enough to leave her sickbed.

Jessie felt almost exultant at the news. She would have thrown her arms around the doctor and given him a big hug, had she not felt he would be embarrassed at such a display of feelings. She gave him a wide smile instead.

"I was beginning to think I was doomed to live out my life in this bedroom, Dr. Lassiter."

He was bent over the bed, examining the wound on her forehead, but at her words, his gaze met hers and he returned her smile. "Impatient to be up, are we?"

"I don't know about you, but I most certainly am."

He chuckled; then his expression became serious again. "I admit I kept you down longer than I normally would have, Jessica, even for a gash like the one on your forehead. But the wound, coupled with extreme dizziness and your loss of memory . . . they tell me something's not right there and we'd best proceed with caution."

His words of warning did nothing to dim her smile. "I feel wonderful, Dr. Lassiter. Not a sign of stiffness or bruises. Except for the injury on my head, of course." She traced the long gash on her forehead with a fingertip and grimaced wryly. "I suppose this is going to leave a permanent scar."

"I imagine so. But I stitched it real close. In time there should only be a thin line and you can cover that with your hair." His eyes became warm, almost teasing. "It would take more than that gash to mar your beauty, Jessie."

She blushed at the compliment, then immediately frowned as a sudden thought occurred. She had no idea what she looked like, had seen no mirrors in the household, which seemed very unusual.

"What's wrong?" Doc Lassiter asked. "Some pain you haven't told me about?"

"No. I just realized I have no idea what I look like."

He lifted a dark red eyebrow. "You haven't been curious enough to look in a mirror?"

"I hadn't thought about it before. Anyway . . ."—she looked pointedly around the room—"there are no mirrors in here. Not even on the dresser."

"Well, I'll be Johnny. You're absolutely right. But there should be one over the dresser. I wonder what happened to it. Never mind, though. There has to be one around somewhere." He crossed the room to the doorway and raised his voice. "Karin!"

When there was no answer, Jessie said, "I haven't heard her since you arrived. Nor Sissy, either. I think she must have gone outside."

He looked back at her. "She told me Sissy was napping. And, come to think of it, I believe she said something about gathering the eggs. More than likely, she's in the henhouse. I'll just go outside and call her."

"It's not that important," Jessie protested. "I'm not so vain that I have to see myself this very moment."

"It's not vanity that I'm trying to satisfy, Jessie," he said gruffly. "There's a good chance seeing your face might bring back your memory, at least some of it. And I'd rather be here when that happens."

"Oh. I never thought of that."

"No, I don't expect you did."

Dr. Lassiter left her alone then, and moments later, she heard him calling Karin again. A distant voice answered, and soon the two of them entered the house together.

"The big mirror on Ma's dresser got broke the day she died," Karin told the doctor as they entered the room. "There's another big one in my room, but we have a hand mirror, too. Will that be big enough?"

"Yes. We just need something large enough for Jessie to see her face."

"I'll get it for you."

Moments later, Jessie was staring at the image in the mirror. A stranger looked back at her. She studied the woman closely. The face was oval, framed by a mass of coppery curls. Thick, dark lashes surrounded green eyes that appeared tremulous with disquiet. Or was it the arch of the auburn eyebrows that made them appear so? Above the eyebrows a thin, slightly puffy redness streaked from eyebrow to hairline.

Was that woman really her? Why did she appear so apprehensive, so fearful? Was there something in the past she was running from?

She studied the gash, held closed by tiny stitches, and suddenly she felt even more afraid. As that feeling persisted, Jessie became aware of a muted sound, a distant roaring that slowly became louder and louder until it drowned out every other sound. Even so, she became aware of a new sound, the high-pitched whinny of a terrified horse.

The horse! The horse!

Oh, God, the horse was almost as terrified as she was. It reared high, pawing at the air with its forelegs as she fought to retain her seat. She felt a dark shadow looming over her, reaching out to tear her away from the horse and she yanked the reins . . . yanked on the reins . . . pulled the reins . . .

"Jessie."

The voice came from a long distance and she felt a hand tugging at her fingers, trying to pry the reins from her fingers, yet she could not . . . dared not . . . give way . . .

"Jessie! What's happening? What do you see?"

"No, no, no, no!"

She closed her eyes tightly, yet she could feel the hand prying her fingers loose and she dropped the reins and heard them crash against the rocks.

"Jessie. It's all right. You're all right."

A hand cupped her face and she pushed it away frantically. "Don't touch me. Don't touch me! Leave me alone."

"All right, Jessie. All right. You're all right. There's nothing here to harm you. Nothing at all."

The voice was so soothing, so soft, that Jessie found her fear dissolving as though it had never been. Slowly, she became aware of her surroundings.

"Open your eyes, Jessie."

The voice was commanding, but she refused to obey it.

"Come on, Jessie. Open your eyes."

She forced her eyes open and looked at the redheaded man bending over her. "That's better. Now tell me what you remembered."

"I don't know," she whispered, forcing her eyes to open and meet his. "I don't know what I remembered."

His brown eyes seemed to see through her. "Think hard, Jessie. You were afraid. Why?"

"I-I . . . didn't see anything."

"Then why were you afraid?"

"It was the sounds . . ."

"What sounds?"

"Roaring. Not loud. Distant, muted. And the horses—or maybe it was just one horse, I don't really know—they . . . it was screaming, as though it was afraid, and it made me afraid."

The doctor's face wavered slightly as though she were seeing him through a veil of water. Only then did she realize tears were streaming from her eyes.

"I'm sorry," she muttered, wiping at her face with the back of her hand. "I'm being a baby, I know, but it seemed so real, as though I was actually there . . ."

"It's more than likely you *were* there," he said gruffly. "That may be how you wound up in the river."

"What do you mean?"

"You mentioned a muted, roaring sound. It might have been the river in flood. And the terrified horse? Well, something could have happened to startle the animal when you were riding near the river. A rattlesnake or mountain lion. The horse, in a panic, may have stumbled over the edge of a bluff with you on his back." His gaze narrowed thoughtfully. "It makes sense."

"What do you mean?"

"You were wearing a riding habit when Rafe pulled you out of the river."

"Yes. So Rafe informed me."

"Is that all you remember, Jessie?" Karin asked in a hushed voice. "You don't remember your name? Or where you came from?"

"No. Nothing more."

"Maybe if you saw your riding habit it would help you remember."

"Let's give her a rest now, Karin," Doc Lassiter said brusquely. "I think Jessie's had enough remembering today." He frowned down at her. "In fact, I'm wondering if you shouldn't stay in bed for . . ."

"No!" Jessie said sharply. "You told me I could leave this bed today. And I'm going to do exactly that."

"Well . . . perhaps that would be best. It's a proven fact that busy hands keep a body from worrying overmuch. So I suppose you can help around the house some. But just remember, young lady, you're not fully recovered yet. If you experience the slightest dizziness, you're to get off your feet immediately."

"I'll remember." She offered him a weak smile, then turned eagerly to Karin, who hovered nearby. "It appears I need my riding habit now."

"No." Lassiter shook his head. "Leave that garment where it is for the moment. I believe Granny Wyatt brought a bundle of clothes for you yesterday."

"I put them in the oak chest." Karin hurried across the room and opened a drawer, extracting several garments which she brought to Jessie. "Granny said these belonged to her daughter—she died a few years back and won't need them anymore." She frowned suddenly. "You don't mind wearing a dead woman's clothes, do you, Jessie?"

"Of course not." Jessie didn't point out that she'd been wearing Gerta's nightgown all this time.

"There's a pair of shoes, too," Karin announced. "They're in the wardrobe."

"Let me put a new bandage on Jessie's forehead, Karin. Then you can help her get dressed."

Jessie grimaced. "I thought I was rid of the bandage for good."

"Not hardly." Lassiter leaned closer and ran a thumb over the wound. "It's too raw to leave open. The bandage will stay until the stitches are out."

"When will that be?" Jessie asked.

"Not more than a couple of days if it keeps improving the way it has."

He tended the wound; then, with a word of warning not to overdo it, he took his leave.

Karin seemed almost as excited as Jessie that she was being allowed up. She turned away while Jessie donned the pantaloons and chemise, then helped her slide the brown gingham dress over her head.

"There." Karin shook the skirt gently to loosen some of the wrinkles. "We managed to get you dressed without messing up the bandage." She eyed Jessie for a long moment. "You look nice, Jessie. Doc Jacob is right. You *are* beautiful. And you know what? I think he's completely smitten with you."

"Nonsense."

"No, it's not nonsense," Karin contradicted. "It's a fact."

Nothing Jessie could say would sway Karin from her belief, and, to Jessie's extreme embarrassment, Karin repeated her words as the family was gathered around the table for the evening meal.

"Smitten, is he?" Rafe's eyes teased Jessie, who sat across the table from him. "Now I wouldn't doubt that for one minute."

"He said she was beautiful."

Feeling a blush stain her cheeks, Jessie lowered her eyelashes to hide her flustered state. "He was only being polite."

Jessie was too aware of Rafe's intense look. She controlled a desire to fidget in her chair. Did he think she was trying to excite his interest? She hoped he wouldn't attribute such actions to her, else he might think badly of her. She lifted her coffee cup to her lips and swallowed convulsively, pretending complete indifference to the conversation.

"I think it was more than just politeness," Karin persisted. "You didn't see the look on his face when you screamed and dropped the mirror. But I did."

Complete silence followed her words. Danny's spoon halted in midair and he flicked a quick look at Jessie. Rafe's eyebrows had drawn into a heavy frown, and his gray eyes were storm-cloud dark, hard and penetrating. When he spoke, his voice had the texture of steel.

"Why did you scream, Jessie?"

"I-I . . . uh . . . don't really know." She looked away from him, unable to hold his gaze. "It was a stupid thing to do."

Seeming to realize Jessie was unable to answer to Rafe's satisfaction, Karin hurried to explain. "It was when she looked in the mirror, Pa. It made her remember how she fell in the river."

"Jessie?"

Rafe's voice had softened considerably, and Jessie forced herself to meet his eyes. "I don't really remember much, Rafe. It wasn't really a memory. At least I don't think so."

"Then what made you afraid?"

Sissy banged loudly on her highchair with a spoon, capturing Jessie's attention, but Danny, as though wanting to hear the answer to his father's question, caught the toddler's hand in his own and shushed her.

Realizing Rafe was waiting for her answer, Jessie said, "It was stupid, really. The sounds frightened me." The words brought the memory surging forth again and she fought the ensuing panic. "The sounds," she repeated, her words coming faster, gushing out as water freed from a bursting dam. "The roaring, the horse . . . horses rearing, pawing at the air . . . screaming, the hands . . . pulling at the reins, trying to . . . trying . . ."

"Pa!"

"What's the matter with her?"

Jessie heard the voices in some corner of her mind, yet they seemed to come from somewhere far away. She tried to focus on the here and now, tried to control her breath that came in short gasps, but her fear was surrounding her, shutting out everything else.

"Jessie! Look at me, Jessie. You're all right. You're safe here with us."

Rafe's voice was close and she tried to concentrate on it—tried, but it began to slip away.

"Look at me, Jessie."

She felt a light slap on her face and tried to focus on the man who knelt before her, but the scent of sweating horseflesh, of muddy water, of flowers . . .

Suddenly, pain streaked through her head and she cried out. The cry was taken up by another, an undulating, wailing sound, as though a baby was crying. She tried to focus on the sound, feeling that if she could follow it, she would find release from her pain. Instead, she succumbed to the enveloping darkness, yielding to the welcoming arms of Morpheus.

Rafe caught Jessie as she slumped into a dead faint. He was vaguely aware of Karin, who was soothing a frightened Sissy. As he gathered Jessie into his arms, he looked at his older daughter over the toddler's head.

"Bring her into the bedroom, Karin. She needs to know there's nothing to worry about."

"Should I go for Doc Lassiter, Pa?" Danny asked.

"He saw her like this, Danny," Karin said. "She didn't faint, though."

"I wonder why he didn't see fit to tell me what happened." Rafe's voice was hard. He'd have an answer from the doctor and it had better be a good one, too.

"He told her not to force the memories." Karin looked away. "It was my fault, Pa. But I didn't mean to make her remember again."

"If anyone's at fault here, it's me." Rafe stretched Jessie out on the bed, then smoothed back an errant curl before he turned to take his youngest daughter from Karin's arms. "Now what's all this crying about?" he asked gently, using a fingertip to catch a stray tear.

"Jessie hurted," Sissy explained, her lips quivering slightly.

"Not really, Pumpkin. Jessie is just having trouble with her memory. And she's scared right now. But we're going to take care of her so she'll know there's nothing to be afraid of. Right?"

Sissy knuckled her eyes and heaved a shuddering sob; then she gave a watery smile. "Right," she agreed. "We take care of Jessie."

"We sure will." He patted her rounded bottom, then gave her to Karin. "Now the lot of you finish your meal while I sit here with Jessie."

"I can do that, Pa."

Karin looked so forlorn that Rafe almost agreed to allow her to stay, yet he found himself unable to do so. He wanted to be with Jessie when she woke, needed to be with her. And yet, he wondered at that need, worried that he was becoming too attached to her, that when she left them he would mourn that loss.

It was more than an hour before Jessie's eyelashes quivered and lifted. She sighed deeply and stretched her arms above her head as though she'd just awakened from a long sleep. Then, as though becoming aware of him, she swiveled her head and looked at him.

"Rafe."

She smiled at him, and his heart gave a jerk, then fluttered wildly, as though a thousand butterflies were trying to escape from beneath his ribcage.

"Hello." Her voice was warm, soft, as she pushed herself to her elbows. "What are you doing there?"

"Watching you." He managed to keep the anxiety from his voice. "You look as innocent as a newborn babe when you're sleeping."

"Is that a compliment?"

Her eyes smiled at him, warm, almost loving. He chided himself for the thought, for wanting to believe it was so. The only excuse he could offer was that he'd been too long without a woman. He had denied himself too long, he knew, when the first beautiful woman who appeared on his horizon had his body standing at attention.

"It's only the truth," he said. "You must know how beautiful you are without me telling you so."

Beautiful. The word caught at her memory and she could feel the color draining away from her face. "We were having supper when that memory came again, didn't it? Oh, Rafe, I'm sorry. I don't know what came over me." She flattened her fingers against her forehead, trying to press away the sudden pain. "My head hurts. It was hurting before. When I . . . when I . . ."

"Don't think about it," he said huskily. "Just lie back on the bed and close your eyes for a minute."

"But I . . ."

"No. Forget the memory." He stroked her hair softly, trying to soothe her. "I was saving something to show you after supper. A surprise."

"You were?" She turned her head to look at him. "What kind of surprise?"

His lips turned up at the corners. "One of the heifers calved today."

"A new calf?"

"Uh-huh. The cutest little calf I ever did see."

"That's wonderful, Rafe. Has Sissy seen it?"

"Not yet. Only Danny knows about it."

"Can we go see it?"

"Later. You need to rest now. You have to get rid of your headache first."

"My headache?" She stared at him, wide-eyed. "It's gone, Rafe. There's no pain now." Her brown furrowed. "Isn't that strange? It was almost unbearable only a minute ago. What in the world . . . ?"

"Forget it, Jessie. Forget the memory, and think only of today. Of what's happening right here on this farm. There's time enough to worry about the rest later." Even as he spoke the words, he wondered if he was doing her a disservice. Was there someone somewhere who mourned her loss, as he had mourned his wife?

A sudden thought occurred. She might even be married. He instantly rejected that. She couldn't be, not and appear so innocent, so unworldly. If he was a gambler, he would bet everything he owned that she'd never known passion, never known what it was to lie in a man's arms throughout the night.

Jessie watched Rafe closely, curious about his expression. His eyelids had lowered slightly, his eyes darkening until they resembled molten steel. She didn't wonder where she'd been to make that comparison, just felt it was so. And the heat from his gaze seemed to reach out and physically scorch her, making her feel as though her bones were melting inside her flesh.

Suddenly, as though mentally shaking himself, Rafe

straightened to his full height. He turned his body slightly away from her before he spoke again.

"Guess I'd better go see how that mother and her calf are doing." Then, before she could say anything more, he left her alone with her thoughts.

Chapter Six

Although Rafe had meant to wait until morning to show Jessie the calf, the children wouldn't hear of it.

"I can help her out here, Pa," Danny pleaded. "Seeing the calf couldn't help but make her feel better. It's such a pretty little thing."

The girls added their pleas to his son's and Rafe found himself unable to ignore their combined efforts. Perhaps because he felt they were right. The tiny calf, with its red and white markings, was bound to lift anyone's spirits. And it was a fact that Jessie needed her spirits lifted.

"You're probably right," Rafe said. "I'll go get her."

"Me and Sissy will come, too," Karin said quickly, scooping Sissy into her arms so she could keep pace with her father.

"Here, give her to me." Rafe took the toddler from his older daughter's arms and, with Karin hurrying behind him, he strode swiftly from the barn.

When Sissy saw Jessie stretched out on the bed, she

bounced up and down in Rafe's arms. "Jessie, Jessie!" The toddler was so excited she could hardly contain her feelings. "Come see, Jessie, come see!"

"Come see what, darling?" Jessie leaned up on her elbows and smiled at the youngster. "The calf? Is that what you want me to come see?"

Rafe deposited Sissy on the floor and immediately the toddler grasped Jessie's fingers with her small, plump hand. "Now, Jessie," she urged. "Come see now."

Before Jessie could reply, Rafe slid one arm behind her shoulder and the other beneath her legs and scooped her against his chest. "Rafe! What are you doing?"

"Taking you to see the calf."

"Oh." She curled her arms around his neck and smiled up at him. "I thought I was supposed to wait until tomorrow."

"Nope. You're supposed to see it now."

Even though she realized she should protest being carried, she settled into the curve of his shoulder and snuggled her head beneath his chin.

Sissy giggled, then muffled the sound with her fist. "Poppa cares Jessie."

"Cares *for* Jessie," Karin corrected, as she scooped the toddler into her arms and hurried after her father.

"No," Sissy said. "Cares Jessie." She curled her arms to her chest as though she carried something in them. "Cares," she repeated.

"Oh." Karin nuzzled her younger sister's nose. "You mean he's *carrying* Jessie." At the toddler's nod, Karin muttered, "That, too."

Jessie had no time to consider her words, because they were inside the barn.

The barn felt cool in comparison to the heat of the day, and Jessie's nostrils were assailed by the pungent smell of hay. Rafe carried her to a stall halfway down the barn and put her down on a bale of hay.

"Look, Jessie," Sissy cried, pointing to the tiny red and white calf nearby. And as she did, the calf made a bleating sound and headed straight for the heifer with swollen udders that stood nearby. As they watched, the calf latched on to one of the teats and nudged sharply to allow the milk to come down. Then it sucked greedily, foam soon appearing on the sides of its mouth.

"I found it, Jessie," Danny said, smiling up from where he knelt in the hay. "The heifer calved in the fields and I carried the calf to the barn."

"You carried it all that way by yourself?"

He ducked his head, his cheeks becoming rosy. "I'm stronger than I look," he mumbled. Then, his pleasure overcoming his embarrassment, he looked at her again, his dark eyes glowing with pride. "Me an' Pa knew the heifer was gonna calve any day. But she still took us by surprise when she did."

"And Bessie's fine now," Karin said. "Even though the birthing must have been hard." She patted the heifer's side. "You did good, Bessie. You did real good."

"See, Jessie?" Sissy looked up at the woman who sat nearby on a bale of hay. "Bessie has a baby." She ran a plump hand across the newborn calf's side, and her expression was one of awe. "Soft . . ." The word was only a tiny breath. "Smoove."

"Yes, Pumpkin."

Rafe's gaze was so tender and loving as he watched the toddler that Jessie's breath caught in her throat.

"The calf's hide is soft and smooth like that because it's a newborn," Rafe said. "Most animals feel like that when they first come into the world." He looked over at Jessie. "We wanted you to see the calf tonight, to share in the joy of birth."

His words, spoken with such tender feeling, brought tears to her eyes. "Thank you, Rafe," she whispered. Then, turning to encompass his little family, she said, "I thank all of you for wanting me here."

"Oh, we do, Jessie."

Rafe's voice drew her gaze to him again, and there was such a world of meaning behind his words that she didn't even try to puzzle it through. Not when he was looking at her with such heat that she felt as though she'd just been branded with a hot iron.

During the next few days Jessie and Karin developed a system of sharing the household chores. Jessie discovered early on that she must tread lightly where Karin was concerned. The girl appeared to resent any attempt to relieve her of her many duties, so Jessie always asked Karin each morning for a list of chores and waited for the girl to portion them out.

Jessie wondered if the girl was afraid their uninvited guest might be trying to replace her mother in the household. Although she wanted to reassure Karin that was not her intention, Jessie didn't know how to go about doing so. She made sure, though, to always ask permission from the girl before making even the slightest change in the household.

They got on well together, so long as Jessie kept firmly in her place, and Karin seemed to appreciate having another female around. They found themselves in agreement over many things—the main one, Corabelle Jones's daily visits.

The woman had a way of getting on both their nerves, and they came to dread her arrival.

One day, as she was readying herself to leave, she reminded Karin of her need for education if she expected to find a decent husband when she was grown.

"Pa needs me here," Karin said quickly. "There'd be nobody to look after Sissy if I went to school every day."

"That's ridiculous," Corabelle snapped. "If your father had any sense of duty, he'd find himself a wife. There's certainly plenty of single women around these parts. In fact"—she tucked a stray curl beneath her hat and preened—"I wouldn't mind being married to Rafe. You might mention that sometimes. If he decides to think about marriage again."

Karin's eyes flashed with temper. "I'm sure if Pa decides to get married again, he'll be able to find a wife without my help."

Corabelle's eyes narrowed sharply. "Your manners have been severely neglected, girl."

Jessie could remain silent no longer. "Her manners are impeccable, Miss Jones. Karin has been courteous enough to welcome you into her home each day, even though you persist in coming here without invitation. Your manners, however, leave a lot to be desired."

"How dare you!" Corabelle was completely incensed. "I shall report this conversation to Rafe without fail. And when he hears how rude you've been to me I'm certain his first thought will be to send you from his home."

Then, whirling around, the woman left them alone.

That evening after supper, Rafe invited Jessie to sit with him on the porch. She was almost certain Corabelle had found him in the barn and informed him of his guest's rude behavior since the carriage was a long time leaving the yard.

Although she'd waited for him to mention Corabelle, he'd remained silent on the subject, perhaps waiting until they were alone.

Finding herself unable to wait for him to find the words to tell her to leave, Jessie decided to save him the trouble.

"It's past time I left here, Rafe," she said, lowering her lashes quickly to hide her expression.

He frowned at her. "Does this have anything to do with Corabelle?"

"Not really."

"Then why now? Why decide suddenly to leave the same day Corabelle comes to me with some story that she's made up about you being a bad influence on my children?"

She sucked in a shocked breath. "She said that? Accused me of being a bad influence?"

"She most certainly did."

"Of all the nerve! She's angry with me because I was sticking up for Karin and besides that, she's afraid that you . . ."

"That I'll what?" he inquired mildly.

"Oh, nothing." She'd almost told him about the teacher's jealousy. "Anyway, that's not the reason I decided to leave. I need to find out where I belong, Rafe. Surely you can see that."

"And where would you stay while you conducted this search?"

"I don't know. I hadn't thought of that."

"No. There's lots of things you haven't thought about." He leaned back in his rocker and watched the sun go down in a blaze of glory. "There's time enough to think about your past later, Jessie. You've only recently recovered your strength. You're certainly in no shape to go wandering all over the place looking for your home."

"We could have the sheriff make inquiries, Rafe."

"I suppose we could," he replied. "But I don't know what all the hurry is about."

"You said before that someone might be searching for me," she told him.

"I know. But if they were, then they would surely have found you by now." He took her hand in his and rubbed his thumb over her palm. "Just leave it lay, Jessie. For a while at least."

"Rafe. I can't keep imposing on you."

"You're not imposing," he growled softly. "We like having you here."

Rafe didn't want her to go, actually dreaded the day she would leave them, but he couldn't tell her that. She might stay just because she felt she owed him; he wanted her to stay because she wanted to, not to pay an imagined debt.

"Corabelle comes out here every day, Rafe. And she never fails to remind me that I'm taking advantage of your goodwill."

"She has no say over what we do here."

Jessie looked away from him. "I think she would like to have a say."

"Yeah. She's made that clear enough. I'm beginning to think nothing will discourage her as long as I remain unmarried." His gaze turned inward, to a time when his family was complete. Yet it was only a momentary thing. Gerta belonged in the past. It was time to begin a new tomorrow.

"Rafe."

Jessie's voice pulled him from his thoughts, and he smiled at her. She was so sweet, so beautiful. So desirable. And the children loved her. And yet, she knew nothing of her past, might have ties that would take her away from them. He dared not allow his emotions to become too involved.

"We can't continue like this, Rafe. It's not just Corabelle. She says people are talking about me being here."

"Talking? Of course they would. Everyone is curious about you."

"How can you be so obtuse?"

He sighed heavily. "Let it rest, Jessie. Forget the gossips. Let's enjoy the sunset together."

Although Jessie fell silent, watching the sun sink below the horizon in a blaze of scarlet and purple, her thoughts were still troubled. Corabelle was right. Rafe's reputation was safe. He was a man. But her reputation would most certainly suffer.

There was no doubt in her mind that she must leave this place where she'd been made to feel welcome. But where would she go? Where did she belong? What past had she forgotten?

Questions continued to torment her as she sought her rest that night, intruding into her dreams until they became host to monsters.

Rafe felt more than unusually restless as he lay in bed beside his son. He listened to the soft sound of Danny's snoring.

Across the room, the full moon cast a silvery light through the window; perhaps it was that illumination that made sleep so elusive for Rafe.

But he thought not.

Sighing, Rafe stirred restlessly. He was tired, had deliberately worn himself out by doing two days' work in one as an excuse to stay away from the house. Little good it had done, though. His turbulent thoughts would not allow him to rest. And it was the woman who slept in his own bed that occupied those thoughts, the woman who had occupied his room now for the past ten days. Ever since he'd pulled her from the flood-swollen river.

He'd never forget the perfection of her body when he'd stripped her sodden garments away. Although he'd tried not to stare, he'd nevertheless been struck by her loveliness. Her pearly white skin had contrasted sharply with her copper hair, long and luxuriant as it spread around her, albeit in tangles. And her breasts had been tantalizing, perfect round globes, standing high and proud as he had slid her chemise away from them. Her waist, so tiny he could span it with his hands, served to complement the taut belly. As he'd gazed at the swell of her hips his lower body had become so taut with need that he thought he might explode. Never had he seen anyone quite so lovely.

Just the thought of her as he'd seen her that night made him want to join her in her bed.

His bed.

Damnation! He was hot! So damned hot! And yet the temperature was cool at nights, as proved by Danny, who clutched the covers around his neck to keep away the cold night air.

But Rafe couldn't feel the cold. Not with his body burning with a heat so great it threatened to consume him.

He'd never felt such need before, not even with Gerta. Jessie had made such a difference in his household. He had yet to come home—since she'd been up and around—when there were no fresh flowers gracing the rough wood table. Funny, though, she hadn't used the vases to hold the flowers—she'd arranged them in fruit jars instead.

He remembered the way she'd looked when he'd entered the kitchen that evening. The room smelled of cinnamon and forget-me-nots and she was seated at the table with Sissy on her lap, playing patty cake with the toddler. Over supper his eyes were continually finding hers and she'd blushed prettily and quickly looked away. She seemed happy enough in his home. She had a habit of singing softly, as though fearful her song would disturb those who might come near enough to hear. Why that should be so he didn't know because she had a beautiful voice, a lilt quite unlike any other he had ever heard.

What was she doing now? Was she sleeping? Or just lying there, stretched out on his bed in her nightclothes. Perhaps she slept in the altogether tonight. The mere thought of such a possibility had his body throbbing with need.

He groaned softly. If only he dared enter that forbidden room. He could go there on some pretense, and could glance her way, casual-like. If she was awake, he could determine by the way she looked at him—sultry with desire, or innocent as a child—whether or not to join her in bed.

Realizing he was being a fool, he silently chided himself. Jessie was innocent, would know nothing of lust, would probably be horrified to know his thoughts.

Wouldn't she?

There's an easy way to find out, an inner voice said. *Just go into your room on some pretense. If she's awake, it would be so easy . . .*

No. He couldn't do that. Not with his children in the house.

He sighed again, yanking his pillow from behind his head to pound and reshape it again as he'd done so many times before. He tried to force his thoughts away from the woman. From Jessie. He had to control himself, could not allow her to affect him so. But it was hard to eject her from his thoughts.

Perhaps she was right. Maybe it was time she left, before his desire for her became too apparent and caused both of them embarrassment.

Come morning he would go to Castle Rock and see the sheriff. Watson would send out inquiries and hopefully they could find Jessie's family. Yeah. That would be best . . . Better put temptation away as soon as possible, before he did something absolutely stupid.

It was happening all over again. Jessie's breath came in short gasps and her heart fought frantically to escape the prison of her ribcage as she struggled to stay on the horse.

Oh, God! He was too strong. Too powerful. She couldn't get away from him. She was doomed. Doomed. No! She couldn't give in. She fought harder, screaming out her terror, struggling wildly, flailing her arms. Her heart was racing and then she was falling . . . falling . . .

Suddenly, hands gripped her forearms and shook her hard.

"Wake up, Jessie. Wake up."

She opened her eyes and saw a man looming above her. She put out a hand to ward off a blow, her body tense as she waited for the first lash of pain.

"What's the matter?"

Although his voice was concerned, when he leaned closer as though to pull her nearer, she flinched. She wanted to flee and it took all her courage to face him.

"It's only me, Jessie. Only me."

Rafe? She tried to speak, but was unable to get a word past the tightness of her throat. He loomed over her, a massive figure, capable of breaking her neck with one quick twist. And he looked almost ready to do it, with his jaw shadowed with a day's growth of beard.

"Did you have a nightmare?"

She nodded, holding her body as stiff as a board.

"Relax," he murmured, pulling her into his embrace.

His breath stirred the fine hair growing near her ear, and he smoothed his hands over her back, soothing her as though she were a newborn colt. "It's all over. You're awake now. Safe. There's nothing to harm you."

She looked up at him, her eyes wet with tears. "I'm sorry," she said shakily. "It's just that it seems so real when I'm having the dream that—"

"Do you want to talk about it?"

"No. At least . . . I can't. It doesn't make sense."

"Tell me anyway."

Chapter Seven

"Pa?"

Karin's voice startled the man and woman locked in an embrace. Almost simultaneously, they turned and saw her standing in the doorway, rubbing her eyes with the back of her hand.

"What's wrong, Pa?"

"Nothing's wrong, Karin," Rafe said gruffly. "Go back to bed."

Karin frowned at them. "I thought I heard Jessie scream."

"She had a nightmare." Rafe felt a guilty need to explain his presence in the bedroom. "I was just trying to calm her down."

"Oh," Karin yawned widely. "Some dreams can be awful scary. Are you all right now, Jessie?" At Jessie's nod, Karin turned away from the door. "I'm going back to bed then. I'll shut the door so your voices won't wake Sissy."

As the door closed behind his daughter, Rafe looked at

the woman in his arms and chuckled softly, his gray eyes glinting with sudden humor. "It was mighty obliging of my daughter to close the door, wasn't it?"

Jessie felt her cheeks grow hot. His face was so close she could see each individual eyelash, could feel his warm breath against her flesh. She sat perfectly still, unable to turn her eyes away from his face. Her fascinated gaze traced the intricate swirls in his ear and she felt an urge to kiss him there, to taste his salty flesh. Startled at that thought, her gaze flickered back to his and she saw him watching her with eyes that glittered with sensual heat.

Her blood flowed hotly through her veins and she felt his palm move slowly down her body, tracing the curve of her waist and hips.

Did he realize what he was doing?

For an instant her lungs stopped functioning and the tightness in her chest was almost suffocating. His eyes darkened slightly as his hand shimmered lightly across her stomach, her abdomen, then lower.

"Rafe," she groaned.

Something passed between them then, something hot and hungry, something so intimate that it shook her to the core of her being. Just when she thought her thudding heart would burst, Rafe moved his hand upward until it came to rest beneath her breast. Her nipples peaked, aching for his touch, but he made no movement whatsoever, just continued to watch her with his heavy-lidded gaze.

Feeling completely dazed, her insides quivering, Jessie found herself smoothing her palms across his wide chest, plucking occasionally at the wiry curls that covered his muscular flesh.

Rafe felt her caress all the way to his toes. His heart was thudding so heavily beneath the palm of her hand that she must be aware of it. Did she know what she was doing to him? Was she aware that his breeches were stretched taut across his hard, aching thighs?

He was so tightly strung, like a bowstring about to snap, that he was afraid his self-imposed restraints would snap at any given moment.

Capturing her tormenting fingers in his hand, Rafe placed a quick kiss on her palm. Then, with a quick, controlling shudder, he gripped her waist and set her aside, effectively widening the distance between them.

"You were going to tell me about the nightmare," he said gruffly.

Her cheeks flushed hotly as she realized her emotions had caused her to act with reckless behavior. She lowered her thick lashes to hide her embarrassment. Then, realizing he was waiting for her reply, she said "I'm almost afraid to talk about my dreams."

"Why?"

"Because it makes them seem more real somehow."

"You have nothing to fear, Jessie. I'm here with you."

"Yes," she murmured, peering at him through the fuzzy screen of her lashes. "And you don't know how much that means to me." She cleared her throat. "I really don't understand the dreams myself, Rafe, but I think they have something to do with my past. And when I try to remember them I have the most awful pain stabbing at my temple. It feels like my head is about to explode."

"Do you really believe the nightmare is part of your past?"

"I think so. Maybe."

"You mentioned hearing sounds. Were they the same ones you told Doc Jacob about?"

She nodded. "Yes. The horses and the roaring water."

Feeling a dull pain thudding near her temple, she rubbed it with her fingertips.

Rafe frowned at her. "I think you'd better forget about

your past, Jessie. At least for a while. Your mind's not ready to deal with what happened."

"That's easy for you to say, but you're not the one with no memory. Oh, God, I'm tired. But I'm afraid to sleep." She arched her back, trying to stretch tense muscles, unaware of the way her nipples strained at the worn fabric covering them.

"No." Rafe was aware his voice had deepened, that it had become husky with longing. "I'm not, Jessie. But I've been wishing I could forget some things."

Jessie's gaze flickered up, met Rafe's, and clung. "What things?" she whispered unsteadily.

"I can't forget the way you looked when I undressed you, Jessie."

"Rafe."

Her voice sounded strangled and she reached out a hand as though to ward him off, but he captured it and drew her nearer.

Rafe knew he should release her, yet he could not. To see her lying there, so close, knowing she desired him as he desired her, was too much to resist. He could smell the sweet scent of her, soft, provocative.

"You have a beautiful body, Jessie. A most desirable body."

"You shouldn't say things like that to me, Rafe."

"I know. It's not a gentlemanly thing to do. But then, I've never claimed to be a gentleman."

His gaze was probing, intense, and Jessie felt her breath quicken, her body begin to tremble.

"I want to kiss you, Jessie," he whispered huskily.

Her body tightened in a wildly responsive way and her head tilted back, her lips parting on a trembling breath as she invited his possession.

Suddenly, he closed the distance between them and laid claim to her mouth. She couldn't breathe, couldn't think, as he kissed her with such exquisite gentleness that it bordered on pain.

Then, he broke the kiss suddenly, his breath harsh and raspy. "I shouldn't have done that, Jessie." He clasped her waist and set her away from him. "I need to get out of here before we both do something we'll regret."

"Would we regret it?"

"You're a guest in my house, Jessie. And you're so vulnerable." He raked a hand through his dark hair. "And, dammit, my children are nearby. They could wake up and walk in here at any given moment."

She blushed hotly. "I never thought about . . . I'm sorry, Rafe. I don't know what got into me."

"You have nothing to apologize for," he said grimly. "I'm to blame for what happened."

"No."

Her expression was so tender that Rafe almost embraced her again. "I'd better get out of here," he muttered.

"Please stay awhile, Rafe."

He groaned loudly. "I can't, Jessie. Surely you can see that."

"You could sit in the rocker," she suggested. "I wouldn't touch you . . . or anything." Her lips curled into a wry smile. "I don't like to ask, but I'm afraid to be alone right now. Afraid I'll go back to sleep and dream again."

His frown smoothed out. "We'll talk awhile then." He moved the rocking chair beside the bed. "What do you want to talk about?"

"Anything," she said. "Tell me about yourself, Rafe. I want to know everything about you. Have you always lived here?"

"No. I grew up in East Texas. My parents owned a farm there. It was a small farm. Only a couple of hundred acres, but it brought us a living."

"Are your parents still there, on the farm in East Texas?"

"No. A drought wiped them out. They lost the farm. Pa tried sharecropping then, but he was never the same after he lost the farm. I remember the winter he got sick. It was the coldest winter in over twenty years, so the old-timers claimed. Pa didn't make it through that winter. He caught a cold and just up and died."

"I'm sorry," she murmured.

"Ma moved us to town after the funeral and she took in laundry. I was only a boy, knee-high to a grasshopper, but I could see her wasting away, day by day."

"She died, too?"

He nodded. "Yeah. But I never shed a tear. Not at her grave, nor at Pa's. I guess I thought if I didn't cry, then maybe, somehow, she'd come back."

"How old were you?"

"Seven."

"Seven?" She wondered how a mother could grieve so much for a husband that she would be willing to leave a seven-year-old child behind to fend for himself. "Who raised you then?"

"My aunt and uncle took me in, but it was obvious from the start they considered me a charity case. I was always being told it was their Christian duty." He sighed heavily. "I ran away when I was fourteen and tramped around some, doing odd jobs and such. Then I met Gerta." His voice changed, became soft and tender. "Gerta saw something in me that nobody else had."

"What was she like?"

His lips curled up with a smile so sweet that Jessie thought her heart would break.

"Gerta was like an angel, with a halo of flaxen hair. So gentle and loving. Exactly what an eighteen-year-old boy needed." His fingers were wound together, his gaze fixed on them. "Karin is very much like her mother. She has that dainty, almost fragile look about her. But Gerta's looks were deceiving. That woman had strength. She had enough grit for the both of us. It was her idea for us to leave East Texas, to venture to the hill country where land was still available."

Jessica found herself wanting to change the subject. She didn't want Rafe remembering his angel wife, possibly comparing the two of them and finding Jessie lacking. But how could she get him off the subject without making him aware of her jealousy? Realizing she could not, she covered her mouth, pretending to yawn, then slid back against the pillow. "I think I won't have any trouble sleeping now, Rafe."

As though he'd just been waiting for her permission to leave, he rose to his feet and headed for the door. With his hand on the doorknob, he looked back at her. "Sure you'll be all right now?"

"I'm sure," she mumbled, clutching the cover tightly with tense fingers. "Good night, Rafe."

"Good night, Jessie."

A moment later he was gone.

The smell of strong coffee woke Jessie. Her nostrils flared at the aroma, and she pushed the cover aside and rose from the bed, padding across the room to the wardrobe for her day dress.

Who was up? Was it Karin who'd made the coffee, or had Rafe awakened early?

In the kitchen she found Rafe shaving. He wore no shirt, only pants and boots, and the sight of his hairy chest brought a flood of memories of the night before.

"Good morning," she mumbled, watching as he raised his arm to scrape the lather from his face.

He flicked her a quick glance before returning to his shaving. " 'Morning, Jessie."

Her gaze was riveted on him, and her feet seemed attached to the floor. She should move, she knew, but she couldn't take her eyes off the straight, hard lines of his smooth, dark skin. As she watched, he raised his arm to scrape the lather from his face.

"Just help yourself to the coffee, Jessie."

A deep, rosy stain flushed her cheeks. Did he know how avidly she'd been watching him?

She swallowed hard and forced her gaze away from him. "You're up early this morning," she said, feeling proud that she'd managed to keep her voice steady. "I hope it's not because I disturbed your sleep."

"You did that, all right."

Jessie felt herself flush right down to her toes. But he couldn't know, because he was concentrating on shaving his jaw, a fact for which she was grateful.

Clearing her throat, Jessie crossed the kitchen and opened a cabinet door. "Have you had your coffee?"

"No."

Pulling two mugs from the cabinet, she put them on the table and forced herself to make light conversation. "You're not much for discussion early in the morning, are you?"

"No."

He wiped the remaining lather from his face and turned to face her. Her hair was shining like polished copper in the shaft of sunlight that streamed through the window. He remembered the way it felt against his bare skin, so soft and silky. While he watched, she lifted the coffeepot from the stove and poured hot coffee into the cups. She smiled sweetly as she handed him a cup, then seated herself at the scarred table.

As she sipped her coffee, Jessie watched Rafe from beneath her lashes. He made no attempt to don the shirt hanging over the back of a chair. Instead, he seated himself across from her. The color in her face deepened to a rosy glow and she kept her eyes lowered to hide her thoughts.

He was much too handsome for his own good, utterly devastating to her senses. Her thoughts turned to the night before, when he'd held her to quiet her fears. She was almost certain the feelings he'd aroused were completely unknown to her, yet how could she be certain? She felt a need to know. "I've been meaning to talk to you, but . . ."

An eyebrow raised inquiringly. "But what?"

"The time never seemed right, what with the children always around and everything."

"They're not around right now."

"I know." She raised her coffee cup to her lips to hide her nervousness. Swallowing quickly, she continued, "Things can't go on this way, Rafe. I have to do something."

"What way?"

"You know." He was deliberately being obtuse. "I'm here in your house, taking your bed while you sleep with your son and . . ."

"Are you suggesting we share the bed?"

"You know I'm not!"

"Do I?"

His gaze dropped and touched on her breasts. It was as though his hands were on her and she could feel her nipples tighten, feel a warmth focus between her thighs.

"Don't tease me like that," she whispered.

"Are you so sure I'm teasing?"

"Rafe, please."

He tensed, his gaze dropped, and his hands clenched around his cup. When his eyes met hers again, they were cool. "Sorry. But you're so easy to tease that I couldn't resist."

She relaxed slightly. "I've always been that way."

His eyebrow rose questioningly. "You have?"

"Yes. My brother used to tease—" She broke off and stared at him, wide-eyed. "I have a brother!"

He leaned toward her and clasped her hand. "Doc hoped this would happen. He said it might, that your memory could just return without you being aware of it. What else do you remember?"

"Nothing," she said, and her eyes filled with tears. "Just that. I saw a face and knew it was my brother."

"What did he look like?"

"I don't know. He was there for only a moment, then as quickly gone."

"Close your eyes and try to get a picture of him in your mind, Jessie. What color was his hair?"

"I don't know."

"Was it red like yours?"

"My hair is not red."

"Never mind that. Think about him. About your brother's hair color. Was it red, black, brown, blond? How old is he? What did you call him?"

"I don't know!" she cried.

"Easy." He squeezed her hand lightly. "It will come back to you. Don't push it and you'll remember more."

"I'm not so sure, Rafe."

"Was this memory like the one before? Did it come with the sounds that frightened you?"

"No. It was different." She frowned heavily. "His face was clear, and then it was gone, as though it had never been. And there was nothing in the memory to cause me pain. My head doesn't ache like it usually does."

"That might mean you're on the point of recovering your memory. Maybe we'll soon know who you are."

"Maybe." But did she really want to know?

"I'm going into Castle Rock this morning, Jessie. I thought I would talk to the sheriff, have him put out some feelers, send some wires to nearby towns on your behalf."

She lowered her head. "That's a good idea. I've imposed on your hospitality long enough."

"You're not imposing. You more than pull your weight around here. The house sparkles since you've come. And meals aren't the same anymore." He sighed heavily. "There was too much work here for Karin to cope with alone. I don't know why I didn't see it before."

"It's not your fault, Rafe. You have so much to do yourself."

"Nevertheless I should have thought of it. The kids are so young and yet they seem to have left their childhood behind. I don't know when it happened. I guess when we lost Gerta. I was so caught up in my own grief that I didn't see what was happening to them."

"You need a woman in your life, Rafe. A mother for your children, a helpmate for yourself. A wife." *Someone like me,* her heart cried.

"I know." He raked a frustrated hand through his dark hair and met her eyes briefly before returning his gaze to his coffee cup. "But it's hard to think about marrying again, Jessie. Gerta and I had something special between us, and it would be hard to settle for anything less. Besides that . . ."—he sighed heavily—". . . there never seems to be enough time for the things that need doing around here, much less courting a lady, something I'd have to do before she'd consent to marry me. There's always fields to plant, stock to tend, and fences to mend, not to mention repairs to the house and barn. There's never enough time for chores, let alone looking for a wife."

Jessie couldn't help but be glad it was so. The thought of Rafe sleeping in the bed she now occupied with another woman caused an ache in the region of her heart.

Rafe sighed again. "Speaking of chores, I hear old Bessie bawling. She needs milking before I put the calf to her." He drained his coffee cup and scraped back his chair. "I'll

get on that while you start breakfast." He eyed her severely.
"And no more talk about leaving before your memory
comes back. You're doing more than your share around
here. In fact, it's going to be hard to do without you when
you leave."

As Jessie watched Rafe exit through the kitchen door,
she wished that she'd never have to leave, but she knew it
was a foolish thought. She couldn't expect him to give her
a permanent home. Anyway, there might be someone out
there, somewhere, who was waiting for her to return. Someone who loved her. The brother, perhaps, but somehow,
something told her that wasn't so. Thoughts of her brother
had been warm, loving, but when she thought about going
home, her feelings were different. She felt frightened, terrified of the unknown.

Why should that be so?

She was pulled out of her thoughts by a stirring in the
girls' bedroom and soon Karin joined her in the kitchen.
The girl stopped short when she saw Jessie seated at the
table. "I thought I heard Pa's voice."

"He was here a minute ago." Jessie picked up the coffee
mugs and carried them to the sink. "He's gone out to start
the chores. I'll make breakfast if you'd like to sleep a while
longer."

Karin shook her head. "I'm already up. You're probably
tired since you had a bad night."

"A little. But there's no way I could go back to sleep."

They worked together in companionable silence and by
the time Rafe had finished milking, breakfast was ready to
put on the table.

"Is Danny up yet?" Rafe asked.

"I am now," Danny mumbled, entering the kitchen.
"What was all that noise last night?"

Rafe and Jessie exchanged glances.

"What noise?" Rafe asked.

"Thought I heard somebody screaming."

"Jessie had a nightmare."

"Oh, really?" Danny's gaze was questioning as he slid his chair from beneath the table. "What was the nightmare about, Jessie? Did you dream of monsters?"

"Wash up before you sit down to breakfast, Danny."

Rafe's words were as sharp as the glance he threw quickly at Jessie. She mouthed a silent "thank you" and he gave a quick nod of acknowledgment. And by the time Danny finished washing, he had completely forgotten his questions, a fact that Jessie was grateful for.

Chapter Eight

As they began the daily chores, Jessie realized the laundry basket was overflowing. After she consulted with Karin they decided it was time to do the family wash. Jessie helped the girl fill the big cast-iron pot that was used to boil white clothes and sheets. Then she built a fire beneath the pot to heat water and went inside the house to strip sheets from the beds.

Jessie's movements were automatic, and her thoughts turned to Rafe and his obvious need for a woman around the house. Although he claimed there was no time to search for a wife, Jessie knew he wouldn't have to look far to find one. Corabelle Jones had made it plain enough that she'd be happy to fill that role, had even insinuated she was already engaged to Rafe, when she'd said there was an "understanding" between them. And yet, Jessie knew it could not be so. She had never seen Rafe look at the woman in the same way he'd looked at her, with that hot, heavy-lidded gaze.

Yet neither had he seemed aware that Jessie might be able, and more than willing, to fill that role in his life. The mere thought thrilled her. To be a mother to his children, a wife to him, would be Heaven on earth.

Had his reaction to her the night before merely been the way any man would have reacted in similar circumstances? She blushed at the thought. She'd been so eager for his touch with never a thought to hide her feelings. If Rafe hadn't pulled away from her they would almost certainly have made love.

How could she have allowed such a thing to happen? She was almost certain she wasn't usually so forward, so free with her favors.

"Are you finished, Jessie?"

Karin's voice jerked Jessie's thoughts back to the present and she smiled at the young girl in the doorway, her arms piled high with dirty laundry. "Almost done." Jessie yanked the pillowcase off a feather pillow and tossed it toward the growing pile of laundry on the floor. "Is Sissy still asleep?"

"No. She's in the parlor playing with Muffy." Muffy was the big tabby cat that lived in the barn. The cat had birthed a litter of kittens two weeks ago, but they had yet to find where she'd hidden them. "I told Sissy I would make her oatmeal soon as the laundry was boiling."

"You go ahead and tend to Sissy while I put the sheets on to boil." Jessie was familiar with the chore, as she'd been with cooking, which probably meant she hadn't come from a monied family.

She smiled at that thought; then her smile faded as she remembered her fear of the past. What could be causing it?

Pushing the fear away, she tried to concentrate on the here and now and this family that she found herself among. If only she could begin her life anew, could start it right now, forget what had come before. But, of course, that was impossible. Events from the past had a way of affecting the future. Old fears—old enemies—could suddenly appear and wreak havoc with her life.

Enemies. Now why should she think of enemies? Had she left enemies behind? Was that the reason for her fear, her abject terror? And would those enemies, if they were suddenly to appear, threaten the family who had come to mean so much to her?

Jessie was still turning the matter over in her mind when Rafe and Danny arrived for their midday meal. Karin had cooked a pot of red beans and baked two pans of cornbread. With apple pie for dessert, it was a meal to be complimented.

Which the menfolk did, around mouthfuls of food. They were lingering at the table while Rafe sipped a second cup of coffee when they heard the sound of a horse being ridden hard.

"Rider coming in fast." Rafe's chair scraped against the wooden floor as he rose quickly and crossed to the kitchen window. "Don't recognize him," he muttered. "Must be a stranger to these parts."

Jessie's mouth dried and the acid taste of her own fear clogged her throat, sickening her. She felt her color drain away as she stood quickly. Why would a stranger come here? It was an unusual occurrence, something that had never happened since she arrived. She fought the urge to run, forcing herself to remain where she was, frozen to a spot beside the kitchen table.

The hoofbeats neared, pounding against the packed dirt in the yard. She heard the sound of creaking leather, the jingle of a bridle. Rafe's hand was on the door, pushing it wide.

No! her mind screamed. *Don't go out there!*

As Rafe's boots slapped against the wooden porch, Jessie was aware of the sound of male voices coming from the yard, but they were too far away for her to understand what they were saying. She waited there, breath bated, a hard knot of fear lodged in her throat until Rafe entered the house again.

"Who is it, Pa?" Danny asked.

"Nobody we know, son." Rafe jerked his hat off the hatrack and jammed it on his head. "Somebody just riding through that's run into trouble."

Jessie forced her legs to move, to carry her to the window. The man was tall and slim, with black hair floating about his narrow shoulders. The beard that covered most of his face was neatly trimmed. He appeared harmless enough. As she made that observation, she felt the fear receding, her muscles slowly relaxing.

Karin joined Jessie at the window, peering over her shoulder. "What does he want, Pa?"

"Says his partner's pinned under their carriage. I'm going to help lift the buggy off. Might be a good idea for you to fetch Doc from town, Danny. There's no telling what kind of injuries he'll have."

"Sure, Pa." Danny plucked his own hat from the hatrack, set it atop his head, and tugged the brim down. "I'll have Doc Jacob there before you can say 'jackrabbit.'"

Jessie felt unaccountably nervous while she waited for the menfolk to return. Several hours passed before Rafe rode in with Jacob Lassiter in tow. She was gathering clothes off the line when Rafe stopped beside her. "Got any coffee left, Jessie?"

"There's some on the back of the stove." She stooped to pick up the basket of clean laundry, but Rafe stopped her.

"I'll carry it for you."

Hurrying into the house, Jessie poured the coffee for the two men, then threw a quick smile at the doctor. "I haven't seen you around here for a while."

"No," he replied, pulling out a chair and straddling it. Propping his elbows on the back, he grinned at her. "I kept waiting for someone to get sick out here so I would have an excuse for seeing you again, but everyone's too healthy."

Jessie flushed at his teasing, aware that Rafe was watching them closely. She handed coffee around, then seated herself across the table from the doctor. "Surely you don't have to wait until someone's sick to visit. We'd love to see you any time." She glanced quickly at Rafe, wondering if he'd think she'd overstepped her bounds, inviting a guest to his home. Although he was unsmiling, his voice was cordial enough when he added his invitation to hers.

"Jessie's right, Doc. You're welcome here any time."

"Then I won't be a stranger."

Jessie felt warmed by the look in the doctor's eyes. "How did you find your patient, Dr. Lassiter?"

"Fair to middlin'," he replied. "He cracked several ribs and sprained an ankle, but it could have been worse. He could have broken his neck." He gave her a warm look. "By the way, don't you think it's time you called me Jacob?"

A blush swept over her cheeks. The doctor was certainly at his most charming today. "If you think so . . . Jacob."

"I do think so." He held her gaze as he reached out a hand and covered hers where it lay on the table. "I think it would be proper for a couple who are stepping out to call each other by their first names."

She lowered her eyes and peeked at him from beneath her lashes. It was obvious he was flirting with her. "Stepping out together? Are we doing that?"

"Not yet. But that's my intention."

"It is?" Jessie was aware of Rafe's gaze flickering between the doctor and herself, and for some reason, the thought of him watching made her smile at the doctor that much sweeter.

"Jessie . . . I've been meaning to . . ."

Before Jacob could complete the sentence, Rafe cleared his throat, capturing their attention. "I've been meaning to talk to you about Jessie, Doc. She's been having nightmares. They keep her awake at night."

Jacob straightened his body, his gaze becoming completely professional as he studied Jessie. A quick frown pulled his brows together. "Why didn't you tell me, Jessie? I have some powders that might help."

"I'd rather not use powders to sleep."

Jacob leaned forward in his chair. "What are the nightmares about?"

"They're not clear enough for me to remember."

"Your mind may be trying to prepare you for your past."

"I thought about that," she admitted. "But if that's true, then there's something awfully frightening in my past. I'm not so sure I want to remember what it is."

"Hmmmm."

Jacob rubbed Jessie's knuckles with his thumb and, although Rafe felt the action was completely unconscious, he couldn't control the jealousy that swept through him.

The doctor's attention was still on Jessie. "Is it sounds you're remembering, Jessie? Or do you remember faces as well?"

"I think I saw my brother's face."

"You did? That's good, Jessie. You're sure the face you saw was your brother?"

"No. Not completely sure. But I think it was."

"Can you describe him?"

"No. Rafe asked me that last night—I woke him up when I screamed—but I couldn't remember his features. Just a feeling . . ."

Jacob Lassiter's gaze swept to Rafe. "You saw her soon after it happened?"

"Immediately after," Rafe replied. "I sleep with my son and there is only a thin wall between the bedrooms."

"I see. She could recall nothing of his features?"

Rafe shook his head. "Nothing."

"Too bad," Lassiter replied thoughtfully. "I'd hoped you'd discovered something while it was fresh in her mind." He shrugged, still playing with Jessie's fingers. "I wouldn't worry overmuch about it." He squeezed her hand. "The memories come easier if you don't force them. You need to relax more, Jessie. Did you hear about the barn raising on Saturday?"

She shook her head.

"There'll be a dance afterwards." He smiled at her. "There'll be folks coming from miles around. I'd be honored if you'd go with me."

Rafe interrupted quickly. "She'll be going with us, Doc. We have to be there early since we're helping to raise the barn."

"We are?" Jessie queried. This was the first she'd heard of it.

"Yes. We are." Rafe's eyes were cold, his jaw clenched. "I hate to deprive you of the good doctor's company, but I volunteered you and Karin to bring food for the midday meal."

"What kind of food?"

"Eating food." His voice was an angry growl, and a muscle jerked in his jaw. "Side dishes, Jessie. Cookies. Pies. Cakes. I was going to tell you before but I completely forgot about it."

She narrowed her eyes and her lips flattened with annoyance. "I wish you'd told me earlier. I'll need some things from the store before I can do all that baking."

"Make a list and Danny can fetch what you need."

Appearing extremely disappointed, Jacob Lassiter shoved back his chair. "I'm sorry we can't go together,

Jessie. But at least we'll see each other there." He smiled gently at her. "You'll save a dance for me, won't you? In fact, put me down for several."

"She'll put you down for one dance, Doc," Rafe said firmly. "Just one, though. It wouldn't be right to monopolize her time."

Lassiter gave Rafe a long look. "No," he finally said, "I guess it wouldn't be right for any of us to do that. Would it?"

The two men went outside together. Just before Lassiter mounted, he turned to Rafe. "Why do I feel like I've been warned off Jessie? Is that what you're doing, Rafe?"

Rafe held the other man's gaze with a measured look. "Jessie's not ready for courting, Doc. You oughtta know that better than anyone. She'd best be left alone until she recovers her memory."

"And what if she never remembers, Rafe? Do you expect her to suspend her life, to go on waiting for memories that may never return?"

"Time enough to worry about that later."

"Are you interested in her, Rafe? If you are, just say so and I'll back off."

"You'll back off anyway, Doc. At least for now, until Jessie shows she's ready for courting." *And when she's ready, then I'll be there first.*

It was with no small amount of relief that Rafe watched the doctor ride away. Then he returned to his work, satisfied that he'd stopped the doctor from pressuring Jessie to accept his attentions.

Jessie, unaware of the men's conversation, sorted through their supplies and made out a list for Danny. When he was on his way, she looked through Gerta's cookbook. There was a cake recipe that looked interesting and could be baked several days early. Realizing the recipe required more eggs than she had on hand, Jessie scooped up the basket and hurried toward the henhouse.

Halfway to the henhouse, she heard a loud wailing that stopped her in her tracks. The sound came from the barn. Was Sissy making that noise? If so, she must be hurt badly.

She hurried into the barn. "Sissy? Where are you, sweetie pie?"

The wailing was louder, looming somewhere above her. "Sissy?" Jessie looked toward the hayloft. The sound appeared to be coming from there.

Upon spying the ladder on the floor, she realized Sissy must have climbed to the loft and, somehow, the ladder was dislodged, trapping her there.

But why wasn't she answering? "Sissy? Are you up there, sweetie?"

The wailing became louder and Jessie, unable to stand the thought of the toddler's fear, tossed the egg basket aside, leaned the ladder against the hayloft, and climbed quickly.

"Sissy?" Jessie's fear for the child was a tangible thing. "Where are you, honey?"

There was no reply except the wailing sound that continued to undulate endlessly. As she left the ladder and searched through the bales of hay, she became aware the sound was not human. A moment later she found Muffy, crying piteously as she tried to pull one of her kittens from beneath a bale of hay that held it trapped.

Relief swept through her that she'd found the cat instead of the child. Then, as the cat continued its pitiful wail, Jessie stooped over the creature. "Oh, Muffy. Is your kitty trapped? Hold on a moment and I'll get it for you."

Jessie wrapped her arms around the bale, but found it too heavy to move. The cat continued to wail out its fear, and Jessie worked harder, trying to lift the bale of hay, but no matter how much strength she expended, it refused to budge.

Deciding she would have to find another way, Jessie looked the situation over. The bale of hay was near the edge of the loft, too close for her to push from that side. And if she pushed from either left or right the kitten would be crushed for sure. That left only one direction. She stooped behind the bale, put her hands beneath it, and with a lifting, shoving motion, she pushed with all her strength. The bale shifted slightly, then moved forward. Jessie shoved harder and the bale of hay jerked, then slid over the edge of the loft. Jessie was caught in mid-shove. She lost her balance and followed the bale of hay, dropping quickly to the floor below where she landed with a heavy thud.

Silence settled around Jessie as she struggled to regain her breath. Dried hay poked painfully at her flesh and dust filled her nostrils. But at least the cat had stopped wailing.

Using her right hand to push herself to her elbows, Jessie spread her left palm against the floor to keep herself upright and felt an immediate jolt of pain streak through her wrist.

"Oh, God," she groaned. "What have I done now?"

She lifted her arm and studied the wrist that had already begun to swell. "It's not like I don't already have enough troubles," she muttered, glaring at the injured joint.

Favoring the one hand, she pushed herself to her feet and picked up the egg basket. The eggs would have to wait until she examined the wrist in a brighter light.

She was in the kitchen, doing just that, when Karin came in with Sissy straddling her hip. "Me and Sissy picked you some flowers, Jessie," Karin said, holding out a bouquet of daisies. "Where do you—what's the matter? What did you do to your wrist?"

"I think I sprained it."

"How did you do that?"

"You hurted, Jessie?" Sissy asked.

"Just a little, honey." Jessie explained what had happened, then grimaced wryly. "Please don't say anything to your father, Karin. I think he is already annoyed with me."

"He is? Whatever for?"

"Never mind." How could she explain to Rafe's daughter that she had deliberately provoked him by flirting with the doctor? "But let's keep this to ourselves, okay?"

"It depends on how bad you're hurt, Jessie. You might need a doctor." She looked at Jessie's wrist. "It's swelling real fast."

"I know. I'll soak it in cool water and wrap it tight for awhile. That should take care of it."

Sissy wriggled to be free and Karin set her on her feet, then went to find an old sheet they could use for a bandage. The toddler went off to play while Karin worked over Jessie's wrist, wrapping it securely. Then Jessie pulled her long sleeve over the bandage so it wouldn't be noticeable and continued her efforts to make the special cake.

That evening, Rafe chided her about encouraging the doctor's attention when there might be someone special in her past. "It wouldn't be right to get his hopes up," he said.

Jessie knew he was right.

As she lifted her hand to brush a curl from her face, her sleeve rode up and exposed the bandage on her wrist.

Rafe's expression became concerned. "What happened to your wrist, Jessie?"

"It's nothing," she said quickly. "Just a small bruise."

"Let me see." He reached across the table and unwrapped her wrist, gently but firmly turning her arm so the deep purple of the bruise was visible.

His intake of breath was audible.

"It's not as bad as it looks," she muttered, pulling away from him. He let go immediately, as though afraid of causing her pain.

Later, he followed her to the porch.

She looks so lovely there with her hair loosened around her shoulders. He stood beside the rocker where she sat, the sweet scent of her drifting into his nostrils, making his head spin.

He caught her slender hand in his fingers and held it gently while his narrowed eyes studied her uplifted face. His jaw clenched, and suddenly he turned his head and, pulling her hand up, pressed his mouth to the bruise.

Jessie's eyes widened as she stared up at Rafe. The feel of his mouth disconcerted her. Her lips parted breathlessly as she met his eyes, and the touch of his mouth on her skin made her innards tremble violently.

Her heart was throbbing. Rafe could see the pulse at the side of her throat, see the lace jumping as she breathed.

Incredible, that a woman so lovely could find him disturbing. It was no act, either. She was all but trembling from just this light touch. His eyes fell to her soft mouth, and he had to fight to keep from pulling her against him.

The look in his eyes made Jessie's breath quicken, caused butterflies to swarm inside her stomach. Her gaze dropped to his chest and that made it worse. His shirt was open, and her eyes lingered on the thick mat of black hair. She remembered the faintly rough feel of it against her soft skin when he'd come to her bed last night.

Oh, God! Just the thought of it caused her cheeks to become hot, caused her breath to jerk as though she'd been running a foot race.

Rafe saw Jessie's reaction and it made his body go taut. He imagined how it might be to have her bare breasts pressed against his flesh and his pulse began to beat a rapid tattoo at his temples.

"Jessie," he said huskily and pressed his mouth to her soft palm.

His eyes closed as he savored the faint scent of her and he knew that she was as helpless as he was. His own vulnerability made him angry even as it stirred his senses to their limit. He realized he should release her and yet he could not. Instead, his teeth nipped at the skin on the heel of her palm, and he opened his eyes and looked down into hers to watch her reaction.

She was stunned by the sensation the rough caress produced in her body. She knew that her eyes betrayed her by mirroring everything she felt and she made a soft sound of protest deep in her throat.

A wail sounded, reminding Jessie of the cat in the barn. It was followed by voices and the sound of the screen door slamming open.

Jessie looked around to see Karin pushing through the screen door with Sissy in her arms.

The toddler's face was scrunched up and she held her chubby arms toward Jessie.

"Jessie," she cried in a tear-filled voice. Her nightgown was rumpled, her eyelashes damp, and her golden curls framed a woeful face. "Jessie."

"What is it, sweetheart?" Jessie was on her feet and at Karin's side in a heartbeat, scooping the toddler into her arms.

"Me hurted," Sissy said in a wobbling voice.

"She fell off the bed," Karin explained quickly, as though fearing she would be blamed for the mishap. "She was bouncing on the bed, and I've told her so many times not to . . ."

"Don't blame yourself, Karin," Jessie said quickly. "You can't be with her every minute."

As though feeling her older sister was getting all the

sympathy, Sissy uttered a high-pitched wail and tears flooded her cheeks. "Me hurted!" she cried.

"I'm so sorry, sweetie pie," Jessie soothed. "Where does it hurt?"

"Here." The toddler's lips quivered and she raised her arm and pointed to a red spot. "It hurts, Jessie," she complained.

Jessie kissed the spot and smiled sweetly at the toddler. "There. Is that better, sweet pea?"

"Uh-huh," Sissy murmured. Then, releasing a shuddering breath, she leaned her golden curls against Jessie's breast and closed her eyes.

Karin was still hovering nearby. "Do you want me to take her back inside, Jessie?"

"No, sweetie," Jessie said. "She's settling down here. Why don't you just leave her with me and I'll rock her to sleep?"

"Okay. I'll turn down her bed so you can put her down without any trouble."

Jessie settled back in the rocker with the toddler, then shifted the child's weight until she was snuggled close against her breast.

Rafe watched the two of them, looking so much like mother and child. Jessie would be a good mother, he realized. And the children were becoming so attached to her that it would be hard on them when she left. The thought of her leaving was untenable, somehow too unbearable even to contemplate.

But he must face the thought that she might one day leave them, unless he could find a way to bind her to them before her memory returned.

Chapter Nine

As the hot Texas sun beat down on the hill country the women on the Sutherland farm labored in an equally hot kitchen preparing food for the barn raising. By late afternoon, when the menfolk made their way home, two cakes and five pies were cooling on a shelf along with two batches of oatmeal cookies. A large batch of sourdough bread was rising in a wooden bowl, while several pans from another batch were baking.

Bending over the oven, Jessie slid a pan of bread from the oven and set it on the table. Then, wiping sweat from her brow, she arched her tired back muscles. "What I wouldn't give for a cold bath," she said.

Karin was busy pumping water into the sink, but she spared Jessie a rueful smile. "Me, too." Then, her smile suddenly widened. "Let's do it, Jessie. I know where there's a perfect swimming hole. You know where the creek joins the river?"

"Yes." Jessie shoved back a damp curl that had escaped

the confines of her bun. "But the water is so deep there, Karin. We couldn't take Sissy with us."

The toddler, who had been playing with her doll on the floor, made it apparent she was listening. "I wants to go."

"You can go, Sissy." Karin looked at Jessie again. "The swimming hole isn't on the river, Jessie. It's on the creek. Just a short distance from where it joins the river there's a waterfall. Under the waterfall is a deep hole that's only ten feet wide or so and nearby, there's a shallow pool where Sissy can play." She looked at the toddler again. "Do you remember, Sissy? We went there last summer. We took you in the cave we found there."

"A cave?" Jessie asked.

"Yes. And it's not just a small one, either. Danny went exploring there one day and he said the cave was real deep. That it went way back into the mountain. Someday I want to explore it, too." Her voice became wistful. "If I ever have time."

Jessie frowned at her. "A place like that could be dangerous, Karin. You shouldn't go there alone. Neither should Danny."

"That's what Pa said. It's the reason Danny hasn't gone back yet. But he will one day. Just as sure as I'm standing here, I know he's going back. He's certain-positive outlaws used the cave to stash away their loot."

"Why does he believe that? Has he found something there?"

"No. But he said the way it's hidden and all, it would make a perfect hiding place. The entrance is low, not more than four feet high, and it's completely covered by a cedar bush."

"I wants to go!" Sissy said again.

Heavy boots thudded against the porch, capturing the toddler's attention. "Poppa!" she cried, leaving her doll on the floor while she hurried to the kitchen door. "Poppa's home."

Jessie gave Karin a rueful smile. "Looks like it's too late for that swim. But maybe after supper's over we can go."

Scooping his youngest daughter up, Rafe entered the kitchen and sniffed appreciatively. "Smells like somebody made fresh bread." His dark brow lifted slightly. "Was it you, Karin?"

"No, it was Jessie."

"They smell delicious." Rafe's gaze swept over the pans of golden-brown bread. "And look perfect. I can hardly wait to taste them."

Jessie blushed rosily, and determined right then to hide the pan she had burned.

"There's cookies, too," Karin said. "And apple pies."

"My, my. The two of you have been mighty busy today."

"I'll taste the rolls for you, Pa," Danny said quickly, reaching to snatch one from a baking sheet.

"Danny, stop that!" Karin ordered. "Those are for the barn raising."

Danny's jaw sagged and he stared at her with consternation. "All of them? I see five pans already baked and more on the counter still rising. And I betcha there's some in the oven, too. You must have enough there to feed an army, and you're tellin' me that we can't eat none?"

"Danny's right, Karin." Jessie pushed a damp curl behind her ear. "There's more than enough rolls here for our meal." She smiled at the boy, who was happily munching on the bread, and added, "And if Danny consumes every one of them, we can always bake more tomorrow."

Karin groaned aloud. "You shouldn't have said that, Jessie."

"Why not?"

"You just gave him permission to gorge himself. More'n likely we'll have to roll him away from the supper table."

Jessie threw back her head and laughed, the sound tinkling like crystal chimes in a gentle breeze. And when the sound drifted away, she became aware of the silence around her. It was absolute. Everyone stood motionless, as though frozen in time, their eyes fixed on her.

She raised an auburn brow and her gaze flickered from one face to another, finally stopping on Rafe. "Why is everyone staring at me?"

"That's the first time we've heard you laugh."

"Oh, but surely . . ."

Karin, apparently determined to cover an awkward moment, clapped her hands sharply. "Everybody clear the kitchen while we get supper on the table."

Danny frowned at his sister. "Why should we leave the kitchen?"

"Because you're in the way, dummy. Besides that, you have to wash up."

"I can do that in here."

"You could set the table, too," she said grimly. "And you will if you don't leave."

"You're gettin' mighty big for your breeches, Karin." Danny glared at his sister. "Telling me I can't eat the bread that's cooked in our own kitchen when Jessie made enough to feed an army."

"More'n likely there'll be enough people there to make an army," Karin replied.

"They won't neither. They'll only be a few neighbors there at supper. The rest won't come to work—they'll just be there for the party."

Jessie wondered why Rafe didn't put a stop to the argument between his two oldest children. He had seated himself at the table and was still watching her, albeit surreptitiously.

"Don't you remember what Mr. Getty's barn raising was like?" Karin asked her brother. "There were people crawling all over his place. Hardly nowhere a body could go to be private."

Danny's lips curled in a mischievous grin. "That didn't keep people from looking though, did it? I saw you and Johnny Walker behind the house an' he was—"

"You shut up!" Karin hissed, her cheeks splotching with sudden color and eyes flaring with rage. "Don't you dare say another word about him!"

Rafe had been watching Jessie, but the argument between brother and sister had become so angry that it drew his attention.

"Hey, you two. What's this all about, anyway?"

Karin's eyes flashed warning signals at her brother, promising dire retribution if he said another word. He shrugged. "Ask her."

Rafe frowned at his daughter. "Karin?"

Karin stood silent, every line of her body tense. Her lips were pressed tightly together, her hands curled into tight fists.

Obviously deciding he'd get nothing from his daughter, Rafe looked at his son again. "Danny? I want an answer. What were you and Karin arguing about?"

Danny threw his sister an apologetic look. "Johnny Walker," he mumbled.

"Johnny Walker?" Rafe studied his oldest daughter's flushed face, then looked at his son again. "What does the Walker boy have to do with Karin?"

Danny's jaw clenched and he hung his head. "I won't say no more, Pa. You can take me to the barn and wallop me if you've a mind to, but it won't make me say nothing else." He met his sister's eyes and swallowed hard as though something was stuck in his throat. "I already done enough damage," he muttered.

"What in hell is going on here?" Rafe demanded angrily. "I've never seen the two of you act like this before." He lifted his daughter's face and forced her to meet his eyes. "I want the truth, Karin. What does the Walker boy have to do with you?"

"Pa, please." Tears misted Karin's eyes and her lips quivered. "Don't make me say."

His mouth tightened grimly. "I won't leave this alone, Karin. You'll tell me, one way or another. If that boy has been fooling around with you . . ."

Jessie couldn't stand it anymore. "Rafe, please don't . . ."

"Stay out of this, Jessie!" he said sharply. "This is none of your business!"

His words cut Jessie to the quick and her hurt erupted in anger. "Fine!" she snapped, tossing the cuptowel she'd been using for a hotpad onto the counter. "I'll just get out of your way so you can browbeat your children without interference."

Sissy, who had gone back to playing with her doll on the kitchen floor, suddenly made her presence known by scrunching up her face and uttering a loud, frightened wail.

Detouring around Rafe and his two older children, Jessie bent over and gathered the toddler into her arms and stomped out of the kitchen.

The silence left behind was a tangible thing. Rafe looked at his son, so young yet bravely defiant, and his daughter, barely holding back her tears, and uttered a heavy sigh.

"Come here, Pumpkin," he ordered, holding out his arms.

With a cry, she ran into his embrace, wrapping her arms around him and pressing her face against his chest.

"I'm sorry, honey." He smoothed her flaxen hair. "I don't know what got into me. I guess it was the thought of losing my little girl . . ." He gave a shaky laugh. "You're growing up way too fast." Looking over his daughter's shoulder, he met his son's gaze and offered him a silent apology.

Danny nodded his head to show he understood, then left father and daughter alone.

Tipping Karin's chin up, Rafe met her gaze. "Am I forgiven?"

She nodded her head and wiped the tears away with the back of her hand. "Uh-huh."

He released her. "Then I'd better go make my peace with Jessie."

Tears stung Jessie's eyes as she strode quickly toward the corrals, putting as much distance between herself and the house as possible.

Sissy shifted positions, snuggling her golden curls in the curve of Jessie's shoulder, then tilting her face so she could look up at the woman who carried her. "Jessie mad at Poppa?"

The tears Jessie had been keeping at bay spilled over and flooded her cheeks. Her shoulders shuddered with sobs that she tried hard to control, knowing that she was only adding to the toddler's distress.

Patting her cheek, the toddler said, "Don't cry, Jessie. Don't cry. Poppa kiss it better."

"Jessie."

One word, just her name. But it was spoken with such abject tenderness that Jessie thought her heart would break. As Rafe's arms curled around her waist, she couldn't stop herself from leaning back against him.

"I'm so sorry," he said gently. "You have every right to be angry with me." His breath whispered across her cheek, sending shivers down her spine. "So did they." He uttered a heavy sigh. "I shouldn't have got so damn mad"—

becoming aware of his youngest daughter's gaze, he quickly corrected himself—"so *darn* mad. But it wasn't really anger. It was fear. She's only thirteen, too young to be interested in boys."

"She's on the verge of being a woman, Rafe."

"But that Walker boy is almost grown. He must be near six feet tall. Dammit! This is too soon!" His gaze swept to the toddler, who was watching him with wide eyes. "I . . . uh, mean *darn* it!"

Pressing a quick kiss on Jessie's earlobe, he whispered, "Forgive me?" At her nod of agreement, he said, "Let's go have supper before Danny eats every one of those rolls."

Rafe needn't have worried. Danny appeared completely subdued during supper and his appetite suffered for it. In fact, none of them, with the exception of Sissy, who ate as though she were starving, had much appetite.

The table was quickly cleared and Danny took himself off to the river with a fishing pole in hand. He was barely out of sight when Karin offered to show Sissy the kittens in the barn.

"Don't let her go into the hayloft, Karin." As soon as Jessie said the words, she wished them unsaid. Rafe had made it plain enough that she was only a guest in his home.

"I won't, Jessie."

Biting her lower lip, Jessie watched Rafe's daughters disappear into the barn. She was aware of Rafe watching her from his place at the kitchen table.

His hand tightened on the coffee cup. "Don't do that, Jessie."

"Do what, Rafe?"

"Don't stop mothering my children."

"I'm not their mother, Rafe. You pointed that out quite effectively."

He rose quickly and his chair turned over with a loud

clatter that startled Jessie. Before she could move, his arms surrounded her, pulling her close against him.

Lifting her head, Jessie met his gaze. His eyes resembled molten steel. Hot, fiery. His head dipped low, his mouth hovering mere inches above hers. She waited breathlessly, knowing that all she had to do was rise to her tiptoes and . . .

The clip-clop of hooves brought Jessie back to reality.

"Somebody coming," Rafe muttered, immediately releasing her. "Sounds like a carriage."

Only then did Jessie hear the sound of wheels mingling with the jingle of a harness. She followed Rafe outside and watched the carriage draw nearer. It looked suspiciously like the one that belonged to Corabelle Jones.

"Oh, no," she groaned aloud, pushing quickly at unruly curls as she attempted to tidy her hair.

"Now what in hell brings Corabelle out here this late in the day?"

Jessie was wondering the same thing. Corabelle's visits were usually earlier in the day, although she'd been conspicuously absent the last two days.

Corabelle hadn't come alone this time. There was another woman in the carriage with her. Although the teacher was hatless, the other woman wore a wide-brimmed hat with flowers nestling on the brim.

After the two women were seated on the porch, Corabelle settled her long, brown skirt around her and tucked a stray curl into the braids she wore around her head. The action made Jessie feel dowdy by comparison, since several of her own wiry curls had escaped the confines of the bun at the nape of her neck.

Corabelle smiled up at Rafe. "You know Lucinda Walters, don't you, Rafe?"

"Yes. We've met." He nodded at the woman. "How are you, Miss Walters?"

"I'm doing well. How are your lovely children?"

Rafe leaned against the porch rail and crossed his arms over his chest. "Just fine. Danny's gone fishing. Karin and Sissy are in the barn playing with the kittens Muffy delivered a few weeks back."

Neither woman had acknowledged Jessie, and Rafe, finding their rudeness unconscionable, quickly brought her into the conversation. "The kittens took to Jessie right away, but they're more wary of the girls, who are trying their best to remedy that." He smiled at Jessie. "Jessie, I don't believe you've met Miss Walters."

"No." Jessie shook her head.

Lucinda acknowledged the introduction with a nod as Corabelle smoothed a hand over her neatly braided hair, then leaned toward Rafe with a smile. "I guess you're wondering why we came so late in the day, Rafe."

"Not at all," he denied politely.

"Well, it is unusual, you must admit. I believe everyone around here is aware of my dislike of being out after sunset. It gets dark so quick, you know. That's the reason I asked Lucinda to accompany me."

"I see." None of that explained her reasons for coming, Rafe knew.

"Anyway, I came about the barn dance on Saturday. You are going, aren't you?"

"Yes. In fact, we're helping raise the barn."

"Oh." Her expression was disappointed. "So I guess you'll be going early then."

"That's right."

She leaned back with a sigh. "I guess I'll have to ride with somebody else then. I was hoping we could go together."

"I'm afraid our buggy will be full anyway." The woman's high-pitched voice was getting on Rafe's nerves.

"But surely Jessie doesn't plan on attending the dance!"

"And why not?"

"Well, I would think with the kind of injury she has that she would want to stay here and rest. Anyway . . ." Her eyelids lowered as though shyly, then swept up to allow her to meet Jessie's gaze. "Oh, dear. I don't know how to put this delicately, but . . . I would hate to see you embarrassed, Jessie."

"Why should she be embarrassed?" Rafe questioned.

"Isn't that just like a man?" Her gaze flickered between the two women before meeting Rafe's. "Just look at her, Rafe. That gown must be twenty years old. Even if it wasn't threadbare it's completely out of fashion. It would be cruel to insist Jessie attend a function where everyone will be dressed in their finest garments."

Jessie blushed hotly, but she managed to hold the other woman's gaze. "My intention is to help the other women," she said stiffly. "And I hardly think my appearance will matter to the workers."

"Oh." Corabelle smiled like the cat who'd just found the bowl of cream. "Then you intend to come back before the dancing starts. In that case, I'm sure Rafe wouldn't mind fetching me from town."

"Jessie won't be coming home until the rest of us do." Rafe's words were clipped, his tone stiff as he held Corabelle's gaze with cold eyes.

"But surely you can't mean to embarrass the poor woman," Corabelle protested. "She wouldn't be comfortable wearing Granny Wyatt's castoff dresses to a party."

"You need not concern yourself with Jessie's appearance, Corabelle. She always manages to look beautiful whatever the occasion. Now . . . if you ladies will excuse me, I have some unfinished work to attend to." He nodded politely at the two women and stalked off toward the corrals.

Corabelle's lips were tight as she watched him leave. The moment Rafe was out of sight, she stood abruptly, shaking the wrinkles from her long skirt, then turned to Lucinda Walters. "It's getting late, Lucinda. I think it's time we went home."

Since Jessie was in complete agreement, she remained silent.

Shortly after the two women left, Rafe saddled up and rode off toward Castle Rock. Jessie wondered why he hadn't told her he was leaving. It was so unlike him. No sooner had the thought occurred than she realized the anger he'd exhibited earlier was also unusual.

Knowing work would help keep her troubled thoughts at bay, Jessie entered the house and gave the kitchen a thorough cleaning. By the time she'd wrung the last drop of water from the mop, the girls had joined her.

As they entered the parlor together, Sissy shivered. "I cold, Jessie," she complained.

"Are you, sweetie pie?"

"Uh-huh."

Pulling the knitted throw off the settee, Jessie wrapped it around the toddler, then built a fire in the fireplace to keep away the cold night air.

The fire was blazing when Danny joined them.

"Did you catch any fish, Danny?" Jessie asked.

"Nah. But that old catfish I've been trying to catch for the last hundred years took my bait every time I threw my line in the river." He sounded completely disgusted. "Don't know why I keep on trying to catch him, neither. I'm beginning to think that old fish is smarter than me."

Karin laughed. "I never thought I'd hear you admit a fish might have more sense than you."

Danny frowned heavily at his older sister. "You know I didn't really mean it, Karin. Ain't no fish alive that's got more brains than me."

"No fish, maybe," Karin teased. "But there's animals that have more brains."

"Ain't neither."

"I'll bet old Bessie has more brains than you."

His eyes narrowed and his hands fisted. "I got more brains than you give me credit for, Karin. Maybe sometimes I don't put 'em to good use, but they're there anyway."

Jessie realized a real argument was about to occur and spoke quickly. "Sissy looks like she's about to fall asleep. I think it's past her bedtime."

Karin was immediately diverted. "You're right, Jessie. I'd better get her to bed."

Lifting the toddler, she left the parlor.

"Thanks, Jessie," Danny said softly.

"For what?"

He ducked his head. "For putting a stop to a stupid argument."

She smiled at him. "You're quite welcome." She was silent for a long moment, then asked, "Danny, do you know where your father went?"

"Said he was going to Castle Rock." He fidgeted for a while, then spoke again. "I didn't mean to get Karin in trouble, Jessie."

"I know, Danny. And you didn't."

"Sure looked like it for a while. I didn't expect Pa to react like that. Anyways, I was just teasing."

"Did you make your apology to Karin?"

"Yeah."

Jessie smiled gently at the boy who had wedged himself firmly in her heart. "Then best leave it alone now."

"Yes'um."

They talked awhile together; then Danny stood and stretched, arching his back. "Guess I'll go on to bed now. Tomorrow's gonna be a long day."

"Good night, Danny."

" 'Night, Jessie."

After Danny retired, silence settled around her. Finding

herself unable to relax, Jessie crossed to the window and stared out into the darkness.

Questions tormented her.

Why had Rafe gone to town so late, something he'd never done before? What business could he possibly have there that he could conduct at night?

Was it business he'd gone for? Or had he gone to see a woman?

Knowing she'd never be able to sleep until he returned, Jessie dug through her basket of darning and found one of Rafe's socks that needed mending. She was threading her needle when he entered the parlor.

"Rafe!" she exclaimed. Her hand went to her throat and her heart skipped a beat. "I didn't hear you come back."

"I walked the horse," he admitted. "Thought you might be asleep and didn't want to disturb you." He tossed a brown paper parcel in her lap.

"What is this, Rafe?"

Although his expression was grim, he appeared embarrassed as well. "It's for you," he muttered.

"For me?" Her fingers fumbled as she opened the package and lifted out a green silk gown decorated with lace of the same color. The color matched her eyes.

"Oh, Rafe. It's a beautiful gown. But you shouldn't have bought this for me."

"I damn well should have! And before that woman had a chance to embarrass you like that." He raked his fingers through his dark hair. "I'm sorry, Jessie. I never even thought about your clothes. I didn't even wonder where you got the ones you wear."

Karin came into the room at that moment. "Sissy's asleep, Jessie, and when—Pa! I didn't hear you come—" She stopped abruptly as she saw the dress in Jessie's lap. "Oh, my goodness!" she exclaimed, bending over Jessie to finger the soft fabric. "It's beautiful, Jessie. Where did you get it?" She looked at her father. "Did you buy the dress for her, Pa?"

"Yes," he muttered. "And there's new dresses for both you and Sissy, too. I left the package on the kitchen table."

Karin squealed with delight and headed for the kitchen.

"Thank you, Rafe," Jessie said softly. "I was going to mention a new dress for her tonight . . . after we'd finished supper, but . . ."

"I know. I messed things up good and proper, didn't I?"

Karin returned, holding a ruffled blue dress against herself. "Look, Jessie. Isn't it the most beautiful dress? And the color matches my eyes." She looked at her father. "I can't believe you bought me a dress, Pa. Thank you!" She flung her arms around his neck and hugged him tight. Then, clutching the dress in her hands, she ran out of the room.

Rafe watched the flames writhe and dance in the fireplace for a long moment. "I've been blind, Jessie. A dress is such a simple thing to make her so happy, and I wouldn't even have bought the damn thing if that Jones woman hadn't come here and taunted you."

"Don't blame yourself, Rafe. You're a good man, a good father to your children."

He laughed harshly. "No, I'm not, Jessie. I don't know a damn thing about raising kids."

"You've done a good job, Rafe. No one could have done more."

Rafe crouched before the fire, stirring the coals with a poker and watching the logs spark and spit. Then he stood and faced her. And when he spoke, his voice was harsh with longing. "I need a wife, Jessie. I didn't know how much until I pulled you out of that river. And the kids need a mother. It's time I faced that, and past time I did something about it."

Jessie swallowed past a lump in her throat as her gaze locked with his. She wished she could be that woman. His wife. A mother to his children. But she was a woman with a forgotten past, a woman who dared not give her heart, lest the giving bring sorrow.

"I know, Rafe."

Rafe felt his gut wrench with pain. It had been so long since he'd made love to a woman, so many years that he'd lived like a monk. But he didn't want just any woman. He wanted Jessie, desired her so much that he ached with the wanting.

Jessie saw the longing in his eyes, and her heart felt as though a giant fist was squeezing it. "Rafe," she said huskily, "I'd give anything to remember my past. To know what I've left behind me."

"I know, Jessie. So would I."

Then, with a look that burned into her soul, Rafe left her alone with her thoughts.

Chapter Ten

The morning sun burst over the horizon, touching the tops of the cedar trees with a bright burst of color as Rafe reined the team of horses up beside the line of carriages left in the Jenkinses' back yard.

"Hey!" Danny exclaimed, his gaze lingering on the carriage beside them. "Ain't that Doc Lassiter's buggy, Pa? I didn't know he'd be here. Did you?"

"No," Rafe replied grimly. "And I'm surprised he found enough time to come."

"Oh, he's got plenty of time. He don't have many patients yet." Danny jumped down from the buggy and went about unhitching the team.

"We'll have to remedy that," Rafe growled.

As Rafe joined the menfolk gathered around a pile of lumber, Jessie turned her attention to the food they'd brought.

"Hey, Jessie!"

Spinning around amidst a flurry of skirts, Jessie saw

Jacob Lassiter approaching. His suit had been replaced by a red-checked shirt and bib overalls.

"How do you like my outfit?" he inquired.

"If you were trying to look like a farmer, then you've succeeded, Jacob. Here, take this." She handed him a box loaded with baked goods, then scooped up two large bowls of cooked vegetables. Eying the house uneasily, she caught her lower lip between her teeth. "I'm afraid I don't know anyone here. Perhaps you can show me where they're putting the food."

"It would be my pleasure, Jessie. And take that frown off your face. I'll stay with you until you become acquainted with the womenfolk."

She smiled up at him. "Thank you. I must admit I'm a little nervous."

"No need to be. Mary Jenkins is a wonderful woman who never met a stranger. And her daughters are just like her. Jewels, every one of them."

After Jessie was introduced to the women, she found herself in complete agreement. Mary Jenkins made her feel welcome the moment they entered the house. By the time they were laying out the noon meal on the makeshift tables, Jessie felt as though she'd known these women all her life.

Mary's people were Comanche, a fact that might have kept her from being accepted by the community had it not been for Al Jenkins's big heart. There were very few people around the area who had not, in some way or another, benefited from his generous nature. It was the reason so many people had come to help build his new barn.

Rachel Jenkins resembled her father, with her brown hair and brown eyes. She was tall and slender, with curves in all the right places. She enjoyed life to the extreme, a fact that was made obvious with almost every breath she took. Laughter was her constant companion and she teased her younger sister, Victoria, unmercifully.

Victoria, on the other hand, was basically shy. She took her looks from her mother, with her black hair, black eyes, high cheekbones, and short stature.

When the men left their work to fill their bellies, Victoria busied herself in the kitchen, away from the crowd.

After the meal was finished, the work on the barn continued. The sound of hammers rang out, mingled with shouts and occasional laughter. By mid-afternoon Jessie watched a wall being raised. Then another one went up, and another until all four walls were standing upright.

The women gossiped in groups until the barn was near completion, then worked together to get the evening meal on the tables. By the time supper was finished the evening guests were arriving. And, at Mary's urging, the ladies who'd helped throughout the day retired upstairs to ready themselves for the dance.

In the bedroom assigned to her, Jessie attended to Sissy, dressing her in the frilly pink dress Rafe had bought her and brushing her silken curls until they resembled a golden halo. She was tying a pink ribbon to one of the curls when Karin entered the room.

"What do you think, Jessie?" She twirled around, her long, blue skirt rustling as it flowed around her ankles.

"You look beautiful, sweetie." Jessie reached out and tugged a long, flaxen curl. "You're growing up fast, Karin. I predict you're going to leave a lot of broken hearts behind before you find a man to love."

Karin's expression became solemn. "I wish Pa would realize that."

Jessie arched an auburn brow. "What? That you're going to break hearts? I'm sure he does know that, sweetie."

"I wasn't talking about the broken hearts, Jessie." She

caught her lower lip between her teeth. "I just wish he would realize that I'm almost grown. I wish he would . . ."

"He knows, honey." Jessie tucked a curl behind the girl's ear, a caressing gesture. "But you must realize it's hard on your father. He dreads the day he'll lose you to another man."

"Johnny isn't—" The words had barely left her mouth before she clapped her hand over her mouth. Her cheeks became rosy with color.

"Oh, ho, so it's Johnny Walker we're discussing now, is it?" Jessie smiled gently at the girl. "Just go easy, will you, sweetie? Boys are different from girls. Their passions are easily aroused and, sometimes, very hard to subdue."

"I know." Karin flicked her a quick glance, then lowered her eyes to hide her expression. "But Johnny is different. He's not like the other boys who try to steal kisses. I think he likes me a lot, though, even if he does keep his hands to himself."

Jessie wondered how she should react to that comment. This was a rare moment between them, one not to be taken lightly. "Then Johnny Walker hasn't stolen a kiss from you?"

"Only the one time, when Danny saw us behind the barn. And even then Johnny kept his hands to himself. He just leaned over, real quick-like, and gave me a peck on the lips. But it felt real good, Jessie, and my heart almost stopped and I got a funny feeling in my stomach." Her brow furrowed. "Do you know what I mean?"

"Um-hum. I know." Didn't Rafe make her feel the same way, only more so?

Sissy fidgeted on the dresser stool. "I wants down, Jessie."

"I'll take her to Granny Wyatt. She offered to look after the little ones." When the toddler started to protest, Karin quickly said, "Ruthie May is with her, Sissy. Don't you want to play dolls with her?"

"Uh-huh." Sissy slid off the stool, snatched up her rag doll, then held out her hand. "Come on, Karin."

Once she was alone, Jessie hurried to get herself ready for the dance. When she was done, she stared at her reflected image in the mirror, wondering about the woman she saw there. Had she stood like this before, gazing into a mirror before some big event? She couldn't remember doing so. She watched the woman's face, then looked at the gown where the rounded neckline dipped low enough to show off the creamy swell of her breasts. The deep green of her gown matched her eyes and contrasted sharply with russet-colored hair that she had pulled smoothly away from her face into a cluster of curls at the nape of her neck.

She appeared calm, poised, and sophisticated. Everything she was not. Her insides were churning so much that she almost wished she'd begged to be taken home. But she had not. Nor could she now. To do so would spoil the rest of the family's enjoyment.

A knock at the door caught her attention and she turned just as the door opened, allowing Mary Jenkins to enter.

"You look lovely, Jessie," Mary said admiringly. "I'm sure Rafe will consider you well worth waiting for. He's been pacing the parlor for the last half hour."

"I'm ready now." Jessie felt nervous about joining the festivities, yet excited at the thought of dancing with Rafe. She followed Mary downstairs.

Rafe had changed, too. He wore a gray suit with an embroidered vest. When he saw her, he stepped forward and took her hand in his. "You look beautiful, Jessie."

An unexpected warmth suffused her and she lowered her eyelids to hide her expressive eyes. "Thank you," she replied, blushing hotly beneath his gaze.

"Absolutely beautiful," he said, rubbing his knuckles

across her hot cheeks. "Are you ready to join the crowd?" At her nod, he placed her hand on the crook of his elbow and led her toward the newly completed barn.

As they crossed the yard they heard the muffled sounds of boisterous conversation and loud music. Jessie clung tightly to Rafe's arm, trying to alleviate her nervousness.

There was a warm intimacy within the vast confines of the barn, created by the kerosene lanterns hung on nails at intervals around the cavernous structure.

A raised platform had been built earlier in the day and the musicians were tuning their instruments, preparing to liven up the crowd.

As the band began a lively tune, Rafe held out his hand. "Dance with me, Jessie?"

She nodded and put her hand in his. She could feel the tension in him and wondered at the reason. She held herself stiffly in his arms, wanting nothing more than to melt against his strength, but knew she dared not lest she give away her feelings toward him.

"Rafe! Jessie! Over here!"

They looked around to find Corabelle frantically waving her arms above her head.

"Oh, God, no," Rafe groaned.

"We can't just ignore her, Rafe. Everyone is watching."

Reluctantly, Rafe and Jessie joined Corabelle, Lucinda, and the man who stood beside them, a tall man with sable-brown hair that framed an angular face with a cleft chin.

"So this is the lady with no memory," he said, studying Jessie intently.

Rafe introduced them. "Jessie, this is Sheriff Watson. Lucas, this is Jessie."

Jessie smiled at the lawman. "Hello."

Although he had a stubborn jaw, his smile was warm and his brown eyes glittered with humor. "Heard a lot about you, ma'am. Fact is, folks was getting hard up for something to talk about until you come along."

"Come on, Lucas," Rafe said. "You'll give her the wrong idea about us."

Lucas Watson lifted an inquiring brow. "And what wrong idea would that be?"

"She'll think everybody around these parts is gossiping about her."

Lucas winked at Jessie. "That's not a wrong idea, Rafe. Everybody *is* gossiping about her."

"I was afraid they were," Jessie said tightly, feeling her cheeks flush with shame.

"Now, ma'am," he drawled. "All the talk going on ain't nothing to worry your pretty head about. Folks are just naturally curious when a beautiful woman with no memory is fished out of the river. They'll naturally speculate as to where she came from and who she is."

Corabelle moved closer to Rafe, curling her fingers around his forearm. "I'd love to dance, Rafe."

"I'm afraid I had already asked Jessie for this dance, Corabelle. But I'm certain the sheriff would be more than happy to oblige you." Rafe's lips tightened grimly. "Wouldn't you, Lucas?"

"It would be my pleasure." Although the sheriff offered his arm to the teacher, his eyes flashed his displeasure at Rafe.

Jessie's heart skipped a beat as the band played a waltz and Rafe led her onto the crowded dance floor. As he pulled her into his arms, Jessie instinctively placed her palm against his chest. He smiled down at her and she caught her breath.

The small sound caught Rafe's attention and he narrowed his line of vision, tracing a path from her neck to the swell of her bosom.

"Rafe," she whispered. "Don't."

"Don't what?" he muttered, noticing how the gown strained over her nipples.

"Don't look at me that way."

His hand tightened over hers and he urged her closer, lifting his gaze to meet hers. His eyes were hot, like molten steel.

"Please," she whispered, her eyes dark with emotion. "Don't hold me so closely. Everyone is watching."

Immediately, his hold loosened. "Sorry," he apologized gruffly. "I didn't realize."

"I know." And she did know. He was obviously in the grip of some strong emotion and unaware of his actions, of how they would appear to those around them.

"Jessie." His voice grated harshly between them. "We need to talk. There are things I must say, things that need clearing up between us."

"All right, Rafe. We'll talk when we get home."

Home. When had his home become hers? And how long would it remain so? Was that, perhaps, why he wanted to talk to her? Was he going to ask her to leave? That thought was almost more than she could bear.

Suddenly, she couldn't stand being in his arms, couldn't abide his nearness because it made her so aware of how much she would lose when they parted.

She sighed with relief when the dance ended, hoping to find a place where she could be alone with her thoughts.

But it wasn't to be. Jacob Lassiter had been waiting for her.

"Will you dance with me, Jessie?" he asked.

"It would be my pleasure, Jacob." Although she mustered a smile for him, it didn't quite reach her eyes.

Out of the corner of her eye, Jessie watched Rafe approach Rachel. He bowed at the waist, then took her hand and swung her onto the dance floor.

Blinking away her tears, Jessie allowed her gaze to wander around the room. She saw Karin standing beside the door where several teenagers lingered. One boy stood almost a head taller than the others . . . the boy who was bending over to hear what Karin was saying.

Who was he? But even as the thought occurred, Jacob spun her around, causing her to lose sight of the teenagers while bringing Rafe and Rachel into view again.

As Jessie watched, Rachel threw her head back and laughed gaily. She looked so pretty and flushed as she and Rafe swayed to the lively tune. They seemed taken with each other, too wrapped up in each other to notice the other occupants of the room.

Suddenly, Rafe caught Rachel up and swung her around again and again, laughing as he did so, making Jessie wonder if he had already decided on his wife.

Rafe wasn't so occupied as he appeared. He watched Jacob and Jessie out of the corner of his eye, and he wasn't happy with what he saw. He had never seen her laugh so much as she did with the other man and he found himself stricken with jealousy. She had held herself so stiffly in his arms, and yet, she appeared totally relaxed with Lassiter.

Why? What did she find wrong with him?

The dance ended and, as he started toward the punch bowl, Danny waylaid him with another boy in tow. It was the Jenkins boy, Alvin.

"Pa," Danny said. "Alvin wants me to stay the night. Would it be all right?" His gaze pleaded with his father. "I could come home early to do the milking and I—"

"No need for that, Danny," Rafe said. "Of course you can stay."

Only moments later, Karin approached him, followed closely by Susie Walker. "Pa! Susie wants me to spend the night at her house. Would it be all right?"

"Not you, too?" he chided.

"Me, too?"

"Danny just asked permission to stay with Alvin."

Her expression dimmed. "I guess I have to go home then, right?"

"Why?" Susie cried. She had neatly braided black hair framing a cherubic, innocent face. Her wide gray eyes pleaded with Rafe, making him feel like an ogre for depriving his daughter of pleasure. "Oh, please, Mr. Sutherland. Let her come home with me. We could have her back early. I promise. Just let her come this once and I'll never ask again."

"You won't?"

Her eyelids lowered. "Well, not much," she muttered.

Rafe studied his daughter for a long moment. He knew she didn't get much pleasure out of life and he wanted this for her, but with Danny gone would it be proper for him to be alone with Jessie, with only Sissy to chaperone them? He thought not.

"Pumpkin, I hate to turn you down, but—"

"Oh, Pa . . ."

"Please, Mr. Sutherland!" Susie pleaded.

"I'm sorry, Pumpkin. Danny's already asked to stay with Alvin and it wouldn't be fair to leave all the work to Jessie, now would it?"

Karin flushed, and the light died from her eyes.

"What's going on?" Jessie asked from behind him. "Everybody looks so serious here."

"I'll fetch you some punch, Jessie," Jacob said, nodding at Rafe before he headed for the punch bowl.

Karin and Rafe remained silent, but Susie spoke quickly, feeling as though an ally had arrived.

"I wanted Karin to spend the night with me, Jessie, but Danny already asked to stay with Alvin. And Mr. Sutherland said they can't both be gone at the same time because you'd be left with their work."

"Oh, but I don't mind, Rafe." She met his eyes, pleading

with him. Couldn't he see how much this meant to Karin, to be with girls her own age? "If it's just the work, then please let her stay. I can do whatever is needed. I can even milk the cow. The children deserve some pleasure now and then."

Damn. She made it sound like he enjoyed depriving his children. His mouth tightened grimly. "I know they deserve a little pleasure. I wasn't trying to keep them from enjoying themselves. After all, they are *my* children."

"Then please allow them to stay with their friends." She squeezed his arm gently. "I don't mind doing their chores tomorrow, Rafe."

Rafe gritted his teeth. She still didn't understand. So to hell with it! And the consequences!

"All right, Karin. *Jessie* thinks you should stay with Susie."

Karin looked up at him and when she spoke her voice was hesitant. "If you want me to go home, Pa, then . . ."

"No, by all means, go with your friend." Realizing the tone of his voice was still too gruff, making his daughter believe he was displeased with her, he chucked her under the chin and said, "I mean it, Pumpkin. Jessie is right. You get very little enjoyment out of life. You go with Susie. I'll come after you tomorrow afternoon."

She flung her arms around his neck and kissed him on the cheek. "Thank you, Pa," she whispered. "I'll work extra hard when I get back home."

He watched her run off to join the young people who waited by the door; then he swallowed hard and turned to Jessie. "I'm not an ogre, Jessie. I want my children to be happy. But you obviously forgot a few things."

Her gaze was puzzled. "Like what?"

"With both kids gone, there's only Sissy to chaperone us."

"Oh, God!" Her face flushed hotly. "I forgot—didn't

mean . . . Oh, you should have explained, Rafe. Now what do we do?"

"Nothing. Just hope nobody mentions it."

Jacob returned and handed Jessie a glass of punch and, thirsty from exertion, she drank it quickly, unaware of the potent addition to the innocent-looking drink.

"Would you allow me another dance, Jessie?" Jacob asked quietly.

Rafe threw the doctor a quick grin. "I'm afraid that's not possible," he said cheerfully. "It's way past Sissy's bedtime and we have to be leaving now."

"Why don't I bring Jessie home?"

"Waste of time," Rafe said, curling his fingers around her hand. "Come on, Jessie. We'd better pick up Sissy before she goes to sleep." He nodded at the other man. "See you later, Jacob."

But Jacob wasn't so easy to ignore. He followed them across the floor. "I was wondering, Jessie. Could I call on you next Sunday?"

"Sundays are usually busy around our house," Rafe said quickly. "Jessie doesn't have much free time."

Lassiter's lips tightened and his eyes flashed with anger. "She's not hired help, Rafe."

"No, she's not. You might keep that in mind."

Rafe's grip was firm as he hurried Jessie toward the house, leaving the other man gazing, tight-lipped, at them.

Jessie tugged at her hand, but Rafe's grip tightened. "Rafe," she protested. "Why did you do that?"

He stopped abruptly and glared at her furiously. "Did you want him to call on you?"

She was shocked at his anger, unable to speak.

"Well, did you?"

She shook herself mentally. "I guess not," she muttered.

"Then stop hem-hawing around, Jessie. It's past time Sissy was in bed."

They arrived at the house an hour later and together they put Sissy to bed. Jessie tucked the toddler in; then after leaning over to kiss her cheek, she sought her own bed. Quickly donning her nightgown, Jessie crawled onto the bed and pulled the covers over her and leaned back against the pillow. But she found herself tense, unable to sleep. When the knock sounded, she jerked with surprise.

Leaning up on her elbows, she called out, "Yes? What is it?"

Jessie wasn't prepared for the opening door, nor for the sight of Rafe. Just before he entered the moonlit room, he stopped abruptly when he saw her. "I'm sorry, Jessie. I didn't know you were already in bed."

"Is there something wrong, Rafe?"

He was silent for a long moment. "I thought we should talk, but since you . . ."

"No, that's all right," she quickly interrupted. "Just give me a minute to dress and I'll join you."

"No. Don't bother to get up," he said gruffly. "This won't take long."

"It's no bother."

As though she had not spoken, he crossed the distance between them, stopping beside her bed to frown down at her. His unwavering stare made her nervous.

"Is Sissy all right?"

"Yes."

His gaze was fixed on her as though he was a starving man looking at his next meal. She scooted up against the headboard and crossed her arms over her breasts.

"I don't mind getting up, Rafe."

"No."

He appeared distracted and she swallowed convulsively as he seated himself on the edge of her bed. "What do you want, Rafe?"

"I came to apologize, Jessie."

His reply startled her. "Whatever for?"

"Jacob Lassiter."

"Why didn't you want Jacob to come?" she asked softly.

He hesitated for a long moment; then his mouth thinned. "The reason is a simple one." His voice was harsh, grating, his eyes glinting silver. "I was just plain jealous."

"You were?"

"Yes. I was."

Jessie licked her lips as though they'd suddenly become dry and the action caused Rafe's groin to tighten uncomfortably. He silently cursed his body for betraying him, even as he drank in the sight of her. God, she was beautiful, with her hair billowing around her face and shoulders in a glorious cloud of burnished curls. He wanted to slide his fingers through the silky strands, wanted to feel the curls winding around his fingers.

His gaze shifted lower, became glued to the vee of her neckline where the quilt had slipped down just below the swell of her breasts.

Dammit! Did she realize how much he wanted her, how painful it was for him to see her this way?

The heat from Rafe's eyes warmed Jessie's flesh. She hadn't realized the quilt had slipped down and left her upper body exposed. Although she was decently covered, she'd left several buttons undone on her nightgown and that part of her had captured his attention.

"Rafe."

The sound was almost a moan and he reacted instantly. With a muttered curse, his arms snaked out, wrapping around her and yanking her against him. His mouth, hot and hungry, covered hers.

It was like setting spark to tinder. The banked coals of desire she'd been fighting that glowed and crackled just below the surface had flamed at the first touch of their lips. Jessie had no thought for resistance. Her arms slid around his neck and she gave herself over to his kiss. When his tongue circled her lips, she gasped at the heat coiling between her thighs. Immediately, she felt the swift thrust of his tongue intruding on the moistness within and the heat became a burning flame.

Their tongues dueled together as the burning kiss went on, and on. Nothing mattered to either of them except the incredible need that only the other could satisfy.

A fever burned in Jessie's blood. Her heart pounded and her pulse raced as his kiss became more passionate, making her senses reel dizzily. She had no will to resist him, nor did she want to do so. It was like a dream come true, being in his arms at last. When his mouth finally lifted, she groaned, her arms tightening around his neck as she tried to pull him back again.

His eyes glittered with unrestrained passion.

"I can't fight this anymore, Jessie." His voice was low and guttural. "Lord knows how I've tried, but I need you too much. Say you need me, too."

"I do, Rafe." She felt on fire, frantic with need. He lowered her on the bed, stretching out beside her, his fingers fumbling with the buttons at her neckline.

"I want to see you," he whispered huskily.

He opened her nightgown, exposing her breasts to his sight, and Jessie blushed hotly, then gasped as he pressed his face to her exposed bosom.

"Rafe!" she cried, feeling completely shocked.

He drew back slightly then, moving his mouth to her shoulder, tracing her collarbone with his tongue.

"Oh, God," she moaned, shuddering with pleasure. "I never knew it would feel this way. Never guessed how wonderful it would be."

She arched her back as he took one nipple into his mouth and sucked on it hard. Her fingers curled into his

dark hair and she tried to pull him closer, needing more
of some nameless something that was being denied.

"Please," she begged shakily. "Oh, please, Rafe."

He lifted his head and she saw his flushed face.

"Please what?" he asked softly, his eyes gleaming darkly
at her.

She tugged at him, trying to pull him closer and yet still
he resisted.

"Tell me what you want," he insisted.

Jessie was on fire, frantic with need. "I want you," she
cried, digging her fingers into the hard flesh of his shoulders.

He leaned closer, his breath hot and moist on her neck
as he teased her taut nipples. "You want me where, Jessie?"

"Oh, God," she moaned again, trying to reach his
mouth with hers. "Don't make me say it, Rafe."

"You're burning up, aren't you, Jessie?"

"Yes." She arched her body against him. "Make it stop,
Rafe. Help me."

"Just say the words, Jessie," he whispered. "Tell me
plain. I want to hear you say it. Tell me where you want
me."

"Inside," she moaned. "I want you inside me."

With a triumphant look, his mouth fused with hers.
Reality fled as he stoked the fires of passion until there
was only sensuous pleasure and the grinding urgency of
desire.

The feel of his rough hands sliding over her skin as he
shoved the hem of her nightgown higher was so sensual
that she was barely aware when her flesh was bared to his
view.

His gaze flared hotly as he tossed the nightgown aside,
then covered her breasts with his callused palms.

She shuddered beneath his touch, sucking in a sharp
breath as his thumbs grazed across the hard, pebbled

crests. And then his lips replaced his hands, his flicking tongue stroking and circling one taut nipple while his hand tormented the other.

"Rafe, please," she moaned, shivering with desire.

"Soon," he muttered, raising himself slightly to fumble with his belt buckle.

A shrill scream pierced the night and it was like a douse of cold water. Jessie felt her blood chill. Her head jerked toward the door where the scream had suddenly given way to a loud wailing cry.

"It's Sissy!" she said. "I'll go to her."

She left him there, and her last look just before she left the room was of Rafe slumping down on her bed.

She found Sissy in a tumble of bedclothes and took her into her arms. "It's okay, honey," she soothed, smoothing down the baby's golden curls. "Jessie's here with you now." She placed a soft kiss on the baby's forehead. "Did you have a bad dream?"

Sissy sniffled, her wide eyes puddled with tears. "Bad, bad dream," she said.

"It's all gone now, baby," Jessie crooned. "You're safe here with me."

Sissy nodded, then wrapped her chubby arms around Jessie's neck. Jessie sat in the rocker and held the toddler while she sang softly to her. She heard the kitchen door open and then close again and knew that Rafe had left the house.

Chapter Eleven

The water sparkled and shimmered in the moonlight, but Rafe was unaware of the beauty of the night. His body was hot, his passion aroused, yet he could not assuage that passion. Not with the woman he'd left behind. And no other woman would do.

His thoughts turned inward and he cursed himself roundly. Dammit! She was a virgin, innocent of the ways of men, and yet he'd almost taken that innocence. If Sissy hadn't awakened with the nightmare it would have been too late. He would have shamed Jessie.

Hell! He'd shamed himself by his own actions!

Feeling totally enraged with himself, he dove into the water and emerged farther out in the river, moving through the stream with the skill of an accomplished swimmer. The water rippled turbulently around his muscular body as he cut through it with powerful strokes. His mouth was drawn into a thin line as he tried to ease his frustration by tiring himself out.

*   *   *

Jessie was turning bacon in the iron skillet the next morning when she heard Rafe's boots thudding against the porch. As the kitchen door opened she pushed a loose curl behind her ear and bent to open the oven. The biscuits were crusty brown.

Folding a dishtowel to protect her hand from the heat, she slid the pans out of the oven and put them on the back of the stove to keep warm.

The short hairs on the back of her neck suddenly prickled and she knew that Rafe was watching her. He crossed the room to her side and her body became rigid . . . until the milk bucket scraped against the dry sink as he set it down.

"Breakfast about ready?" he asked gruffly, opening the cabinet door to extract a cup.

Her eyes met his for the briefest moment, then flickered quickly back to the half-cooked bacon. "Almost done."

Hoping he would attribute her flush to the heat from the stove, Jessie turned the bacon over. "D-do you want gravy this morning?"

He closed the distance between them and her breath caught in her throat. Her body trembled. *Oh, God, please don't let him mention last night.*

His long arm snaked out, curving past her, brushing against her breasts. She shivered at the unexpected contact and her startled eyes flashed up to meet his with a wounded expression.

"Don't look at me that way, Jessie!" he snapped. "I'm just after a cup of coffee!"

His fingers fastened on the granite coffeepot and he carried it to the long, wooden table and set it down with a heavy thump.

Oh, God, why was she so vulnerable to him, so pliant to his slightest touch, so unable to control her reactions?

She flicked a quick glance at him. He looked so angry, so unapproachable.

After pouring coffee into a cup, he pulled out a chair and straddled it, his gaze fixed unwaveringly on her.

Her hands trembled as she reached for plates and forced herself to turn around, to cross the distance and set the table. She could feel his eyes on her, could feel her cheeks burning hotly with shame.

"Jessie," he said gently. "Look at me."

"I c-can't," she stuttered. "I feel so awful. So terribly ashamed."

He sighed heavily. "It's not you who should feel shame. It's me. I owe you an apology . . ."

It was obvious that he was sorry he'd ever touched her, that he'd caressed her and kissed her. How could she stand knowing that?

Keeping her eyes lowered so he wouldn't see the tears forming in her eyes, she whispered, "There's no need to apologize. It was my fault. I sh-shouldn't have been so sh-shameless."

She turned away quickly, but his lean hand shot out and caught her small wrist in a hot, strong grasp. She gasped and stared at him with wide, wary eyes.

He scowled at her reaction. "Of course there's a need," he snarled. "And it was not your fault. You're an innocent, Jessie. And I took advantage of you."

"No, you didn't." She twisted nervous fingers in the skirt of the plain brown and white gingham dress she'd donned that morning. If anyone had been taken advantage of, it was him. She could have made him leave the room easily enough. All she'd had to do was ask. But no. What she'd asked for instead made her shrivel up inside. What she'd begged for made her cringe. She was no better than a loose woman. And deserved no more consideration.

Rafe was having his own problems. He felt like a low-down skunk, lower than a snake's belly in a wagon rut. He had destroyed her confidence in him by taking advantage of her. Why in hell couldn't he have controlled his passion?

"Jessie . . ."

She looked at him then. His powerful body was tense, his expression watchful.

"Please, Rafe, do we have to discuss this? What's done is done. I'm just sorry it happened."

Sorry it happened? Dammit! He didn't want her to be sorry; he wanted her to—what?

His gaze searched hers and she felt her body heat at the expression she saw there. Could it be desire? An intense longing?

She stood before him, feeling completely helpless, unable to move, to speak, to hide her own feelings.

"Jessie . . . I didn't mean to . . ."

Oh, God! He was apologizing again.

"Please, Rafe," she whispered. "Don't say anything more. Just leave it alone. I just want to forget what happened."

Forget? How in hell was he supposed to forget the way she'd felt in his arms, the way she looked at him, her eyes slumberous with passion? He'd damn well never forget that. And he suspected that she wouldn't, either. But if she wanted to pretend they could, then so be it.

"All right," he said stiffly. "If that's what you really want. Should I get Sissy up for you?"

"No. She had a long night, Rafe. I think she needs to sleep a while yet."

They sat together over breakfast, neither of them showing any appetite. Finally, Rafe broke the strained silence.

"Have I ruined everything, Jessie?" His voice sounded

rough as gravel and it felt that way in his throat. "Are you going to abandon us now?"

Abandon us. She wondered at his choice of words, and yet, to her, leaving Rafe and the children would feel like abandonment. She realized then how totally committed to the Sutherland family she felt. "I wouldn't know where to go, Rafe. I don't know where I belong."

He hated the thought of her leaving, yet he didn't want her to feel she was being forced to stay. *Oh, God, what have I done?* He'd only meant to talk to her, to make her aware of his feelings. Instead, he'd allowed those feelings to control him, had treated her like a two-bit whore.

He sighed heavily. "If you really want to go, Jessie, then I'll give you the money you need."

Oh, God, it's worse than I thought. He wants me to leave so bad that he's willing to pay me to go.

She blinked away the tears that flooded her eyes. "I-I couldn't take money from you," she whispered.

"Don't be foolish, Jessie." His knuckles whitened around his coffee cup. "You've worked hard around here and you haven't asked for a dime. I owe you."

"You saved my life, Rafe. That's a debt I can never repay. I won't take money from you."

Suddenly he slammed his fist on the table. "If you won't take my money then you'll damn well have to stay here!" he roared.

He sounded so angry. When she met his gaze for a brief moment, his eyes were so hot, so glittery, that she felt as though she'd been burned with a hot poker. Was he angry at his inability to be rid of her?

She forced words around the obstruction in her throat. "I . . . could probably find a position in town, Rafe."

"Doing what?" he growled.

She fiddled with her fork, turning it over in her hand and pretending great interest in the design. "I don't know." Her voice was almost a whisper. "Perhaps I could teach."

"We already have a teacher."

"Maybe a waitress then."

"The Wileys have the only eating place in town and they have two teenage daughters to wait on tables." He shook his head. "No, Jessie. You're stuck with us, at least for a while." Then, as though he'd settled everything to his complete satisfaction, he slid back his chair and straightened his long length. "It's past time I started the chores."

"But Rafe, what about . . . ?"

"Forget it, Jessie," he growled. "It's settled. You're staying." Like the coward he was, Rafe strode quickly away before she could renew the argument.

Moments later he was gone.

It was mid-morning before Sissy woke and Jessie used the time to give the house a thorough cleaning. She felt the need to keep busy, to work hard in order to keep memories of Rafe's loving at bay. Little good it did, though, for the memory of his mouth on her was too fresh, too strong in her mind. She couldn't forget the intimate way he'd kissed her, nor her feelings when his tongue caressed her flesh. Couldn't forget the way he'd laved her nipples and the hot moistness between her thighs.

Oh, God, she would never forget!

And somehow, her regret for that loving was fading fast. Now she wanted only to hold on to the memories, for they might be all she would ever have.

Lunch was a silent affair, broken only by an occasional word from Sissy. When it was over, Rafe hitched up the buggy and rode away to fetch his two oldest children. Jessie watched him leave from the kitchen window, then went outside with Sissy to tend the small vegetable garden behind the house. She was down on her knees pulling weeds when she heard the clip-clop of hooves on the hard dirt road that led to the house.

It couldn't be Rafe. He'd taken the buggy. And it couldn't be Jacob Lassiter, either. He used a carriage.

Consternation raced through her as she realized how alone they were, how isolated from their neighbors. As the rider drew closer, Jessie felt the first stirrings of real alarm. She looked at Rafe's youngest daughter, who knelt nearby using a stick to dig at a root, which was her way of helping to weed the garden.

"Sissy!" The toddler looked up. "Come with me."

Almost always biddable, Sissy rose and curled her plump fingers around Jessie's.

Clip-clop, clip-clop.

The sound was louder now and, unable to adjust to the toddler's pace, Jessie snatched the youngster up and hurried into the house. She couldn't explain her fear, only knew that it was suddenly overpowering. She swept through the house like a whirlwind, sliding the bars across both the front and back doors, pushing the windows down and locking them in place.

"I want a cookie, Jessie," Sissy piped up.

"Just a minute, sweetie."

Jessie hurried into the kitchen and plucked several cookies from the large mason jar, hoping that would keep the youngster quiet until she could discover the identity of their visitor. "Take the cookies and play in your room with Dolly."

Clip-clop. The sound was in the yard now.

"Be real quiet for me, okay?"

"Okay."

Jessie carried the child to her room and handed her the rag doll. Then she hurried back to the parlor and peered outside. She started then, as though an unseen hand had reached out of the past and slapped her. She knew him.

The jolt of recognition told her it was so. Yet she could not remember where—or when—she'd seen him. The man who dismounted wore a slouch hat atop greasy, black hair. An ugly scar slashed across his left cheek. It was a face she wouldn't soon forget, a face that caused her vision to blur, made her knees wobble like wet noodles.

She struggled to recall where she'd seen him and pain wrapped around her skull, squeezing it tightly. Her heart thumped like a hammer and her breath came in quick, short spurts.

Sweat beaded her upper lip and fear gripped her heart. Her stomach churned and she fought the blood-chilling dread threatening to consume her.

Scarface dismounted and stepped onto the porch.

Jessie drew back quickly to keep herself from being seen. Fear gripped her heart and she tasted the bile that rose in her. Forcing it back with a hard swallow, she waited for discovery.

He rapped on the door loudly with his knuckles and, although Jessie had been expecting the sound, she gave a quick jerk. The knocks came again; then his boots sounded as he walked around the porch to the back door.

Oh, God, had she locked that door? She couldn't remember. She hurried into the kitchen and stopped short. Sissy stood in the middle of the room, staring first at the barred door, then at Jessie's ashen face.

As the toddler opened her mouth to speak, Jessie quickly placed a finger over her own mouth and hoped it would be enough.

Tiptoeing across the room, Jessie bent and scooped Sissy into her arms. Then, pressing her lips against the youngster's ear, she whispered, "We must be very, very quiet, Sissy. Don't make a sound."

The knock sounded again and Sissy's expression was suddenly eager. "Comp'ny?" she inquired.

"Not company, Sissy," Jessie whispered. "We don't know him. And since Poppa's not here, we must be real quiet so he doesn't hear us."

Sissy's eyebrows pulled together. "It's bad man?"

"I don't know, Pumpkin." Jessie unconsciously stroked the child's back. "But we aren't going to take any chances. Shhhh." Jessie searched for a way to keep the little girl quiet. "We're playing hide-and-seek," she whispered. "We mustn't make a sound or he'll find us."

"Okay," Sissy whispered.

Jessie's gaze was fixed unwaveringly on the door, wondering if Scarface would try to break into the house.

He rapped again. Louder. "Anybody home?"

Sissy stirred restlessly and Jessie put a finger across her mouth. The child smiled and returned the gesture. Oh, if only she could be like the baby, so unaware of danger, so sure that those around her would always offer protection. Jessie knew, though, that there were some things a person had to go through alone.

Boots stomped across the porch and thudded on the dirt as the stranger walked away. Hurrying to the window, Jessie shielded herself against the curtain and watched him. He stood near his horse, his gaze traveling around the yard; then, seeming to shrug his shoulders, he mounted and rode away.

Slowly, the fear drained away, as did her strength. Jessie returned to the parlor and slumped down on the rocker, shifting Sissy into the curve of her arms.

"I need to rest for a minute." She managed a shaky smile for the little girl. "Would you just sit here with me for a few minutes so we can rock together?"

"Okay," Sissy said, relaxing against Jessie's breast. "Sing to me, Jessie. Sing a song."

Softly, Jessie began to hum a tune, and as she did, the tension slowly drained away. She laid her head back and continued to rock, singing a soft lullaby until she heard the jingle of harness and the steady clip-clop of hooves mingling with rolling wheels.

Realizing that Rafe must be returning, she looked down at Sissy, who was sound asleep, her lips moving softly. Jessie gazed tenderly at her. If only she could stay forever, could be a mother to the children, a wife to Rafe.

She looked up as a voice called out, "Jessie, where are you?" It was Karin.

Before Jessie could move a thud sounded against the front door. She jerked upright so fast that Sissy's eyes flew open.

Karin's voice sounded again. "It's locked, Pa!"

"Go around, then!"

Jessie hurried into the kitchen just as a pounding began on the back door. "Jessie! Open the door!" The voice became muffled as Karin apparently turned away to speak. "This one's locked, too, Pa."

Jessie's hands trembled as she slid the bar aside. She'd barely done so when the door was flung open and she looked up into Rafe's blazing eyes.

"What in hell is going on, Jessie? Why was the door locked?"

"A bad man comed," Sissy cried, her gaze fixed on her father's face. "We hided."

Rafe scowled. "What's she talking about, Jessie? Who was here?"

"I don't know," she replied, stooping to put Sissy on the floor. The child immediately ran to the door. "Sissy, don't go out there yet."

"Why not?" Rafe asked. "There's nobody out there." He gripped her chin and turned her face up to his. "Did something happen to frighten you while I was gone?"

Noticing they had Karin's full attention, Jessie tried to make light of her fears. "Nothing happened, Rafe. It was my own foolish caution that made me bar the door. A stranger came and since we were alone here I thought it best to stay out of sight."

"Sissy said he was a bad man."

"Probably because we were hiding in the house. We stayed real quiet so he wouldn't know we were here."

Rafe appeared to accept her explanation for what it was. "You have no idea who he was?"

"No. He was just a stranger. I guess I'm a coward, Rafe."

"You're no coward," he said abruptly. "It's always better to err on the side of caution. Anyway, if it was something important, then whoever it was will come back again."

Jessie feared he was right and could only hope she wasn't around when Scarface returned.

Deciding it was time for a change of subject, Jessie turned to Karin. "Did you have a good time at Susie's house?"

"Oh, yes," Karin said and her eyes began to shine. "It was so much fun. Joe Bob Thompson was there. But he didn't stay long."

"Who is Joe Bob Thompson?"

"He's our neighbor. We're planning a hayride for next Saturday." She looked at her father quickly. "Pa already said I could go." She took Jessie's arm. "Do you think you could make me something to wear for the hayride, Jessie? Pa said I could have some new material. And we could buy enough for you, too."

"Oh, I don't think—"

"Oh, please, Jessie. I can help you make the dresses."

"Of course I'll make you a dress, Karin. I just meant I don't need one."

"Yes, you do. I could cut out the pieces for both. I could use my old blue dress for a pattern. I know exactly how I want mine made." She took Jessie's arm. "Do you remember that frock in the Montgomery Ward catalog? The one with tucks on the bodice and lace on the neck?" She pulled

Jessie along and they quickly became embroiled in plans for the new clothes.

It was late that evening when Sissy had been put to bed and Danny and Karin were busy with their own pursuits that Jessie found herself alone with Rafe. He sat beside the fireplace while she mended one of his shirts.

"Do you want to tell me why you were so afraid today?" he asked quietly.

She had been expecting his question. "I recognized that man, Rafe. And I was more frightened, I think, than I've ever been before."

"You recognized him?" His gaze narrowed. "Has your memory returned?"

"No. But I remembered his face. The scar. And it made me afraid. I tried to force the memory, but the pain it caused was too bad. It felt like someone was squeezing my head."

"Don't try to force the memories, Jessie. I'm beginning to believe they are best forgotten." He was thoughtful for a long moment. "Maybe I'd better stay close to the house for a while. Just in case he comes again."

"You can't stay around the house, Rafe. You have field work that needs doing."

His brow furrowed as he studied her face, still pale from her fright. There was something in her past that caused her fear, and that something could be dangerous, not only to her, but to the whole family. Until they knew what they were faced with, he wouldn't leave her alone. But how could he convince her of that without frightening her even more?

"We've about finished planting, Jessie. There's nothing in the fields that can't wait a while." He studied her for a long moment, wondering what words to use that would cause her the least anxiety. "We don't know how you came to be in that river," he said slowly. "It might have been accidental, but we don't know that."

Her face paled instantly, making him wish the words unsaid.

"I don't believe it was an accident, Rafe. I believe someone pushed me in the river." Her eyes were wide with fear. "What could I have done that was so terrible that someone wanted me dead?"

"Whatever the reason, Jessie, you shouldn't blame yourself."

"How can you know that?"

"I know you, Jessie."

"No. You don't."

"Yes." He leaned toward her, his unwavering gaze fixed on her. "I do know it, Jessie. I'm not blind. I have eyes that see. And they watch you." His voice became softer, almost caressing. "If you could see from these eyes of mine you'd understand. I've seen the way you treat my children. No mother could be more tender, more loving with them. Sissy turns to you for comfort, Karin looks to you for understanding, for female companionship. And Danny . . . my God, Jessie. My son has grown by leaps and bounds since you've been here. I never realized how far a little praise could go. He struts around the farm like he's the barnyard rooster responsible for the sun rising each morning. How could I have been so blind to my own children's needs?"

"You're not being fair to yourself, Rafe. You've been a good father."

"I've done my best, Jessie. But it hasn't been enough."

"Nonsense."

"No. They need a mother." His eyes glittered. "And I need a wife, Jessie." He turned away from her. "I need you."

Even though his last words were spoken softly, slightly muffled, she understood them perfectly. She choked back a reply and captured her lower lip between her teeth. It would serve no purpose to speak of her own needs. Not when her past remained hidden from her conscious mind.

Chapter Twelve

The wind was unseasonably warm against Rafe's face, carrying a hint of newly turned earth. He could hear the sound of crickets beneath the bushes, could hear the hoot of an owl—a mournful sound—as it went about its business of hunting for food.

But Rafe was barely aware of these sounds as he leaned his arms against the top rail of the corral. Nor was he that aware of the sorrel mare and the colt confined in that corral. His thoughts were occupied with Jessie.

Jessie.

Just the thought of her could make his body hard with need that was harder to fight with each passing day. Was he wrong to keep her here? She had been frightened by the stranger, certain that she'd once known him and that he was a danger to her. If she was right, then he might be exposing his children to that danger.

Dammit! This was his home. It had always provided safety

for him and his family. But that safety could no longer be taken for granted.

He sighed heavily. Jessie was certain the man was looking for her and that if she left, there would be no danger to his family. But he couldn't send her away. She had no place to go. And even if she did, he didn't want her to leave. He even found the thought physically painful.

And what of his children's needs? They depended on Jessie, had come to love her.

No. He couldn't allow her to leave. Wouldn't allow it. Why did life have to be so hard?

The sound of squeaking hinges caught his attention; he turned to see the kitchen door open and the woman who occupied his thoughts step onto the porch.

Rafe straightened his long frame and watched her, expecting her to seek him out. Instead, she turned toward the nearby woods where a path led to the creek that flowed into the river.

His brow furrowed. Where was she going? Did Jessie feel a need for time alone to sort out troubled thoughts? If that was her reason for leaving the house alone, he wouldn't disturb her.

Then, suddenly remembering the stranger who'd frightened her so, Rafe turned to follow her.

The house was dark and silent as Jessie, finding herself unable to sleep, finally rose from her bed and left the house. The night was unseasonably warm, but a quick dip in the creek should cool her and make sleeping easier.

The full moon lighted her way as she crossed the yard and found the path leading through the woods to the creek. It was a well-worn path, tromped down daily by the Sutherland family as they played or fished in the stream. Watercress and wild onions grew in profusion there and had become a daily addition to the family meals. Wild plum bushes grew in abundance along the path and the green fruit was watched daily so they could gather what they wanted before the wild creatures found them.

As Jessie neared the creek, the tall cedars that lined the trail gave way to cottonwood and willow trees. She heard the croaking of frogs mingling with the sound of rushing water just before she emerged from the woods.

She seated herself on a stump and allowed the peace of the night to wash over her. She could stay here forever, she knew, with Rafe and the children and be completely happy. If she were allowed. But the stranger who came among them was someone from her past. She was certain of it, and certain, too, that he was an enemy.

The thought of him brought a frown to her face as she watched the water flow softly and tried to regain that sense of inner peace she'd known only moments before. The feeling proved to be elusive, though, as the stranger—Scarface—continued to intrude on her thoughts.

A sudden prickling at the base of her neck made Jessie uneasy. She felt as though eyes were on her and turned her head quickly, her gaze searching the woods for an intruder.

A sudden screech jerked her head around and her body upright. Her heart beat erratically. She was poised to take flight until she heard the flurry of wings beating through the forest and saw the owl swooping through the trees toward some unseen prey.

Although Jessie laughed softly at her fears, she continued to feel uneasy. She was anxious to take her bath and return to the house.

Rafe had no thought of intruding on Jessie's privacy; he had only meant to watch, to keep her safe. But that moment in time when he'd been distracted by the owl had worked against him. When he turned his attention to Jessie again it was too late. He stood frozen to the spot as her nightgown puddled softly at her feet, leaving her beautiful body bare.

He knew he should turn away. An honorable man would have done so, but he couldn't move. His feet were frozen to the ground, his eyes glued to her sweetly curved body, her thrusting breasts as she raised her arms over her head and arched her back.

Rafe's gaze remained riveted on her as she waded into the stream and lowered herself into the cool water. His breath quickened as she sucked in a sharp breath, then quickly stood upright again, the silvery drops glistening on her breasts as she stood in waist-deep water.

Then, as he watched, she tilted her head back and ran her palm over her neck and down her body, smoothing over her breasts in a leisurely motion that made Rafe's breath quicken and his loins tighten as he imagined his own hand taking that same path, gliding over those same curves that made his body burn and pulse with need.

Jessie didn't know how long she'd been enjoying her bath when she suddenly realized she was no longer alone. She looked up to see Rafe occupying the same stump she had used only a short while ago.

Her eyes drank in the sight of him, seated on the stump, wearing nothing but his breeches.

She knew she should sink into the water, hide herself from his eyes, but her body refused to obey her mind. Instead, she watched him silently until he rose from the stump and strode toward her, his hand on the buttons of his breeches.

Jessie could have stopped him, she knew, with only a few words. And yet those words remained unspoken.

She watched as he stripped the breeches away and kicked them aside. Her eyes were glued to his lower body as he waded into the water and joined her.

Their eyes met and held for a long moment. Then he reached out and gently touched her cheek. She closed her eyes and turned her head into his palm and kissed it. His arm snaked out then and he drew her fiercely to him, his mouth closing over hers, fiercely, possessively, insistent.

Jessie's heart beat rapidly, the sound pulsing in her ears as his tongue probed the corners of her mouth. Helplessly, she opened her mouth to grant him entry. His tongue thrust quickly inside, dueling with hers as he sought the sweetness there. It was only the need for air that finally broke the kiss.

"God! I want you," he muttered.

His tongue swirled in her ear as his hands roamed urgently over her back and her hips.

"I want you, too," she moaned. "But we must stop. We can't do this."

She gasped as he lifted her and pressed his face to her bosom. And then his tongue trailed along the creamy flesh and his mouth latched onto one nipple.

With a sharp gasp, she clutched at him, twining her fingers through his dark hair while he sucked gently.

Suddenly his hands were everywhere, searching, leaving a trail of fire wherever they touched. He whispered in her ear, his breath sending shudders of pleasure through her body as she moaned low in her throat.

She felt her breasts swelling, thrusting into the palms of his hands, begging for his touch. Her nipples were taut, eager for his possession. He kissed her eyelids, her cheeks, her nose, her chin. She moaned again, trying to capture the lips that so carefully evaded hers.

"Open your mouth," he whispered.

She had no thought of disobeying. The taste and feel

of him made her helpless in his arms, unable to stop her mindless response.

When her mouth opened he deepened the kiss, inserting his tongue into her mouth. She trembled and yielded helplessly, her body pliant in his embrace.

Jessie's lower body began to throb sweetly and her hands clenched tightly in the hair at his nape. She was aroused beyond bearing and he seemed totally aware of that fact.

Her head was spinning, her body felt feverish. She wanted him in the worst way. As though sensing her hunger, his hands slid to her hips and he ground her against his lower body. She gasped at the feel of his manhood, throbbing against her thigh.

The unfamiliar touch of his aroused body brought a thread of sanity and she tried to latch onto it. She must stop him while there was still time, must deny her own body, but oh, how could she bear it, when she wanted him so badly.

She placed her palms against his chest, pulling her head away from him.

"No," she moaned. "We can't do this. We have to stop."

He lifted his head and looked at her, his eyes fixed on her swollen lips and flushed face. She wanted him, he knew it, could see it in her eyes and, he wanted her—with every fiber of his being, he wanted her. She was a fever in his blood, a fire that would never be quenched until he claimed her for his own.

"I can't," he said hoarsely. "I want you too much." His mouth dipped down again and claimed her lips, his tongue intruding into the wet, moist cavern and pushing in and out as he imitated a rhythm as old as time.

She shuddered beneath him as her body caught fire again, but still she pushed at him, refusing to allow the feelings that swamped over her.

Jerking her mouth away, she protested, "Please, Rafe.

We have to stop." Even as she said the words her body
yearned for him.

"You want it, too, Jessie," he said hoarsely. "Don't try
to deny it."

"I'm not denying it, Rafe. But until we know what's in
my past we can . . . What if I have a husband?"

A husband. The words had the effect of a bucket of ice
water being dumped over his head. His eyes flashed down
at her, angry, furious. Damn her! She couldn't have a
husband. Not when he had only to touch her and she went
up in flames.

His breath came in ragged gasps as he tried to control
himself. As her eyes moistened, he jerked backward, fling-
ing himself away from her. Then he turned away, diving
into the deeper water.

She watched him swim away from her, his arms cleaving
the water furiously as he moved swiftly across the creek,
seeming intent on putting as much distance between them
as possible.

Not until he reached the other side did she wade out
of the river, silently mourning what might have been.

The next morning Jessie avoided Rafe, putting breakfast
on the table, then quickly escaping to the henhouse with
a muttered explanation that she wasn't hungry. He allowed
the lie although his gaze told her he knew her reason for
absenting herself. She realized he was just as anxious to
avoid a confrontation as she was.

They managed to keep apart until the evening meal.
When they were seated and platters were being passed
around, Rafe turned to Danny and engaged him in conversation.

The children seemed unaware of the strain between the

adults. Karin claimed Jessie's attention as they discussed the frock they would make for the upcoming hayride.

Supper was over and they were clearing the table while Rafe lingered over a third cup of coffee when a knock sounded on the kitchen door and startled them into silence. Jessie tensed, her gaze flickering to Rafe. Had Scarface returned?

Rafe read the fear in Jessie's eyes and muttered a silent curse. She was obviously afraid Scarface had returned. Rafe hoped she was right. If Scarface had returned, and if, as Jessie thought, he was someone out of her past, then he'd damn well have some answers for them.

A heavy scowl marred Rafe's features as he scraped back his chair and strode swiftly to the door. His narrowed gaze settled on the dark-haired boy who waited on the front porch.

Disappointment deepened his frown as he glared at the boy, who leaned against one of the porch columns. "Yeah?" he growled.

The newcomer's glance slid over Rafe, then to the kitchen behind him where his family stood waiting quietly. During that moment, recognition dawned. "You're Sam Walker's boy, aren't you?" When the boy nodded, Rafe asked, "Is something wrong over at your place?"

"No, sir," the boy replied, straightening his body to its full length, which was only a few inches less than Rafe's six feet.

Rafe frowned at the boy—who was almost a man—while a memory teased at his mind. Then suddenly it slammed his memory like a door that had been kicked open. This was the boy Danny had teased his sister about. This half-grown pup, from the looks of him, would have the strength of two men twice his size. His fear for his daughter erupted in anger.

"What do you want here?"

"Pa!" Karin gasped, moving quickly beside him. "That's not polite." She looked at the newcomer. "Would you like to come in, Johnny?"

"Uh, no." He moved backward, out of the lamplight streaming through the doorway, into the deeper shadows. "I just thought, uh . . ."

Jessie realized Rafe was making Johnny Walker uncomfortable with his penetrating stare. She joined him at the door and gripped his upper arm.

Rafe started at Jessie's touch. He looked at her and saw the warning in her green eyes.

"Please come in, Johnny," she said sweetly. "We've only just finished supper but there's still plenty left if you're hungry."

"Uh, no, ma'am. But thanks anyway." Johnny's gaze shifted to Rafe as he forced himself to brave what he obviously considered the enemy. "I come to see Karin. But if she's busy then I . . ."

"I'm not busy." Karin threw a grim look at her father, then stepped outside and took Johnny's hand and led him toward the corrals.

"Karin!" Rafe's voice grated harshly in the silence.

"What?" Karin turned to glare at her father.

"Rafe. Please." Jessie spoke softly, warningly, and her voice had the desired effect. She could feel a slight lessening of the tension that held Rafe in its grip.

Realizing Karin was still watching him warily, Rafe cleared his throat. "Don't go far, Karin. The snakes are out tonight."

"All right."

A moment later his daughter and the Walker boy were only shadows that blended with the night.

Rafe turned to Jessie. "I shouldn't have let her go out there with him. She's too damn young to have callers. For God's sake, Jessie! She's only thirteen years old."

"And he's only sixteen."

"Damn near a man," he growled. "Did you see the size of him?"

"They've only gone to the corrals, Rafe. They're near enough she could holler for help if there was need."

"Shoot!" Danny said from behind them. "Johnny Walker wouldn't do anything to hurt Karin."

Rafe turned on his son. "What do you know about that boy, Danny?"

"What do you mean, Pa?"

"What do folks say about him? What kind of reputation does he have? Does he make a habit of sweet-talking young girls?"

The questions shot at Danny with the rapidity of a repeating rifle and his face mirrored his confusion. "Folks don't say nothing about him, Pa. And he ain't got no reputation that I know of. And, heck! Johnny ain't never had a girlfriend before. Leastways not that I know of. He sure ain't in the habit of doing none of that."

"None of what?" Rafe demanded.

"None of that sweet-talking stuff."

"Oh." Rafe turned away from his son and peered outside again. "She's too young for this," he muttered. "She knows nothing about men. Not a damn thing!" He looked at Jessie. "Why did they have to go outside? Why couldn't they use the parlor?"

"Because you made Johnny uncomfortable, Rafe."

"If he touches her then he'll be more than uncomfortable," he grumbled. He raised his voice. "Karin?"

Her voice came out of the darkness. "What is it, Pa?"

Rafe peered into the shadows at the silhouettes near the corral. "You stay close by, you hear?"

"I hear."

At Jessie's gentle prodding, Rafe reluctantly turned away

from the door and allowed his daughter to visit with her company without prying eyes.

Outside, his elbows leaning on the top rail of the corral, Johnny sighed with relief. "Your Pa doesn't like me, does he?"

"Why wouldn't he?" Karin bent and found a piece of straw and stuck it in her mouth. She turned then to study the horses in the corral.

"I dunno. Unless he thinks I might like you a little too much."

She glanced his way, trying to remain casual. She hoped Pa was right, that Johnny did like her, that he liked her more than any other girl. But why should he? She was three years younger than her, and he was so good-looking with his raven hair and gray eyes.

"Why did you come to see me?" she asked gently, hoping he would reveal his feelings.

"Susie asked me to come to the hayride."

Karin knew he was avoiding her question, but couldn't make herself ask again. "Are you going?"

"I dunno." He picked up a stone and threw it against the side of the barn. She heard it thud against the wood. "Are you going?"

"Yeah." Her gaze flicked shyly to him, then slid away again. "Jessie is making me a new dress."

"That's nice." He glanced down at her. "But you don't need dressin' up to make you look pretty, Karin. With the moon shinin' on your hair the way it is . . ." His hand reached out and wound a long, flaxen lock around his finger. "Your hair looks like a moonbeam, Karin, and it feels that soft."

She flushed rosily. Nobody had ever talked to her that way before.

"Karin!"

Rafe's voice caused her body to jerk and she turned to

see her father standing in the doorway again, the lamplight streaming out from behind him.

She sighed deeply. "I'm coming, Pa," she called out, wishing he would leave her alone for a few more minutes. She turned back to Johnny. "I guess I have to go inside now. Maybe if you come back tomorrow when it's daylight we could talk some more."

"I can't," he said gruffly. "I got too many chores in the daytime." He turned away and she caught his arm quickly.

"Johnny?"

"Yeah?"

"Are you going on the hayride?"

"Maybe. I want to go since you're gonna be there. But sometimes chores run late."

"I hope you come," she said softly. "It would be more fun if you were there."

"Then I'll be there, Karin. There won't nothing stop me from coming on that hayride."

Johnny flicked a quick glance toward the kitchen doorway where her father waited. He appeared to hesitate; then, wrapping a long arm around her waist, he pulled Karin to the deeper shadows of the barn and dipped his head, covering her mouth with a kiss so sweet that it made Karin's chest ache.

Karin stood on shaky legs, her lips tingling from his kiss as she watched Johnny fade into the darkness of the night. And then she turned toward the house where her father waited with, she was almost certain, questions that she wouldn't want to answer.

Chapter Thirteen

The next few days passed in a flurry of activity. Jessie and Karin worked together to finish the household chores by noon so they could work on the frock the girl would wear to the hayride.

Jessie picked the seams out of one of Karin's old blouses and spread the pieces on the brown paper wrapping she'd saved for that purpose. Then, allowing room for the girl's developing figure, Jessie made a pattern for the new frock.

They knelt together on the parlor floor, spreading the pattern pieces on the new material while Sissy played nearby with her doll. As the last piece of the bodice was pinned in place, Karin voiced her thoughts.

"Jessie . . . I was wondering . . ."

Jessie sensed the girl's embarrassment and pretended to be totally absorbed in her work, hoping that would help alleviate those feelings. "Hmmm?" She flicked a quick look at the girl. "Would you hand me the scissors, sweetie?"

"Oh, yeah." Karin reached for the scissors and handed

them across. "Jessie . . . do you think thirteen is too young for a beau?"

Jessie made the first cut in the material. "That's hard to answer, sweetie. Some girls, at thirteen, are incredibly young emotionally. Definitely too young for a beau."

"Mary Lou Renner married when she was only thirteen."

"Married!" Jessie paused and met Karin's eyes with a long look. "Thirteen is definitely too young for marriage, Karin. For anyone. Marriage is a big responsibility. With it comes a husband's needs. There would be meals to cook and the house to tend, clothes to wash and babies . . ." Her voice trailed off as she realized she was reciting the chores the girl had been performing since her mother died.

She reached out a hand and cupped the girl's face. "Karin, honey. You're so young and yet you're almost a woman emotionally. But please, sweetie. Don't set your sights on one boy right now. It could lead to so much heartache in later years."

"What do you mean?"

Jessie thought of Rafe. "Someday you might meet that perfect someone who was made for you. And if you're tied to another man when it happens then you'd be honor bound to stay with him." *As I could be.*

"How do you know, Jessie? How can you be sure if he's the right one?"

"Your heart will know." Jessie sighed and returned to her work. Then, afraid she'd done more damage than good, she added, "Please take your time, sweetie. You have years ahead of you before you make a decision like that." She looked up again. "I'd like to see you in school. You and Danny both."

"Most people say women don't need an education."

"Don't you believe it. A woman has a better chance in life if she's educated."

"You must have had an education, Jessie. You know so much more about things—letters and ciphering and such—than the other ladies around here."

"I think maybe I did."

"But you don't remember going to school?"

Jessie had a vision of a four-storied white house where several young women dressed in some kind of tunic frock played croquet on a wide, green lawn. But it was only a momentary thing, gone as quickly as it came.

"No. I don't remember."

"You've gone pale," Karin said with alarm. "Are you all right, Jessie?"

Jessie rubbed her temples. "Just a headache," she muttered, closing her eyes against the pain.

"Maybe we better stop for a while."

"Just a minute, maybe," Jessie agreed, laying aside the scissors.

As she leaned her head back against the settee the kitchen door opened and boot heels thumped across the floor.

"Jessie!"

Realizing Rafe was looking for her, Jessie opened her eyes and was on the point of rising when he entered the parlor. His sweeping gaze found Jessie and his body tensed.

"What's wrong?"

"Jessie had another memory," Karin said quickly.

"Jessie?" He knelt before her. "Are you in pain?"

"Just a headache."

"Dammit," he growled. "I told you not to push it."

Weak tears squeezed past her eyelids and spilled down her cheeks. Oh, God, she couldn't take his anger. Not when her head felt as though it was being squeezed by a giant hand.

Rafe muttered another curse. "Stretch out on the settee,

Jessie, and I'll get some of those headache powders Doc Lassiter left for you.''

"You don't have to wait on me."

He pulled a hanky from his back pocket and wiped away her tears. "Hush. Just keep still while I get the powders."

"I'm sorry, Jessie," Karin said. "I didn't mean to make a memory come."

Sissy rose and came to Jessie. "Are you hurted, Jessie?"

"Leave Jessie alone, Sissy." Karin reached for the toddler, but Sissy quickly evaded her sister. "Come on, Sissy," Karin scolded. "Jessie's head hurts. We need to be real quiet."

Sissy leaned over Jessie and planted a wet kiss on her forehead.

"Thank you, Pumpkin," Jessie said. "That's much better now."

The little girl went back to her doll, satisfied that Jessie would soon recover from her pain.

Jessie swallowed the medicine Rafe brought her, then, leaning on him to steady her wobbly legs, stumbled to her bed to sleep away the pain.

In the parlor Rafe questioned his daughter, intent on learning what had brought about Jessie's latest memory flash, hoping it would provide a lead to her past.

"It was nothing really, Pa," Karin said. "We were talking about school and how women needed an education these days and I asked her if she remembered going to school and she got real pale and her face had that look she gets when she remembers something and then the pain came."

Disappointment swept over Rafe. There was probably nothing in the flashback that would help them in their search. Unless Jessie retained something from that memory. And what if she did? Would asking her about it cause that terrible pain to come again?

How were they supposed to learn anything about Jessie if every memory was kept hidden from her conscious mind?

He thought about what she'd said at the swimming hole, and, try as he might, he couldn't reject the possibility of a former commitment, of a husband waiting somewhere in her past. And that thought was slowly driving him crazy.

Sighing heavily, he went to the kitchen and poured himself a cup of coffee from the pot left warming at the back of the stove. It was thick as mud and just as strong but he liked it that way. He was still there when Jessie joined him in the kitchen.

"What are you doing up?" he asked, eying her grimly. "I told you to go to sleep."

"I'm all right now, Rafe." She poured herself a cup of coffee and joined him at the table. "The powders you gave me took the pain away." She eyed him across the rim of the cup. "You came to the house for a reason. What was it?"

"I need to go to town. I was wondering if you needed anything."

She shook her head. "I don't think so. Unless, maybe . . ." She eyed the pantry thoughtfully. "I was going to bake cookies for the hayride but we're low on sugar. Maybe you could . . ."

"Yeah. I'll get some from the general store."

"Pa." Karin stood in the doorway. "If you're going to the general store, could you get me some wide, blue ribbon? Get the satin stuff, not the ribbed."

"Why don't you come along and pick it out yourself?"

Karin raised the flaxen braid that had fallen across one shoulder and flipped it behind her head. "I don't know, Pa. I hate to leave Sissy for Jessie to . . ."

"Nonsense," Jessie said quickly. "You go on, sweetie. I feel fine now. Maybe I'll even get your frock cut out while you're gone."

"Leave the damn thing alone, Jessie," Rafe said. "You need to rest a while. You've got all week to finish that damn frock."

"Stop fussing, Rafe," Jessie said. "Just go on about your business and leave me to mine."

"You're getting mighty sassy these days." He finished his coffee, then scraped back his chair. "Hurry along, Karin. I want to be back here before nightfall."

Karin didn't have to be told twice. Moments later, Jessie stood in the kitchen doorway watching the wagon holding Rafe and his two oldest children roll away.

True to her word, Jessie finished cutting out the pattern. Then, after putting Sissy down for her afternoon nap, she seated herself in the rocker to stitch the darts in the bodice. When every dart was finished, Jessie turned her attention to the side seams, working her needle in and out in neat, tiny stitches that would hold longer than the material lasted.

She was lost in her thoughts when she heard the clip-clop of hooves on the lane leading to the house and realized Rafe and the children must be coming home.

Even as that thought occurred, she became aware of the absence of wheels and the jangle of a harness and realized a single horseman was approaching.

Hurrying to the window, she saw the horse and rider in the distance. Jessie didn't have to distinguish the features to know the rider's identity. The blaze on the gelding told its own story. It was Scarface. The man from her past.

She didn't wonder at her sudden terror. She just reacted.

Hurrying to the girls' bedroom, she snatched Sissy into her arms, security blanket and all. "Be real quiet, sweetie," Jessie said. "We have to go outside."

"Dolly," the toddler muttered, squirming around, reaching chubby arms toward the rag doll.

"Okay, honey. Dolly comes, too."

She shoved the doll into Sissy's arms; then, with the child riding her hip, she hurried out the back door toward the nearby woods, knowing the house would provide cover for her escape.

Jessie shifted Sissy in her arms to make her more comfortable. "We're going to play a game," she told her.

"Game?" Sissy squirmed until she sat upright and her arms slid around Jessie's neck.

"Yes, honey. We're going to play hide-and-seek. Would you like that?"

Sissy nodded quickly, her blond curls bobbing in the wind. Her smile was wide, her blue eyes glowing.

"Shhh. Be real quiet, sweetie. We don't want anyone to hear us. If they found us too soon the game would be over."

Drawing a quick breath, she held the child tightly against her as she raced toward the woods.

Elation filled her as she reached the cedar thicket without the shout that would mean they'd been seen.

A quick glance backward told her Scarface was circling the house; a shiver of alarm swept over her. She had expected him to spend time knocking on the doors and wondered now why he hadn't.

Had he seen her leave?

That thought sent her deeper into the woods, over the thick layer of cedar needles that carpeted the path and muffled her footsteps. As it would muffle anyone's who followed them, she realized suddenly.

With that thought in mind, she left the trail and circled around bushes and fallen debris, working her way into the denser areas of the woods where each step would reveal the presence of anyone pursuing them.

A crackling sound ahead froze her in her tracks. Her heart leapt wildly, pulsing through her eardrums as she waited for attack.

The noise came again, followed by a dark blur low on the ground. Jessie stifled a scream before it erupted as she realized the blur was a small, furry creature with long ears. She identified the rabbit just before it scurried beneath another bush.

Then silence reigned.

"Jessie . . ."

"Hush, baby!"

Jessie willed her heart to stop beating so rapidly as she strained for the sound of hoofbeats that would mean Scarface was leaving. But the sound she heard drove terror into her soul. Brush crackled and popped beneath booted feet. Scarface was hot on their trail.

Oh, God, how could he know where they were?

Jessie hurried farther into the woods, winding her way through cedars and massive oaks and saplings that grew thick and unchecked and ivy that twined with the bare strings of grapevines and thickets of thorn.

The sun set in a blaze of glory, making the treetops look as though they'd been set aflame, but Jessie had no thought for the beauty surrounding her. Her ears were attuned to the man who followed them, the man who, she was certain, presented a danger to both herself and Sissy.

An owl hooted, a mournful sound, and goose bumps rose along Jessie's arms. Sissy cried out and buried her face in the crook of Jessie's neck.

"It's all right," Jessie crooned, soothing the little girl's fears. "It was just an owl, baby. Just a hungry old owl looking for his dinner."

"Jessie, I want to go home."

"I know, sweetie," Jessie whispered. "And we'll go soon. But let's play the game just a little bit longer. Okay? Just because Jessie is having so much fun?"

Jessie shifted the child, trying to settle her in a more

comfortable position on her hip. The youngster seemed to grow heavier by the minute.

Jessie's arm muscles quivered from the strain of supporting the toddler and trying to shield her from the branches as she cut through a bunch of willows.

Willows. Jessie realized suddenly that she must be near the creek. If she could find the cave it would provide a hiding place until Rafe returned from town.

"Jessie!"

Jessie's head jerked around at the sound of the masculine voice. Had Rafe returned? Oh, God, it must be Rafe!

"Jessie. I know you're there. You might as well come on out." The voice was masculine, deep and rough. But it was not Rafe's voice.

It was Scarface.

Clutching Sissy against her, she ran blindly, crashing through the forest with no thought except to escape her pursuer. She heard his triumphant yell before he gave chase.

Jessie broke through the woods and stumbled to a stop beside the wide stream. Which way to go? Which direction was the waterfall?

Knowing she dared not linger, Jessie headed upstream. Moments later she saw the waterfall that flowed over the rocky ledge. Then she began her search for the cave.

Fear held her in its grip as she searched the bushes around the cliff. As she pushed aside another cedar bush she could hear the snap, crackle, pop of branches as her pursuer drew closer.

Spinning quickly around, she was on the point of leaving when the ground suddenly gave way beneath her feet and she fell on her backside with a thump that knocked her breath away.

"Jessie!" Sissy cried out.

"Shhh! It's okay, honey. We're okay." She struggled to

regain her balance and her hand pushed at the rock behind the bush and found an empty space.

God be praised, she'd found the cavern.

Holding the toddler closer against her, Jessie crawled into the hole and moved quickly back into the passageway.

Sissy whimpered, becoming restless in her arms.

"Be real quiet, honey," Jessie whispered. "We don't want to be found."

They were in a dark, cool place and the air smelled musty. Jessie's eyes turned upward, toward the light that slanted in from a long crack high above her.

She realized then that it wasn't exactly a cave, but more of a crevice between two huge boulders, a space that measured only five feet or less in width.

Becoming aware of Sissy's gaze, she turned her attention to the child, while trying to keep her ears attuned for approaching footsteps. She had to keep the youngster quiet. "I just thought of something, sweetie," she whispered. "Wouldn't it be fun to take a nap together? Out here in this lovely cave?"

Sissy yawned again. "Uh-huh."

Jessie stretched out on the hard, rocky ground with the blanket-wrapped youngster held in the crook of her arm. "Nighty-night," she murmured, hoping the toddler would go to sleep immediately.

Jessie lay still, her heart beating fast, her ears straining as she listened for the sound of pursuit. If she could just hide out until Rafe returned, he would surely search for them when he found them gone.

Wouldn't he?

A sharp snap caught her attention. Then she heard the sound of cursing. A moment later a voice rang out. "I'm gonna find you, Jessie. And when I do you're gonna be dead meat."

Oh, God, she had been right. He did know her! And he meant to kill her!

Jessie looked at the toddler who cuddled against her and felt a surge of fierce protectiveness. She couldn't let Scarface find Sissy. A man like that would have no qualms about taking the life of an innocent child.

She had to stop him. Had to keep him from finding Sissy. If she waited until he left the waterfall, she could leave the cave without being seen. Then perhaps she could lead him back to the house where, hopefully, Rafe would be waiting.

Scarface continued to mutter threats but his voice was farther away now. Jessie knew it was time to act, and yet she continued to hesitate.

Perhaps if she lingered a while he would give up the chase and go away. Yet, could she take the chance that he might return and find the cave?

No. She could not. Sissy's life might depend on her leading Scarface away from the cave.

Quietly, Jessie crept out of the cave and made her way several yards downstream across the bluffs that lined the creek. Then, deciding she was far enough away from her pursuer to outrun him, she stepped on a branch and heard it snap.

She waited for a long moment, but heard nothing. She stepped on another branch, then yelled, "Ouch!" as though she'd been hurt.

The response was immediate. A loud crashing sounded near the cave and her heart jerked frantically. But he was leaving that area, making his way toward her as fast as he could.

Deliberately, Jessie led her pursuer farther downstream, and when she considered the distance was great enough from the cave, she walked on the fallen cedar needles to quiet her footsteps.

The creek that flowed twenty feet below her widened considerably as it entered the river and, from her vantage point, she could see the silhouette of the farmhouse.

Her hopes dimmed at the sight of the dark windows. Rafe had not yet returned.

Her attention was focused on the house so hard that she never heard the footsteps coming behind her.

She didn't feel the strong hands grab her . . . until it was too late.

Chapter Fourteen

Rafe was so absorbed in his own thoughts that his movements were automatic as he turned the team off the main road onto the lane leading to his home.

He was later than he had expected but, with Jessie there, he was sure to find a hot meal waiting for his family.

Jessie. How had they managed without her?

A smile tugged at the corners of his mouth as he remembered the surprise he'd brought her. It was a simple thing, and yet he knew she'd appreciate the musical powder box he'd found hidden in a corner of the general store. Although Karin had appeared surprised when he'd suggested they purchase the music box for Jessie, she had heartily approved.

It was such a little thing to give her when she had given them so much of herself. He couldn't give her money, though—she'd already refused it—so the gift was a way of expressing his appreciation for all she'd done for them.

His stomach growled at the prospect of the supper he'd

be eating within the hour. Had Jessie made apple pie again? Or would she have chosen to use the jar of apricots she'd been saving? It made no real difference to him. The prospect of either pie set his stomach to growling again.

The shadows had lengthened considerably by the time he reined the team up near the back door and waited for Karin to get out with her packages. He frowned at the dark kitchen window. Jessie had a habit of waiting as long as she could before using the lamp to save the oil. He would have to scold her again as he'd done so many times before. But he refused to do so tonight.

He frowned as he remembered her headache. It had been bad. He wished she'd stop trying so hard to remember her past.

Karin climbed down from the wagon and reached for her packages. "Jessie didn't light the lamp yet, Pa."

"I know. We'll have to scold her for being so thrifty at the expense of her eyes, won't we?"

She nodded. "Not today, though."

"No. Not today."

"You want me to unhitch the team, Pa?" Danny asked.

"No," Rafe replied. "But you'd better go ahead and milk the cow. I imagine Jessie has supper about ready." He threw a quick look at the window that had become even darker as the lengthening shadows blended into the surrounding darkness. "Wonder why she's so bent on leaving the light off so long?"

The thought continued to worry him as he urged the horses toward the barn. He was unharnessing the team when he heard a shout and looked up. Alarm streaked through him as he saw Karin running toward him.

"Pa! Jessie's not here! And neither is Sissy!"

The fear in her voice echoed his own. "Dammit! I shouldn't have gone off and left her alone!" His long strides carried him swiftly into the house where he searched rooms his daughter had already searched before him.

Jessie couldn't remember a time when she'd been so afraid. Rough hands trapped her wrists in an iron grip while foul breath washed over her.

"Let me go!" she cried, struggling with the scarfaced man who held her prisoner. "Turn me loose!"

"Not on your life," he snarled. "You got away from me once, but you ain't gonna do it again. This time I'll make sure you're dead before I leave."

"Why are you doing this?" she cried. "What have I ever done to you?"

He laughed harshly. "You don't remember, do you? I heard that about you in town but I didn't believe it. But it's true, ain't it? You don't remember nothing."

"Yes, it's true!" she cried. "I have no knowledge of my past. It's a complete blank."

He became still, yet the strength of his hold did not weaken. "Now ain't that a nice howdy-do?"

"Then you'll release me?" she asked hopefully.

His grin was evil. "I didn't say that. It don't make no nevermind whether or not you remember nothing about your past. The fact is you're still alive and I gotta come up with a dead body."

She sucked in a sharp breath. "Why? For God's sake, tell me why you want me dead?"

His grin widened, became a smile that chilled her blood. "Money, Jessie. It all boils down to money." His head bent lower. "But before I arrange this little accident I'm gonna do something I been wanting to do for a long time."

As his open mouth descended, washing her with foul odor, Jessie gagged and fought furiously, her body squirming, her head turning this way and that as she tried to evade his mouth.

They were getting closer to the edge of the bluff, she realized, but she couldn't free herself. *God, help me!* she cried silently. She continued to struggle with the scarfaced man even though she knew his hold was too strong. As her foot slipped off the edge of the bluff she saw a flash of light out of the corner of her eye and jerked her head around. A light had appeared in the window of the farmhouse.

Rafe was home.

Too late, though, she knew, when she felt the push that sent her over the edge of the bluff. The scream that erupted was involuntary, jerked from her throat by the horror of death as she plunged toward the creek below.

A scream echoed over the valley, pulling Rafe's head around and causing terror to pound through his veins.

"Pa!" Danny cried. "Did you hear that?"

"I heard!" Rafe set off at a dead run.

Danny lingered long enough to grab the rifle off the gun rack in Rafe's room before he followed his father. As he ran he listened for another scream that would lead them to Jessie but there was only the sound of their own presence, their boots crashing over brush and fallen logs and debris as they raced through the woods toward the creek that seemed so far away.

Jessie struck the water with a hard splash and a feeling of doom as she waited to be crushed against the bottom of the shallow stream. But luck was with her, at least momentarily. The water was deep where she'd fallen and although she struck the bottom heavily with her feet, she felt no injury as she kicked hard and surged upward.

As her head cleared water again she sucked in air, choking around the water that had filled her lungs. She coughed and choked as she trod water, trying to expel the liquid from her lungs. Then she searched for the nearest bank and realized darkness had descended on the valley, leaving only the moon to light her way.

Jessie swam in a circle, trying to orient herself. Moonlight glinted off the slime-slicked rocks that lined the nearest bank and she turned that way, her arms aching with every stroke, her muscles protesting the strain as she cleaved slowly through the water.

Her mind felt completely numb as she reached the bank and clutched at the slick rocks. Her hands slipped clumsily as she groped desperately for a handhold, finding a tiny break in the rock and holding on.

There was no strength or breath left in her body to pull herself out of the water so she clung to the rock, sucking air into her aching lungs as she tried to gather enough energy to drag herself out of the creek.

Suddenly she heard a crackling sound nearby, as though someone had trod over brush.

Rafe. With hope lighting her face, she looked up . . . and saw a man leave the darkest part of the woods nearby.

"Rafe?" she whispered.

Silence was her only answer as the man moved closer, leaving the shadows and stepping into the moonlight. Jessie sucked in a sharp breath as she saw the scar that streaked across his face.

Her horror erupted in a shrill scream.

Scarface laughed. "Thought you got away from me, didn't you, Jessie? Good thing I come down here to make sure you didn't survive the fall off that ledge."

Jessie pushed herself off the rock, kicking out to carry

her body into the stream, knowing it was the only way she'd ever escape him.

He laughed. "You might as well give in, 'cause you ain't gonna get away from me. They ain't no way I'm gonna be leaving here until you're dead. And then I'll take your body back with me."

Not if she could help it, Jessie thought grimly. She stroked through the water, putting distance between them as she made her way toward the other bank. And then she heard a splash that told her he was coming after her.

Jessie put all her effort into the strokes that brought her closer and closer to shore. Her heart was pounding so heavily that she couldn't hear the man who pursued her, but even so, she knew he was there.

Her feet touched sand and she waded through water that seemed intent on holding her back until she reached the shore. Only then did she turn around.

Oh, God, he was right behind her!

Knowing her only hope was to outrun him, she raced along the riverbank, her heart racing as fast as her feet, her breath coming in short spurts as she tried to outrace the man who was just as determined to catch her.

A quick glance around showed her he was in hot pursuit, that she was only moments away from being caught. Up ahead, the woods grew thickly along the bank. Should she enter those woods and take a chance on losing him that way?

Even as the thought occurred she remembered that she hadn't been able to elude him in the woods before. She would be safer on the other side of the creek since it was nearer to the farmhouse . . . and Rafe.

Realizing she'd never be able to swim fast enough to escape him, she knew she had to fool him into thinking she'd gone into the woods.

With that thought in mind, she raced around the bend

and entered the woods with a deliberately loud crash over the underbrush. Then, with only moonlight to guide her, she worked her way through the trees until she reached the creek again and slid silently into the water.

Jessie was almost across the creek when she heard the shout of discovery followed by a splash. Scarface had found her again. Her time had run out.

A calmness settled over Jessie as she realized she had no strength left to fight. As Scarface overtook her and pushed her beneath the water, Jessie realized nobody knew where Sissy was!

That was her last thought before she lost consciousness.

Rafe emerged from the cedar thicket near the river's bend, his son keeping pace beside him. The acrid taste of fear burned his throat as he wondered which direction to take. There were three directions to choose from: north, which led upriver; south, which led downstream; or west, which led up the creek that fed into the river at this point. The wrong decision might be fatal for Jessie and his daughter.

Oh, God, what should he do?

Scream, Jessie! he pleaded silently. *Help me find the way.*

"Pa . . ."

"Quiet!" Rafe listened for a sound . . . a footfall, a snap . . . anything that would give him direction. But there was nothing. Not even the croaking of frogs that were usually heard near the water.

"Pa!" Danny whispered again. "I hear water splashing."

Rafe stopped breathing to quiet the sound of his own heartbeat. And then he heard it, too. More like a swishing instead of a splash.

"Pa! There's somebody in the creek."

Rafe's head jerked around and his sweeping gaze found

the dark silhouette in the water several hundred yards away. In the darkness the object could have been mistaken for a pumpkin bobbing up and down had it not been for the wet hair that trapped a silver moonbeam.

"Jessie!" he shouted.

A deep voice muttered a harsh string of curses as a dark head jerked toward them. Then a pale hand thrust upward, followed by a slender arm that rose, flailed out, then went under again.

Horror seized Rafe as he realized what he was seeing, just as Danny's terror-stricken voice cried out.

"Pa! That's not Jessie! It's a man. And he's holding something under the water!"

With his heart in his throat, Rafe sprinted forward, then made a quick, clean dive into the water with enough force that it was only moments before he cleared water beside Jessie and her attacker.

Knocking aside the man who held her down, he lifted Jessie upward and felt relief as her head cleared water. But that relief was short-lived because her head lolled sideways as though her life force had completely drained away.

He had to get her ashore, had to breathe life into her. He'd done it once before, and he'd do it again. *Oh, God, please let her live,* he prayed silently as he plowed through the water with the woman who meant so much to him.

Something heavy plowed into him and he went under, taking Jessie with him. Hands gripped his shoulders and the weight on him appeared to grow as he struggled to escape their grip. His feet struck the sand and he kicked hard, bringing Jessie and himself to the surface again.

"I got her, Pa!"

Rafe saw the blur of a pale face surrounded by russet hair before he felt water closing around him again. But that one glimpse was enough to know that his son would do whatever he could for Jessie. Now it was up to Rafe to make certain her attacker couldn't interfere.

He struck out at the man holding him under, but the water made the blow sluggish, too slow to have any effect on his attacker.

Rafe's lungs began to burn—he had to have air. His fists were proving useless in the water.

Desperation lent him strength as he kicked at the other man. Rafe's attacker leaned forward and Rafe quickly wrapped his legs around the man's waist and leaned back hard. The movement made his attacker lose his grip and jerked him beneath the surface. With his legs tight around the other man, Rafe twisted his body until his head was above water, filled his lungs with air, then twisted again until his fingers could circle the man's neck.

His lungs burned for air, his chest felt as though a sharp knife was slicing through it, and still he refused to release the other man. Then, when he could hold out no longer, he surfaced and sucked in huge gulps of life-giving air.

A shout caught his attention.

"Pa! I can't get Jessie outta the water."

Jessie! The water cascading over Rafe's face blurred his vision as he swam toward his son and the limp figure that he held against the rocks. His breath tore through his lungs and his shoulder, arm, and leg muscles ached badly, yet he could not give in to the pain, not when a precious life hung in the balance . . . No! *Two* precious lives.

My God! Sissy! In the struggle, he'd forgotten his youngest daughter.

As he reached the creek bank, he saw the woman lying against the rocks and felt despair surge through him. She appeared lifeless. He turned her over and searched for a pulse.

"She's alive," he told his son. "Jessie." He patted her face. "Jessie!" When she didn't respond, he slapped her lightly and was rewarded by a soft moan. "Jessie! Open your eyes."

She moaned again. Her eyelids flickered. "Rafe?"

"Jessie!" Rafe slapped her harder. "Jessie! Come on! Open your eyes."

Her eyes opened and she stared up at him. "Why did you slap me, Rafe?"

"I have to know what happened to Sissy," he said gruffly.

"Sissy?" She looked around. "Why are we in the water, Rafe?"

"Where's Sissy, Jessie? What did you do with my daughter?"

Fear closed around Jessie as memory returned. "Scarface! He—"

"He can't hurt you now," Rafe said quickly. "Jessie. I need to know where my daughter is. What happened to Sissy?"

Tears flooded Jessie's eyes. "She's in the cave, Rafe. Sleeping. And she'll be so frightened if she wakes up alone."

"Cave? The cave near the waterfall?"

She nodded.

"I'll get her, Pa. I know where she is." Danny scrambled over the slick rocks and soon disappeared into the darkness.

"Where's Scarface?" Jessie asked fearfully.

Rafe turned his head. Moonlight glinted on the water, but not a ripple marred its surface. "He's gone, Jessie. He won't be bothering you again."

"Gone? Where? We have to find him, Rafe. He knows who I am. He could tell me . . ."

"He's done answering questions, Jessie."

Before Jessie could ask what Rafe meant, Danny returned with Sissy in his arms. She yawned and stretched, then smiled down at Jessie. "I want to swim, too, Jessie."

"No, Sissy," Rafe said. "It's too cold for swimming." He looked at his son. "She's all right?"

"Yeah," Danny replied. "She was sound asleep."

"Thank God." Rafe heaved a sigh of relief. "Take her back to the house, Danny. Have Karin feed her and put her to bed."

"I'm not sleepy, Poppa!" Sissy protested loudly.

"All right. You don't have to go to bed yet. But go with Danny. And be a good girl."

"I want to go swimming," Sissy said loudly.

"It's too cold, Sweetie," Jessie said. "I'm freezing in here."

Jessie shuddered as a chill swept over her.

As Danny carried the protesting toddler away, Rafe dragged himself out of the water and reached for Jessie. When they were both on dry land again, he wrapped her in his arms for a long moment.

"Let's go home, darling," he said gruffly.

Home.

The word brought a sense of peace to Jessie. And, with Rafe's arms lending her strength, they made their way, together, toward the log cabin that had become home to her.

Chapter Fifteen

At the first light of dawn, Rafe saddled his horse and rode into Castle Rock. The door to the sheriff's office was locked, but Rafe had expected that. He crossed the street to the cafe where Watson always ate his morning meal. As Rafe shoved the door open, his nostrils were assailed by the aroma of fried meat, hot coffee, and baking bread, which made his stomach rumble appreciatively.

Rafe's narrowed gaze traversed the room, stopping on the sheriff, who occupied his usual table that kept his back against the farthest wall.

Lucas Watson's eyes narrowed as he watched Rafe approach. "Howdy, Rafe," he growled. "You looking for me?"

"How'd you guess?"

Lucas grinned. "Saw you outside my office." He motioned to the young, blond waitress. "Martha, bring Rafe some hot coffee."

Rafe jerked out a chair and joined the sheriff at the

table. "Steak and eggs, too, Martha. And a couple of hot biscuits."

Watson's lips curled up at the edges. "I take it you missed breakfast."

"Yeah. Jessie had a rough night."

"Time was when you did your own cooking out there . . . with a little help from Karin."

"Yeah. Time was." Rafe removed his hat and tossed it onto the chair beside him, then watched Martha pour his coffee.

"Your breakfast will be right out, Rafe. Cook's working on it now."

Rafe nodded. "Thanks, Martha."

Over coffee, Rafe told the sheriff why he had come.

Sheriff Watson listened silently until Rafe stopped talking. Then, lifting his cup, he sipped his coffee and allowed his gaze to travel over the other occupants of the room. "I don't suppose he coulda just been some stranger who was passing through and happened to see something he wanted?"

"No. He was definitely after Jessie. She said he spoke her name and made threats."

Lucas Watson's lips flattened and his eyes were hard as marbles. "Made threats? What kind of threats?"

"Hell, Lucas! I don't know exactly what he said. Jessie was naturally upset. Scarface nearly killed her. I didn't ask for details."

"Scarface?"

Before Rafe could reply, the waitress slapped a large plate down on the table in front of Rafe. "Steak and eggs," she said. "And *four* hot biscuits."

Rafe looked at the steaming plate and picked up a fork, but before he could dig in, Watson spoke again. "Why did you call him Scarface?"

"That's what Jessie called him. She didn't know his

name, but he had a scar. Ran sorta like this.'' Rafe slashed his finger across his cheek.

Sheriff Watson was thoughtful for a long moment. ''Beats me why anybody'd want to hurt that little gal. She couldn't have done nothing to make somebody want to do her harm. From what I hear she don't even know how to frown.'' He fixed cold eyes on Rafe. ''You sure he's dead?''

''No. I'm not sure. But I think he might be. I was so worried about Jessie ... thought at first he'd drowned her.'' He shoved back a stray lock of hair. ''And when I finally remembered the son of a bitch there was no sign of him, no sign of the water having ever been disturbed. Jessie was shivering something fierce so I took her home, then went back to the river and looked for him.'' He sighed heavily. ''For all the good it did me.''

''I suppose she's mighty upset.''

''You're damn right she is. And she's trying to hold it all inside. She'd do better to let all that emotion out, to scream and yell and kick stuff.'' He sighed heavily. ''But that's not her way.''

''No. I guess it's not. Rafe ... I spoke to Doc Lassiter the other day, and he mentioned Jessie. Says he thinks there's a reason her memory's still gone. That there might be something she don't want to remember.''

''Yeah. He told me that, too.'' Rafe laid his fork beside his plate. ''I guess I'm not so hungry after all.''

''You worried about what she's not remembering?''

''I've thought on it some.''

''Figures.'' Watson reached for his hat. ''Give me enough time to round up a posse and we'll ride out with you.''

Rafe slid back his chair. ''I need to go on home, Lucas. I don't like leavin' Jessie alone with nobody but the kids for company. Not when she's so strung out. Just let me know when you're ready to search the river and I'll join you."

"No. You stay with Jessie and the kids. There'll be enough folks to look for that scarfaced man."

When Rafe reached for his wallet, Watson shook his head. "Put that away, Rafe. Breakfast is on me." He grinned widely. "You shoulda ate it."

Jessie was washing dishes after the noon meal when Karin reminded her of the upcoming hayride.

"I know my dress isn't finished yet," she said hesitantly. "But they won't be coming for me until after dark and since there's only the hem to be done I thought maybe you could show me . . ."

Looking up from the dishpan, Jessie noticed the girl's anxious expression. "I forgot the hayride was tonight, Karin. Don't worry about your frock. I'll finish it this afternoon."

"Oh, no," Karin said quickly. "Pa said I wasn't to bother you about it."

Jessie summoned up a smile for the girl. "Don't worry so much, sweetie," she said softly. "I'll handle your pa."

Karin's eyes puddled and her lips trembled. "Am I being selfish, Jessie?"

"Oh, no, honey," Jessie assured her. "Of course not. Why should you even think that?"

A tear spilled over and slid down Karin's face. "Because it feels like somebody just died."

Jessie dried her hands and wrapped her arms around the girl. "I'm sorry, Karin. I'm responsible for this heavy atmosphere. And I didn't mean for it to be that way." She pushed the girl back and gripped her face between her palms. "There's no earthly reason you shouldn't go out with your friends and enjoy yourself, Karin. Not even one.

Now you stop worrying so much about what happened last''—she swallowed hard, then continued—''last night, and go out and enjoy yourself.''

Karin threw her arms around Jessie's neck. ''I'm so glad you're here, Jessie. Please don't ever go away!''

''I hope I don't ever have to,'' Jessie murmured, smoothing her palm over the girl's back.

As though suddenly embarrassed by her emotion, Karin released Jessie and stepped away. ''I've been thinking about that plum thicket, Jessie. You reckon there's any ripe plums on it yet?''

''I don't know,'' Jessie replied. ''It may be too soon.''

''I think I'll have a look at it this afternoon. If you don't need me here.''

''No!'' Jessie said sharply. Then, softening her voice, she said, ''I wish you'd stay close to the house until those men have completed their search.''

''All right,'' Karin agreed. ''I can look at the plum bush later.''

Jessie knew the girl felt confined in the house, knew as well that there was no real reason to keep her there. And yet, until they knew the fate of Scarface, knew for certain he wasn't hiding somewhere nearby, she felt a need to keep the children within shouting distance.

''Do you have something I could do?'' Karin asked hesitantly.

''Well . . .'' Jessie searched her mind for something to keep the girl busy, then remembered Rafe saying they needed to give some of the kittens away. ''You could pick out the kittens you want to keep,'' she suggested.

''We can't keep them all?''

''No. I thought your pa would have told you.''

Karin placed her hands on her hips. ''Well, he didn't! And there's only six. I don't see why we have to get rid of—'' She broke off and her eyes became round with horror. "He's not going to drown them, is he?"

"Oh, no, honey. He wouldn't do that." Jessie knew that some of the farmers did exactly that. But surely not Rafe. No. He would find the kittens a good home. "He said you can keep two of them."

"Just two?" Karin wailed. "How can I pick just two?"

Jessie's lips twitched. "I imagine it will be hard, but I feel certain you'll manage somehow. Sissy might be able to help."

"She'll want to keep all of them. But I'll take her with me anyway." She eyed Jessie. "This could take all day, you know."

Jessie knew—and hoped it did. At least Karin would have her mind off the searchers that continued to scour the riverbanks for the scarfaced man who had tried to drown her.

She was in the parlor, working on Karin's frock, when she heard the sound of hooves accompanied by the squeak of saddle leather. She set aside her work and looked out the window. It was Sheriff Watson.

He dismounted by the corral where Rafe waited and the two men spoke together for a long moment, then headed for the back porch.

Jessie was gathering cups from the cabinet when they entered the kitchen. She looked at the two men, but when she found their expressions unreadable, she directed her attention to the coffeepot on the stove.

Sheriff Watson shifted his weight, then reached up and lifted his hat. " 'Afternoon, Jessie."

"Sheriff." Jessie poured coffee into the cups. "Please sit here. Would you like a piece of pie to go with your coffee?"

Rafe noticed Jessie's wan features, the tense way she clutched the coffeepot as though using it for a shield. He was worried about her. She'd been quiet all day. Too quiet. And, with each passing hour, she seemed more distant, as though afraid if she allowed her feelings to show they would completely overwhelm her.

It wasn't a good situation. He didn't like the thought of Lucas questioning her. Not in her frame of mind. Yet Rafe knew they needed answers. Perhaps if they spoke of other things for a while, just a general conversation so she could relax, then maybe the memories would be easier for her to handle.

Lucas cleared his throat. "I didn't come for coffee and pie, Jessie," he said gruffly. "I came to—"

"You get pie first, Lucas!" Rafe growled. "Set yourself down there." He pulled out the chair across from Watson and turned to Jessie. When he spoke again, his voice was gentle. "Here, Jessie. Join us, please. I'll bring another cup."

Jessie slid into the chair and waited quietly while Rafe poured another cup of coffee, then brought plates, the apple pie, and three forks.

Sheriff Watson lifted his cup and took a long swallow. Then, with a determined look at Rafe, he set the cup down again. "Jessie . . . I need—"

"I said *later!*" Rafe snapped. "You just got here, Lucas. Now eat!" He shoved a large wedge of apple pie toward the sheriff and handed him a fork.

Watson cut into the pie and shoved a forkful into his mouth. He chewed slowly; then a genuine smile curved his lips. "That's some kinda apple pie, Jessie. Reckon it's about the best damn pie I ever ate."

"You aren't through with it yet," Rafe growled.

Without a protest, the sheriff shoveled more in his mouth and washed it down with a hearty swig of coffee. He sighed heavily and flicked a quick look at Jessie, then at Rafe, who was eying him severely.

"It's all right, Rafe," Jessie said. "I have to talk about this." She met the sheriff's gaze. "You didn't find him?"

"No. But that don't mean he's not dead, Jessie," Watson said quickly. "He could be caught in some brush or debris somewhere, or he might even be so waterlogged he's at the bottom of the river."

"Or he could have survived."

Rafe's hand covered hers. "No, honey. He couldn't have survived." Rafe was sure of it. He had felt the man's neck between his fingers, had felt the life go out of him, but he wasn't about to tell her that. "He's dead, Jessie. Believe me."

There was real fear in her eyes when she met his gaze. "I can't believe it, Rafe. I dare not. He could be out there now. Waiting."

"I think Rafe's right, Jessie. We'll alert folks along the river downstream, tell them to keep a sharp eye out for a body that might wash up." He ran a finger around the rim of his cup. "How's Sissy taking all this?"

"Just fine," Rafe replied. "She has no knowledge of what took place. Jessie made a game of the whole thing. Told Sissy they were playing hide-and-seek."

The sheriff arched a brow. "And Sissy accepted that?"

"Yeah."

"That's good." He tapped a long finger against the oak table and cleared his throat. "I hate to bother you with details, Jessie, but I need to know what he said to you. His exact words. He might've let something slip that would explain why he was after you."

She shook her head. "No. There was nothing."

"Tell me anyway. Everything. Start at the beginning."

Jessie told him what happened from the moment she'd recognized Scarface. When she had finished, the sheriff was no wiser than he'd been before. With a heavy sigh, Watson pushed back his chair.

"What are you going to do now?" Jessie asked.

"Not much I *can* do, Jessie. I'll have Cal Conroe contact you. He's an artist—he'll draw a picture using your description. I'll send it around the county and see if anything comes from it." The sheriff rose to his feet. "Whatever that man's reasons were, he won't be telling us." He eyed Jessie sympathetically. "Don't worry no more about him. I reckon his days of causing trouble are over. And the world is better off for it, too."

Rafe saw the sheriff out, then returned to Jessie. She sat in her chair, pleating the material of her skirt, smoothing it out, then pleating it again as though completely unaware of what she was doing.

Squatting down beside her chair, Rafe wrapped his arms around her and gently stroked her back.

"The sheriff's right, Jessie. Whatever his reasons might have been, Scarface can't hurt you now. You're safe here with us."

If only she could believe that, Jessie thought. If only she could believe the nightmare was over.

Darkness had settled over the valley by the time the wagonload of laughing young people arrived. Jessie tried to hide her fear as Karin, dressed in her new frock, snatched up the basket of food that had been prepared earlier and reached up to kiss her father's rough cheek.

"See you later, Pa." Shyly, she turned to Jessie. "Thank you, Jessie."

She hurried to the door, then stopped, spinning around in a flurry of skirts. "Whoops! I almost forgot Danny!" Raising her voice, she yelled, "Hurry up, knothead! They're here!" A moment later she joined the laughing teenagers sprawled on the hay-covered wagon.

Danny ran into the kitchen, fumbling with the top button on his shirt. As he passed the platter of cookies left out on the counter he snatched a handful and stuffed them in his pocket. "See you later, Pa . . . Jessie," he called and ran through the door.

Moments later, Jessie and Rafe, with Sissy in his arms, stood together on the porch, watching the wagonload of young people roll away into the night.

Rafe was aware of Jessie's tension as she watched them leave. "Don't worry about them," he said. "They'll be fine. Joe Bob Thompson is a responsible young man."

"He was the boy driving the team?"

"Yeah."

"He looked so young. And they only have lanterns to light their way."

"Joe Bob is nineteen years old, Jessie, and he's been working his pa's farm alone for the past four years. That big old moon above is doing a good job of lighting their way. Those lanterns are only for emergencies." He tilted her chin up so she'd have to look at him and the fear in her eyes smacked him in the gut. "Don't look like that, sweetheart. Trust me. The kids are gonna be fine."

She laughed uneasily. "I think there's something wrong with this conversation."

He slid an arm around her waist. "How so?"

"I imagined I would be the one offering reassurance, that you'd be tense and nervous about Karin going off with them, but it's the other way around, isn't it? You're the one holding me up."

"It's the circumstances, honey. You're still nervous because of last night." *Dammit! Why'd he have to go and remind her about that? She'd been relaxing against him until he'd opened his big mouth.*

"I wish they'd found his body, Rafe."

"I am tired, Jessie," Sissy said, rubbing her eyes and

reaching plump arms toward Jessie. "I want to go to sleep now."

"Jessie's tired, Pumpkin," Rafe said gruffly. "I'll put you to bed."

"Uh-uh." Sissy shook her golden curls and stretched farther.

"It's all right, Rafe. I really don't mind."

Maybe I do, though. Rafe felt a momentary burst of jealousy, then realized how useless that was. And stupid. Jessie had taken a load off him when she'd taken over Sissy's care. Karin, too. This time last month his oldest daughter wouldn't have asked to go on the hayride. She'd have crawled into her bed, exhausted from her day's work, while her friends had fun. Hell! Karin had no friends before Jessie arrived.

Jessie had done so much for them, more than he could ever repay, and when she joined him in the parlor, he intended to let her know how much he appreciated her efforts.

But Jessie didn't join him. She stopped momentarily to make certain he was waiting up for his children; then, claiming fatigue, she told him she was retiring.

Rafe sat a while in the parlor, hearing Jessie toss and turn through the thin wall that separated them. Then, unable to relax with her so near yet so far away, he went outside. He'd only been there a short while when he heard the sound of hooves and the creak of saddle leather. Moments later Lucas Watson reined his horse up beside him.

"Thought you might be awake," Watson said, dismounting easily.

"What brings you out this way, Lucas?"

"I was worried about Jessie. She okay?"

"I guess. She's mighty nervous, though."

"That's the reason I didn't wait until morning. We found him, Rafe."

"Alive?"

"Nope. He was dead. Just like you figured. One of the Reynolds boys found him."

Reynolds. Rafe knew the family. The Reynolds farm was almost five miles downriver. "Much obliged to you for coming out tonight, Lucas. Jessie's in there tossing and turning, worrying about that skunk coming back here. Maybe now she'll be able to relax."

"Hope so." Lucas sighed and arched his back. "It's been a mighty long day, Rafe. Reckon I'll mosey on home now. You folks have a good night."

A good night might be possible now, Rafe silently told himself. Then he went back into the house to give Jessie the news.

Chapter Sixteen

Rafe had his fist raised to knock on the bedroom door when a sudden thought stopped him. Jessie might have gone to sleep. If so, he didn't want to disturb her. He listened quietly, but heard no sound.

He turned away from the door, then stopped again. Even though he'd heard no sound she might be awake, lying on the bed, worrying about the skunk who'd tried to drown her.

Needing to make certain, yet unwilling to disturb her sleep if she was resting, Rafe gripped the doorknob and eased the door open. A shaft of lamplight streamed through the doorway, reaching the four-poster bed. Jessie was crouched against the farthest wall, her green eyes wide with fear, her fist jammed against her mouth to stifle a scream.

"Jessie, sweetheart." He strode quickly across the room and reached across the bed, pulling her trembling body into his embrace.

Her arms twined around his neck and she buried her head against his chest.

"It's okay, love," he whispered, stroking her hair gently. "Everything is fine."

"I'm sorry to be such a coward," she whispered, "But I heard somebody ride in and when I saw the door opening I thought he'd—"

"Shhhh!" he whispered. "Shhhh." He rocked her back and forth. "He's dead, honey. They found his body. Scarface won't be bothering you again."

She lifted her head and stared up at him with wide, green eyes. "Dead? They found his body?"

"Yes. The Reynolds boy found him."

She started crying then, the tears flowing like water over a dam. Her body began to shake uncontrollably. Rafe didn't know what to do except hold her. And he did, pressing her head against his chest, and murmuring soothing words as she cried away the fear that had held her in its grip for so long.

As the tears slowed, Jessie became aware of the harshness of Rafe's breath, of the echo of his heart, so close to her lips. She felt the tension that spoke of his control, tenuous at best, and felt a fierce need for him overwhelm her.

"Rafe," she whispered, tilting her head to gaze up at him with tremulous vulnerability.

Rafe's need for her overcame his good sense. He lifted her chin and slanted his mouth across hers, kissing her hungrily. His fingers were rough and the thunder of his heart pounded through his eardrums.

Jessie's arms twined around Rafe's neck, her fingers sliding through his thick hair. The solid wall of his chest both tormented and comforted her. But it was not enough.

"Open your mouth," he muttered. "I want to taste you."

Her mouth opened beneath his and she felt the quick intrusion of his tongue as the fire he had ignited exploded into flame. She groaned, her hands seeking the ridge of his chest muscles. She wanted to touch him, needed to feel his flesh beneath her fingers.

As their tongues fought a duel, her fingers worked frantically at the buttons that fastened his shirt. Her senses reeled as she felt the tickle of hair against her fingers, the security of his warm flesh.

His mouth was insatiable, his body impatient with need. He pressed her back onto the bed, covering her body with his own; she could feel the tautness of his thighs as his hips raked against hers, his legs insinuating themselves between hers. Her body was a riot of sensation, her breasts aching with need. He tugged her nightgown up and his hands covered her breasts, caressing them.

"Oh, Rafe," she groaned. "What are you doing to me?"

He lifted his head and looked at her. "Loving you, Jessie," he muttered harshly. "I'm loving you."

His eyes glittered with passion in the light streaming through the door. *The door.* They had forgotten the door was open.

As Rafe's head bent to her breast again, she struggled against the feelings that swept over her.

"The door, Rafe. Sissy might wake up."

Rafe moved swiftly, closing the door and wedging a chair beneath the doorknob. Then, he turned back to her, shedding his clothing as his quick strides carried him to the bedside again. As his breeches dropped to his ankles, he kicked them aside and stood before her, a magnificent man, capable and ready.

Then he was beside her again, smoothing her gown away, tossing it aside to join the garments that puddled on the floor. When he came to her again, she sighed with pleasure. Her body was entwined with his as he tasted her breasts again, filling his mouth with first one and then the other, suckling, caressing, nipping until Jessie could stand no more.

She raked his back with her fingernails, silently pleading for him to stop the aching need that continued to grow in her lower belly. He delighted in tormenting her. He nibbled her earlobe, tasted her chin, the inside of her elbow, until she sobbed with need. When his fingers found the hot core of her she thought he was intent on satisfying that need. Until his fingers dipped into her.

His touch was almost painfully exquisite, the feathering of his caresses agonizing. Jessie clutched at him, raking her hands across his back, bucking her body beneath his as he stoked the fire that threatened to consume her.

"Please, Rafe," she cried urgently. "I can't stand any more."

He lifted his head and watched her avidly. "Do you want me to stop?"

"No! Yes. No! Don't stop! Don't ever stop."

She was on the knife edge of something important. A wave that lapped her body, threatening to wash over it, deep, hot, so close that she couldn't go back, could only go on to whatever awaited her.

Rafe moved above her, positioning himself between her legs again, and she felt a probing between her thighs. His hands tangled in her hair as his mouth covered hers in a deep, probing kiss. And then he plunged into her. Jessie felt a momentary pain that was quickly gone; then there was only the feel of him, slick and hot and sweet. He was still for a moment, then began to move within her. A shudder swept over Jessie as he began to stoke the fire again, plunging deeper than the fire, deeper than the need.

Arching against him, Jessie clutched his shoulders as his tongue mated with hers and his hands worked his magic on her breasts. She whimpered and moaned and felt her body tremble, begging for release. But Rafe was patient, stroking her body as he worked to bring the flame of desire higher and higher.

Jessie knew she couldn't stand much more. It was a pleasure that bordered on pain as the fire continued to build into a white-hot storm. Then suddenly she was there, shuddering on the peak. She cried out, a high, keening sound that went on and on as her body shattered into a thousand fragments. As her body reached completion, Rafe's quickly followed. He threw his head back and, with a hoarse, rasping cry, he gave a mighty shudder and collapsed against her.

They lay quietly together, Rafe's arms tightly around her, his breath shivering against her ear. Jessie looked up and found him watching her.

She blushed hotly and his lips twitched slightly as if he were aware of her embarrassment and was amused by it.

"I like holding you in my arms," he said softly, picking up a long, russet curl and twisting it lightly between his fingers.

"And I like being here," she admitted, lowering her lashes to shield her eyes.

"Then give me the right to keep you here, Jessie."

Her gaze flicked up and met his and she basked in the warmth she saw there. "What do you mean?"

"Marry me, Jessie. Be my wife and mother to my children."

"We don't know about my past, Rafe." Tears moistened her eyes. "There might be . . . ."

"There is nobody important in your past, Jessie. No husband. I think we just proved that."

"We did?"

"Yes." His voice was husky, seducing her senses, doing mad things to her pulse and heartbeat. "We most certainly did."

"And you really know for certain?"

"Yes, Jessie," he said gently. "I know for certain." He traced the line of her mouth. "You're such an innocent."

"Not any more," she said primly. "I think you dealt with that little problem. Quite nicely, I might add."

"I guess I did at that." His eyes began to smolder. "But I wouldn't mind dealing with it again. Just in case."

The hope in his voice was her undoing. A giggle escaped her lips. He was insatiable. Totally adorable.

As if drawn by the sparkle in her eyes, Rafe lowered his lips and he kissed her softly.

Jessie returned the kiss fervently. As her senses began to swim, she twined her arms around his neck and pulled him closer.

He kissed her once again, then leaned back on one elbow to study her flushed cheeks. "You didn't answer my question, Jessie."

"Yes, Rafe."

"Yes, you didn't answer my question, or yes, you'll marry me."

"Yes, I'll marry you. If that's what you really want."

"It is, my love. It's exactly what I want." His mouth found hers again and latched onto it as though he would never let her go. And Jessie found deep contentment in that fact, totally secure in his love. All the problems that would arise in the future, they would handle together. With Rafe beside her nothing would ever frighten her again.

Her world was secure.

The sound of wagon wheels brought them back to reality.

"Dammit!" Rafe growled. "That's the kids coming home."

He jerked to his feet and yanked on his breeches, his fingers fumbling in their haste as the wagon stopped in the yard. They heard the sound of laughter as he snatched up his shoes and shirt and leapt across the room to pull the chair out of the way.

Jessie was bathed in the lamplight that streamed through the doorway and, knowing she'd be seen when the children entered, she slid from the bed and was shoving her door closed as the kitchen door opened.

She stood there, naked, shivering against the closed door, her heart thudding wildly as she listened to the sound of conversation. A question was asked and a deeper voice replied. Rafe. The voices quieted, as though Rafe had hushed them, and then the footsteps faded.

Silently, Jessie returned to her bed, put on her gown, and reached for the cover that had been swept to the floor during their lovemaking. Smoothing the quilt on the mattress, she pulled it back and climbed on the bed. Then she lay there, wishing Rafe's arms were around her again, wishing they could sleep together, that she could wake up in the morning snuggled close in his arms.

But that time would come, she told herself. And soon. Rafe had asked her to marry him, and although she had no memory of her past, she had accepted.

If her memories should suddenly return, and there was something in her past that could not be ignored, then they would face it together.

Together. Such a beautiful word.

Sighing contentedly, she snuggled down and closed her eyes and promptly fell asleep.

Chapter Seventeen

"Jessie!"

Jessie's door slammed open and she jerked upright, her heart skip-hopping in her chest. Karin stood in the doorway in her flannel nightgown, her hair tousled from sleep, her blue eyes glittering with happiness.

"Is it true, Jessie? Is it? Are you really going to be our mother?"

Jessie realized Danny stood poised expectantly behind Karin, as though waiting for the answer with as much eagerness as his sister. Rafe stood behind his son, his hand on the boy's shoulder, his eyes on Jessie, and a smile widening his lips.

They all seemed to be waiting for her to speak.

But before she could do so, Sissy, who was unacquainted with patience, dashed forward and threw herself on the bed and into Jessie's arms. "You gonna be our ma, Jessie?" she asked eagerly.

Jessie laughed huskily and looked beyond the children

to the man who had stolen her heart. "I guess I am, sweetie. Yes. I'm going to be your mother."

"Yeah!" Danny yelled, leaping into the air and twirling around as though he was a ballet dancer.

"Oh, Jessie!" Karin burst into tears and threw herself at Jessie, almost squashing Sissy as she did so. "I'm so glad you're gonna stay."

"I am, too, sweetie," Jessie said, patting Karin on the shoulders, looking helplessly at Rafe, who had turned away from them.

"Stop blubbering, Karin," Danny said. "You been worrying all this time that Jessie's gonna be leaving us and now that she's staying for good you break down and bawl." He turned away. "Girls!" he growled.

"Never mind him," Jessie said, tears shimmering in her own eyes. "He doesn't know the way of things, sweetie. Sometimes it's good to cry."

Karin sniffled, then wiped her eyes with the back of her hand. "I know," she said. "And I'm sorry about waking you up, but when Pa told us I was afraid he was just fooling. And I had to know. I just had to."

"Of course you did. And from the looks of that sun, I'd say it's past time I was out of bed anyway." She shoved back the covers and slid out of bed while Sissy took advantage of being alone on an unmade bed and rolled over and over, giggling all the while.

"How was the hayride?" Jessie asked, crossing the room to extract a day dress from the chest of drawers.

"It was fun," Karin said. But there was something in her voice that caught Jessie's attention.

"But . . ."

"But Danny made himself obnoxious."

Jessie raised an eyebrow. "He did? How?"

"He stuck with me like honey to a bee. When I asked

him politely to leave he was so rude that it made me blush to admit he was my brother.''

"He stuck with you?" Jessie frowned. "But I thought everyone was staying together. You don't mean you separated, do you?"

"Well, for a while." She pleated the bedsheet between her fingers, keeping her eyelids lowered to hide her expressive eyes. "We picnicked at Johnson's Creek, where the kids from town go to swim. And some of us, when we were finished, well, we kind of went off to look at the stars . . . and the moonlight. You know how it is, Jessie."

"Yes. I do know, hon. But maybe Danny knows, too. Maybe that's the reason he stayed close by."

"No, it wasn't!" Karin's eyelids jerked up and her eyes were furious. "It was just because I was with Joe Bob, and he didn't . . ."

"Joe Bob?" Jessie stopped in the act of sliding her dress over her head, her gaze fixed on Rafe's oldest daughter. "You mean the young man who drove the team?"

"Yes."

"You were with him?"

"Uh-huh." Karin's eyes lowered, concealing her expression.

"What happened to Johnny? I thought you liked him?"

"I do. But there's something about Joe Bob that makes me feel funny. My stomach . . ."

"I thought Johnny made your stomach feel funny."

"Well, he does. When he kisses me. But Joe Bob doesn't have to touch me. He can just look at me and goose bumps break out on my arms and my knees get shaky and, well, you know, don't you?"

"Yes, sweetie, I know." She buttoned her bodice. "What about Johnny, Karin? Was he upset when you went off with Joe Bob?"

"No," she said petulantly. "He was with Elizabeth Rollins."

Jessie controlled a grin, knowing it wouldn't be appreciated. "Does Danny have anything against Joe Bob? I mean, maybe he has a bad reputation or something."

"Joe Bob is about the sweetest boy I ever met!" Karin said indignantly. "A lot nicer than Johnny Walker, that's for sure."

"Sounds like Johnny might be in trouble." Jessie frowned at Karin. "But I don't really understand, sweetie. I thought Joe Bob was older, that he had his own farm somewhere nearby."

"He does, Jessie. And he's really proud of it, too. He has a lot of plans for it. He told me all about it while we looked at the stars. He said he's not always going to farm, though. That someday he's going to breed horses. He'll plant some of his fields to raise feed for them. He already has a thoroughbred. A stallion. He's kinda old, Joe Bob says. But he thinks he can get a few colts from him before he has to be put out to pasture."

Karin sounded completely infatuated with the young man and that worried Jessie. He was obviously too old for Karin. Danny had known that, and had reacted accordingly. But how could she make Karin understand? Perhaps, she thought, there would be no need. If she just left it alone, the whole thing might fizzle out.

And if it didn't, then she would deal with it later.

It was mid-morning when a horse and buggy pulled up outside the house. Jessie looked out the kitchen window and saw Jacob Lassiter climbing out of the carriage.

Realizing she hadn't seen Jacob since the barn dance, Jessie opened the door and invited him inside. His expression was one of concern.

"I just heard what happened, Jessie. Are you all right?"

Jessie's engagement was so new, so fresh in her mind, that she thought Jacob was asking about that. "I'm fine, Jacob," she said, laughing. "Quite happy, in fact."

His frown deepened. "So I see. I must admit that comes as a relief. I was afraid such an ordeal would have been too much for your mind."

"My mind?" She stared at him, wondering what he was talking about. Then suddenly she realized he was referring to her encounter with Scarface. "Oh. No. I'm just fine, really. And it's a real relief to know he won't be bothering me again."

"You didn't know what I was talking about, did you?" he asked gently.

"No," she admitted. "Actually, I had quite forgotten the whole thing."

He frowned again. "Sheriff Watson thought otherwise. He said that you were so distraught that he rode out here as soon as the body was found, afraid you wouldn't be able to sleep unless he did."

"Yes." She thought about what the sheriff's coming had led to and blushed hotly. "He did come out, and I haven't thanked him properly yet."

"Is there something else going on that I'm not aware of yet?" he asked. "Has your memory returned, Jessie? Have you remembered who you are?"

"No."

"Then what happened to you? Is that man's death responsible for the blush in your cheeks, for that happy glitter in your eyes?" He tilted her chin and held her gaze. "Tell me, what's going on?"

Before she could answer, Rafe entered the kitchen and stopped abruptly when he saw them together. A muscle clenched in his jaw and his lips flattened and his gray eyes resembled shards of glass.

"I thought that was your buggy out there, Jacob." His voice was harsh and grating as he stopped beside Jessie and circled her waist and pulled her against him, obviously staking his claim. "What're you doing out here?"

"I could ask you the same thing," Jacob Lassiter said grimly. "What *are* you doing out here?"

"I live here, Doc." Rafe's gaze raked the other man, his stance threatening.

"Yes, you do, Rafe. But Jessie is only visiting."

"Not for long."

"What does that mean?"

"Means there's going to be a wedding, Doc. Soon as it can be arranged."

Lassiter's gaze flicked to Jessie. "You agreed to that, Jessie?"

"Of course she did!" Rafe snapped. "Did you imagine I would force her to marry me?"

The anger Rafe generated vibrated through him; his words had suddenly thrown her into a panic. Why should that be? She knew Rafe, shouldn't be afraid of him, and yet her heart had begun to pound and red spots hovered at the edge of her vision.

What was happening to her? She blinked at the two men, her gaze flicking back and forth between them. They were faced off like two dogs, each one protecting its territory.

"Rafe," she whispered unsteadily, gripping his forearm with trembling fingers, but he ignored her completely in his endeavor to face off a man he considered his opponent.

Her head was swimming and Jessie knew there would be no relief from the dizziness unless she could sit down, but her knees were so weak they would most certainly not carry her to the parlor, or even to a kitchen chair.

Rafe seemed totally unaware of her problem, as did

the young doctor whose only interest appeared to be the argument that had sprung up between the two men. An argument that somehow went completely over Jessie's head, because she couldn't even understand their words, much less see their angry faces, which was good in a way, because she most certainly didn't want to carry those angry faces with her into this darkness that had taken hold of her.

She sensed she was collapsing, felt Rafe's arms tighten around her. Then she was swept up into his arms, which sent the rest of her senses to oblivion.

When Jessie regained consciousness, she was on the sofa and Jacob Lassiter was bending over her with his fingers on her wrist, looking anxiously into her eyes.

"What happened?" she asked.

"You fainted."

Jessie saw Rafe's anxious face as he watched from over Jacob's shoulder. She saw the love he felt for her reflected there and summoned up a smile, hoping to ease his strain.

Doc Lassiter opened her gown at the neck, slid his stethoscope against her chest, and listened intently. He lifted her eyelid and peered at her eye, then turned his attention to the other one.

"How do you feel?" he asked quietly.

"I have a headache," she replied.

"Where does it hurt?"

"At the base of my head."

"Not the temples this time?"

She shook her head, then wished she hadn't as hammers began to pound furiously.

He questioned her gently, trying to ascertain when the trouble started. But Jessie didn't know for sure. She thought the argument had set her off, but was tactful enough to keep that opinion to herself.

But the doctor must have guessed, because he didn't tarry long. When he was gone, Rafe took her into his arms and held her tight against him. Everything was all right in Jessie's world again.

Chapter Eighteen

Jacob Lassiter shoved open the door to the sheriff's office and stepped inside. Although the only light in the room streamed through a small window behind the desk, there was enough to make out the craggy features of the man seated there.

"Howdy, Doc," the sheriff said, looking up from the papers he'd been studying. It was a stack of WANTED posters that had just arrived by stagecoach.

"Hello, Lucas." Jacob sat in the chair across from the desk and nodded at the stack of posters. "Anything interesting there?"

"Haven't really had time to look through them yet," Watson replied. "Guess there's no hurry, though. We don't get many strangers traveling through here." He grinned wryly. "And when we do, they seem to wind up dead." His grin widened. "Maybe Castle Rock ain't such a healthy place for strangers."

"Jessie's a stranger."

Lucas Watson's eyes narrowed. "So she is. What of it?"

"I'm worried about that situation, Lucas."

"Worried how? You think Jessie is guilty of something? That she's faking her memory loss and is some kinda female outlaw that's using Castle Rock for a hideout?"

"Of course not!"

"Then what's bothering you?"

Jacob shifted in his chair, feeling suddenly uncomfortable with the sheriff's narrowed gaze fixated on him. "Did you know Rafe is planning to marry her?"

"No. But that don't surprise me none."

"And you think it's all right?"

"Hell, Jacob! It ain't up to me to object! And it ain't up to you, neither." His fingers twined together and he leaned forward. "They're both adults. And it's a fact that Rafe needs a wife and that little gal needs somebody to take care of her." His mouth tightened. "Now, suppose you tell me what's really got you all het up."

"I'm not 'het up,' as you call it," Jacob said stiffly. "But I have to wonder how legal it is for Jessie to marry when she doesn't even know who she is or where she came from."

"There's nothing in my lawbooks that says the wedding can't take place." He glared at the doctor. "And was I you, I wouldn't repeat this conversation to nobody. It might get back to Rafe and I don't suppose he'd be too happy about the whole thing."

"No. I'm sure he wouldn't."

"What did you really come here for?"

"I thought you might put some feelers out, Lucas. Try and find out where Jessie belongs."

"Now that ain't like you, Jacob. You're a kind man at heart, but you ain't acting that way now. In fact, you're acting like a dog that's trying his best to steal away another dog's bone."

"Maybe so," Jacob mumbled, feeling a red tinge creep up his face.

Jacob knew he should be ashamed of himself. It wasn't like him to go behind a man's back like this, but dammit! He knew in his heart that Rafe was taking advantage of Jessie's innocence. And he didn't like it one bit.

It had been three days since Rafe had proposed. Wonderful days. Days filled with much laughter and stolen kisses whenever they found themselves alone—a feat that, somehow, even with three children about, Rafe managed to accomplish on occasion.

The wedding was planned for Sunday, week after next, and Jessie was kept busy with all the arrangements. A wedding gown must be made, new clothes for the children, and invitations sent out.

But Jessie didn't mind the work. Instead, she gloried in it, knowing that when it was over, she would be part of the Sutherland family. And nothing that ever happened, no memory returning, no past catching up with her, could ever change the fact that she was Rafe's wife, mother to his children.

Jessie hummed softly to herself as she gathered eggs in the chicken house. She had been saving part of each day's yield to make the wedding cake.

When she'd gathered the last egg, she carried her basket outside and lifted her skirts to pick her way carefully across the chicken yard. When she was free of the clutter and the gate was fastened behind her, she lifted her face to the sky and laughed exultantly.

Rafe was working in the barn when he heard her laugh. It shivered through his body, turned his bones to jelly, and started a fire in his lower body.

Knowing the children were gone, and unable to resist temptation, he followed the sound outside.

Jessie was twirling around, her head tilted to the sky, laughing like a silly child, when a hand reached out and snagged her wrist and pulled her against a hard, firm body.

"Rafe!" she gasped, laughing up at him. "You startled me."

"That's not half of what you do to me," he teased, pressing her lower body against his.

She could feel the tautness of his thighs and blushed rosily as she remembered the night they'd made love in her bed. His head lowered and he claimed her mouth, probing quickly at the seam of her lips until she opened for him.

Jessie shivered as she felt his tongue dart inside and sweep the inner moistness of her mouth. She clutched the basket of eggs as though they were a lifeline; when his mouth lifted from hers and she stared into their blazing depths, she felt as though she'd been branded with a hot poker.

"Jessie," he groaned. "It seems forever since we were together. I want you desperately."

"The children . . ."

"Are gone. Danny is fishing and the girls went to examine the plum bushes." He tugged at her hand. "Come in the barn with me, sweetheart. I want to make love to you."

"In the barn?" she squeaked.

"Yes. It will be safer there."

They entered the barn together and her nostrils were assailed by the pungent scent of hay. Rafe took the basket of eggs and set them aside, then led her to a nearby stall that had a suspiciously large stack of fresh hay.

Her gaze twinkled up at him. "Did you have this planned?"

"What do you think?" he asked, leaning over to nibble on her earlobe.

"I think you did," she said huskily. "But how you managed to talk the children into leaving beats me."

"Beats me, too." He nipped at her neck as he unfastened her bodice, then pushed it aside. His mouth moved lower, his lips nuzzling at the swell of her breasts.

"Rafe," she said breathlessly. "I don't think this is a good idea."

"Don't think then."

He held her arm out and licked the inner part of her elbow and her legs wobbled, her knees threatening to buckle. As though knowing her reaction, he licked the same place again, then pushed her backward into the haystack and covered her body with his own.

There was no sound in the barn except their breathing.

Rafe's body was hard against hers; his rough hands slid down her body to caress the hillocks of her breasts, and she gasped at the pleasure that assailed her. His hands were eager, caressing, and her nipples grew taut beneath his fingertips.

She felt his heart beating in a rhythm that exactly matched her own. His manhood was hard, throbbing with passion as it pressed against her thigh.

Jessie melted against him, her body arching against the lean hardness of his and her fingers entangled in the thick darkness of his hair. This was her man. Of that she was certain. Their future lay together, and she would be everything to him, would see to all his needs.

"Rafe," she whispered, in unconscious longing as his lips left hers to trail a path of fire down her neck to the curve of her breast.

Ecstatic with longing, feeling light and boneless, Jessie fitted her body to his.

His mouth was moist as it teased first one nipple and

then moved to give the other satisfaction. Moaning low in her throat, Jessie felt delicious shudders quiver through her.

His hands stroked her body, inviting the rhythmic movement of her hips against him. His caress offered a vague satisfaction but not the complete kind that she craved.

"Please," she whispered, wanting him desperately. "Don't stop, Rafe."

She was begging him to make love to her, but she didn't care. Pride had no place in the love she felt for him. He was the man she wanted, the man she'd always waited for.

His hands were on her clothing, fumbling at the fastenings until they were stripped away and she lay naked beside him. Then he moved away suddenly, discarded his own clothing, and came to her again.

Rafe's naked flesh was against hers, his hair-coarsened legs brushing against her. She could feel the rough texture against her smoother flesh. His chest hairs rubbing on her breast drove her wild with desire.

He drank from the dark well of her mouth, plunging his tongue deep inside her, tasting, tempting, pulling panting little whimpers from her as she bucked beneath him.

Jessie was mindless with a pleasure that overwhelmed caution, leaving only this aching need. Caught in a raging tide, she was too besotted even to consider fighting it. When his leg parted her thighs, she felt the burning heat of him against her core.

He probed for entrance, then thrust quickly, penetrating deeply.

Incredible pleasure swept over her as Rafe stoked the fires of passion, driving his shaft deeper and swifter over and over again, until she was moaning involuntarily beneath the burning demand of his mouth.

With her arms locked tightly around his neck, he carried her to those incredible heights again. Rafe continued to stroke her, to kiss her deeply, holding off as long as he could while he built the ache to such an incredible sweetness that it was almost an agony.

They continued to climb together, higher and higher, and when the explosion finally came, her body arched instinctively to prolong the pleasure. The shudders that racked her body were so strong that she thought they might split her asunder.

Jessie's eyes were wide as they gazed into Rafe's. She moved with him quickly to that place where no others could follow. And together, they went crashing down to the other side.

The exquisite fulfillment of their lovemaking stayed locked inside Jessie's mind, even when her body relaxed into exhausted satisfaction.

Jessie lay wrapped in his arms until his even breathing made her aware that he was asleep. She allowed him a few moments' rest before she woke him, knowing they had only a short time alone before the children returned.

Chapter Nineteen

After Jacob Lassiter left his office, Lucas turned his attention again to the WANTED posters. He'd already perused the one on top of the stack, but he looked at the face again. "The Deadwood Kid," he muttered, his lips curling into a wry grin. The face depicted in the drawing held no resemblance to a boy. His dark hair covered his shoulders and a bushy beard covered most of his face. Small, mean eyes that resembled black marbles glared back at Lucas.

The bell over the door jangled suddenly and Watson looked up to see Timmy Carter enter. The six-year-old boy had become a regular visitor of late, and Lucas suspected the youngster had developed a bad case of hero worship.

"Howdy, Sheriff." Timmy stuck his hands in the pockets of his faded breeches and swaggered across to lean against the sheriff's desk.

"Howdy, pardner."

Lucas Watson pushed the posters aside and gave his complete attention to the youngster. The boy had curly brown hair that refused to be tamed and big brown eyes that could make a man feel ten feet tall when they looked up at him. Right now they were focused on Lucas.

"You outta school for the day, Timmy?"

"Yep." Timmy looked longingly at the wastebasket nearby. "You got any work around here that needs doing, Sheriff?"

"Well, pard, let me see now." Lucas rubbed his nose thoughtfully. "I cleaned the rifles this morning. And I swept out the office. But I reckon that trash over yonder hasn't been emptied since yesterday when you were here."

A wide grin split Timmy's cheeks. "You want me to do it now?"

"It's your job, Timmy. I wouldn't give it to nobody else."

The boy needed male attention. Living in a boarding-house that contained mostly women did nothing to instill pride of self, a fact that Lucas did his best to remedy. And that pa of his had certainly been no help. Timmy had only been two years old when his father left town, leaving Martha to raise the boy alone.

Lucas watched Timmy carry the trash outside to the barrel where it would be burned at a later time. When the boy was finished, they talked together a while. The youngster had so many questions that needed answering, questions that were usually answered by fathers, like what was the biggest fish ever caught from Miller's Pond? And, why do worms squirm so much when you put them on a hook? And, why do tomcats prowl at night—a question that Lucas only had vague answers for—and, how far does a rifle shoot? Martha did her best, but a boy needed a man to identify with. And he had chosen Lucas.

As they talked, Lucas kept a careful eye on the clock, knowing the boy was only allowed an hour before his mother would start worrying about him. When that time drew near, Lucas rose to his feet and stretched, like he had done every day since Timmy first stopped by.

"Well, pardner," he said, "guess it's time to make rounds."

"Guess so," Timmy agreed wistfully. "Don't suppose I could go all the way this time?"

"Reckon not," Lucas said. "We get some awful bad hombres around these parts."

"Yeah. An' you might have to arrest somebody. Right?"

"Right."

"I heard you arrested old Charlie the other day."

"Well now, son, I reckon you heard right."

"What'd he do?"

"Old Charlie's got himself a little problem, son. And sometimes it gets so bad he has to have a place to stay so's he can work through that problem."

"And you give him a place to stay?"

"Yep. I sure do that." He ruffled the boy's hair. "Now let's start our rounds or the mayor's gonna be looking for us." *And your ma as well.*

They walked together as far as the cafe; then Timmy shoved open the door and went inside while Lucas continued his rounds. It was more than an hour later when he returned to his office, intent on going through the rest of the WANTED posters before locking up for the day. But he couldn't keep his mind on what he was doing. The need in a small boy's eyes tugged at his heart. He thumbed through several more posters, trying to embed the faces he saw there in his memory, then finally decided to leave the rest for tomorrow. As he shuffled the posters he'd already looked at to the back of the pile, something about the top sheet caught his attention. He looked at it closer . . . and his eyes widened with recognition. It was a woman's face depicted on the white paper. A woman who looked exactly like Jessie.

* * *

The day had been an especially long one for Jessie, with so many things to attend to before the wedding. But she didn't mind one whit, she told herself. Not when the end result would make her Rafe's wife.

Rafe. Her lips curled into a smile as she remembered how he'd pulled her into the barn and made passionate love to her. Neither of them had wanted to leave their love nest—the hay-strewn stall—they had barely donned their garments again when the girls had entered the barn to spend time with the kittens which would soon be going to another home.

A knock on the door startled her, and she dropped the potato she'd been peeling for supper. A quick peek out the window told her Johnny Walker had come visiting.

She greeted him and watched as he shuffled his feet and looked at the ground as though he found something interesting there. "Uh . . . I'm looking for Karin," he mumbled. "She anywheres around?"

"I think she's in the barn, Johnny."

"Thanks," he muttered. Then, spinning on his heels, he took off toward the barn like a scalded cat.

Jessie grinned and returned to her work. It wasn't long before Karin left the barn, her nose reaching for the sky and her chin following closely behind. As Karin entered the kitchen, Jessie could see by her stance that she was angry. Her hands were fisted at her side and her mouth was pulled into a tight line.

"Trouble?" Jessie asked gently.

"Boys!" Karin snapped, as though that explained everything. Then she stalked into the house, slamming the door behind her.

Jessie looked toward the barn and saw Johnny standing beside the wide door, his hands shoved deep into his pockets. He looked so woeful that she felt sorry for him, and yet knew she must not appear so lest he come to her with his problems, which Karin would see as a betrayal of trust.

Casting a hopeful look toward the house, Johnny waited a long moment, then, apparently deciding he could do nothing else, went on his way.

The moment he disappeared from sight, Karin opened the door and stepped out onto the porch. Her blue eyes were fever-bright as she met Jessie's gaze.

"Do you want to talk about it?" Jessie asked softly.

"No," Karin said, then went on to do just that. "Johnny came here to try to make amends for the hayride."

"Make amends?"

"Yes. You know, for choosing to walk with Elizabeth Rollins instead of me." She made a face. "And when I told him I didn't care one whit who he stepped out with, he made ugly remarks about Joe Bob."

Jessie frowned. "What kind of ugly remarks?"

"The usual kind. You know, like, he's wild and can't be trusted around girls because he knows how to say pretty words that turn their heads . . . and that he could never be true to one girl." Her lips flattened and her eyes glittered with anger. "Johnny had better watch himself, 'cause Joe Bob is older and stronger and he'd be plenty mad if he finds out what Johnny's been saying about him."

"Are you going to tell Joe Bob?"

"No." Karin's tone was softer. "No, I wouldn't do that. It would hurt his feelings. Besides, Johnny and Joe Bob are friends. Johnny's just saying that stuff because he didn't like me stepping out with Joe Bob."

"What's this? You stepped out with Joe Bob? When did that happen?"

The sudden intrusion of Rafe's voice startled both of them. His brows were drawn into a heavy frown as he waited for one of them to reply.

"On the hayride, Pa." Karin eased toward the door. "I better go see about Sissy, Jessie. She's with the kittens. You can talk to Pa."

Rafe watched his daughter leave the house, then turned to Jessie with a raised brow. " 'Talk to Pa,' " he said, "as in calm him down before she comes back?"

Jessie laughed and curled her fingers around his hand, and the world suddenly became brighter. "I could get used to this," he said softly, cupping her cheek with a callused palm.

"Used to what?"

"You," he replied, his voice gravel on velvet. "You . . . soothing the savage beast." *Savage.* "Jessie, you don't think Karin is getting attached to that boy, do you?"

Jessie sighed, wondering how to answer Rafe without betraying Karin's confidence. "I think her feelings are innocent enough right now, Rafe," she replied. "But, given time, they might develop into something stronger."

"Maybe I should have been nicer to Johnny Walker."

"I'm afraid it wouldn't have made any difference."

"Wonder if that boy would come to supper?"

She laughed, and the sound was like wind chimes in a rainstorm. Rafe wanted to hear the sound again, but couldn't think of anything funny to say.

"I think you should stay out of it, Rafe," she said gently. "Johnny Walker brought this whole thing about by his attentions to Elizabeth Rollins. He's been here to apologize—without much luck, I might add—and it's up to him to make amends."

"I suppose you're right." He shrugged, as though dismissing the subject, then looked hopefully at the bowl of potatoes she'd been peeling. "Are those for supper?"

"Uh-huh. Are you hungry?"

"Starved." He lifted her hand and kissed the palm, managing to run his tongue over it quickly, an act that sent shivers along her spine and goose bumps along her arms. "For more than food."

"Stop that!" she said breathlessly, drawing her fingers away from him. "The children might see."

"There's nobody here but us."

"They could come inside any time, though."

"Okay. I guess I can wait for a while. But just until the kids are in bed."

"Speaking of the children . . . where is Danny? I haven't seen him for a while."

"Gone fishing," Rafe replied. "But he'll be home for supper. You can be sure of it. That boy's stomach never gets full enough for him." He raked a hand through his dark hair. "How long before it's ready, anyway?"

"About an hour."

"That long?"

"Yes," she replied ruefully. "And it will probably be even longer if you don't go away and let me prepare these vegetables."

"Okay," he laughed. "I can take a hint."

She watched him leave the house, then turned her attention to the vegetables on the table. The potatoes would be boiled and mashed and the squash would be fried. They would be served with biscuits and the roast that was simmering at the back of the stove.

Realizing that she hadn't checked on the roast in more than an hour, Jessie rose to her feet and went to do so.

An hour later they were seating themselves at the kitchen table when the sheriff rode in.

When Rafe extended an invitation to dine, Sheriff Watson immediately accepted, hanging his hat on the deer horn beside the back door and going outside to wash up at the washstand on the back porch. By the time he returned, Jessie had another place set on the table.

"I figured you folks would be done with your meal by

now," Watson said, his gaze on the platters and bowls of food that covered the table. "I can't deny that I'm mighty glad for the invite. I missed the noon meal today and my stomach's been complaining awful loud these last few hours."

"How come you missed dinner, Sheriff?" Danny asked, reaching for the bowl of potatoes.

Watson took the platter of meat and forked a slice of roast beef onto his plate before replying. "Doc Lassiter stopped by about the time I was gonna go. We got to jawing and I completely forgot about it."

"I don't forget something as important as meals," Danny said, taking the platter of fried squash that had made its way around the table to him and placing several pieces on his plate.

"No," Watson replied wryly, directing a pointed look at the food piling up on Danny's plate. "I don't imagine you would forget something that important."

As Jessie listened to the voices around her, she wondered silently why the sheriff had come. Lucas Watson was obviously hungry because he ate two helpings of everything. When he was done, the men went outside to talk together.

They were there for a long time. Jessie felt a deep sense of foreboding, a worry that gnawed at her gut until, finally, Rafe entered the room again. The expression on his face told her she'd been right to worry.

"What's wrong, Rafe?"

"I think you'd better come outside, Jessie."

Karin paused in the act of stacking dishes, her expression suddenly alert, wary. "What's going on, Pa?" she asked.

"Lucas just wants a private word with Jessie." Rafe said gruffly.

Jessie's breath came in short spurts as she followed Rafe toward the corral where Lucas waited. "Do you know why Lucas wants to talk to me?" she asked anxiously.

"He wouldn't say." Rafe's expression betrayed his concern. He was obviously as anxious as she was.

The sheriff's expression didn't do anything to dispel that anxiety. His gaze was sympathetic when he looked at Jessie, and he gave every appearance of being completely unhappy with the situation.

"What is this about, Lucas?" Jessie asked abruptly.

Lucas Watson sighed heavily. "I don't like doing this, Jessie. But the fact is, a sheriff has a lot of things dumped on him that he'd rather not do."

Rafe's body tensed beside her. His hand reached for hers as they both waited for the sheriff to explain the one particular thing that had brought him here today, the chore that he'd said had been dumped on him.

"I know the two of you are planning a wedding soon. Hell! The whole damned county knows. And folks are mighty proud for the both of you, too." He looked at his feet, appearing to study the scuffed toes of his battered boots. "This had to be done, though," he mumbled. "No matter how hard it is. You had to know."

"Know what?" Jessie stared at him. "For God's sake, Lucas! Stop beating around the bush and tell me what you came to say."

"Easy, Jessie," Rafe said, sliding his arm around her waist and pulling her tight against his side. "Just hear Lucas out."

Jessie gritted her teeth and waited.

"WANTED posters come in the mail every so often, Jessie. And a batch of them came in today."

"WANTED posters?"

"Yeah."

"You mean . . . like the posters they make up for WANTED men . . . for outlaws?"

"Yeah."

"What does this have to do with me, Lucas?"

"Fact is, Jessie, your face was on one of them posters that come today."

Rafe made a rude sound and started to speak, but Jessie stopped him before he could utter a word. "*My* face?" she squeaked. "You saw my face on one of the WANTED posters?"

Lucas nodded.

"I'm an outlaw?"

"Don't be stupid!" Rafe snarled.

"Dammit!" Lucas swore. "No, Jessie! Of course you're not an outlaw."

"Then why would my face be on a WANTED poster?"

"Well . . . fact is, Jessie, sometimes one of them posters is made up and sent out by regular folks. Folks that post a reward for family that's gone missing."

"Missing?" A slow pounding began in Jessie's ears and she realized it was the sound of her own heartbeat. "Someone is searching for me? Who?"

"Fella by the name of Lawson. Charles Lawson."

Jessie frowned as she tried to force a memory to attach to the name, but none was forthcoming. "I don't know that name, Lucas. Why is he looking for me?"

"Claims he's your husband."

"Oh, my God!" Jessie reached out to Rafe, who tightened his grip around her, holding her upright when her legs would have buckled beneath her.

Apparently the sheriff had withheld the news from Rafe because he looked like a man who'd been poleaxed.

"That's a damn lie!" Rafe snarled. "Jessie has no husband!"

"How can you be sure of that?"

The look Rafe gave Watson should have struck him dead on the spot. "Jessie has never been married, Lucas. I know that for a fact."

Lucas Watson fell silent, directing his attention toward

the sorrel mare in the corral. Then, seeming to come to a decision, he looked at the two of them again. Jessie leaned against Rafe, whose arm held her tight against his side, binding her as surely as though a rope secured them together.

"I guess there's no more to be said then, Rafe. If you're that positive she's never been married . . ."

"I am!"

"Good enough then." Lucas leaned against the corral and studied the sorrel again. "Mighty fine-looking horse you got there, Rafe. You gonna sell her?"

Rafe relaxed his stance and some of the tension drained away. "I might. If the price is right."

Apparently the two men had completely dismissed the poster, but Jessie couldn't let it go so easily. "Lucas."

His eyes were warm with sympathy as they met hers. "Yeah, Miss Jessie?"

"You said the woman on the poster looked like me."

"Yeah," he agreed laconically. "I did say that. But them posters are hard to make out sometimes. Somebody draws 'em up by hand, you know." He didn't add that the poster in question had been made from a photograph.

"But the woman resembled me?" He had already said so, but Jessie needed to hear him say it again, hoping he might have been mistaken.

"Yeah. Kinda. But that don't make no difference. Rafe said it wasn't possible you was ever married. And I'll take his word on that."

Jessie should have left it at that—would have, except it worried her so. She'd never be able to go through with their wedding if she didn't ask.

"What was the name on the poster, Lucas?"

He sighed heavily. "Already told you, Jessie. It was Charles Lawson. And you said . . ."

"Not that name. The name of the woman." She held his gaze. "Surely Charles Lawson gave her a name."

He cleared his throat and shuffled his feet as though he didn't want to answer.

Rafe's grip tightened around her. "Leave it, Jessie," he said harshly.

"What was her name, Lucas?"

"Hell, Jessie!" Lucas growled. "It don't make no difference."

"It was my name, wasn't it?"

He looked at the sorrel again, unable to meet her eyes. "The name on the poster was Jessica Lawson."

The world swirled around Jessie, and she fought against the darkness that threatened. "It's not possible," she mumbled. "I hadn't been with a man until . . ."

"Jessie, shut up!" Rafe looked at the sheriff. "That's enough, Lucas! The woman on the poster is not Jessie! Not my Jessie. It might be somebody else's Jessie, but not mine. Jessie has never been married before."

"If you say so, Rafe."

"I say so."

"Then consider the whole thing forgotten."

The sheriff turned to leave.

"Lucas," Rafe said softly.

"Yeah?"

"Destroy that poster."

"I'm gonna do just that, Rafe. Soon's I get back to town."

"See that you do."

Rafe held Jessie in his arms as the two of them watched the sheriff ride out. Then he looked at her and she saw the fear in his eyes. He tightened his grip and kissed her hard, as though intent on branding her as his own. When he raised his head there was a new determination about him.

"Forget about it, Jessie. The woman on the poster is not you."

She swallowed hard. "Are you sure, Rafe?"

"We both know you were a virgin, Jessie. Whoever that man Lawson is, he is not your husband."

"But maybe it *is* me he's looking for. Maybe that man, Charles Somebody, just made up the part about us being married, thinking folks would contact a husband who'd lost his wife. If we write to him . . ."

"No! Dammit!"

"But, Rafe . . ."

His fingers dug into her shoulders and he gave her a hard shake. "I said no, Jessie! I don't want him coming anywhere near you. We're going to be married just as we planned. And I don't want anybody coming here trying to interfere with the wedding."

"But what if . . ."

"No!" he snarled. "Let it go, Jessie! I don't want to hear another word about it!"

His mouth came down on hers again and the kiss was hungry, fearful, and she knew he was as worried as she was. And that he'd do everything in his power to keep Charles Lawson from discovering her whereabouts.

But were they doing the right thing by ignoring the poster?

Jessie just wasn't sure. But she was afraid the decision they'd made today would eventually come home to roost, that something would happen to prevent their marriage. And the thought of losing Rafe caused an ache in her soul that even his kiss could not take away.

Chapter Twenty

In times like these, Lucas Watson felt an intense dislike for his job. Being the bearer of bad news was no way to earn a living. Of course, there were other times that compensated, other times when he'd been personally responsible for putting away outlaws bent on wreaking havoc on his town.

Lucas was a forward-looking man, a man who had been able to put his past behind him—at least, most of the time—and all his efforts were concentrated on keeping his town safe. To do that, he had to keep a firm check on his emotions. But sometimes that was hard to do. Sometimes, like today, when he had to deliver bad news to people he looked on as friends, he found his duty hard going.

He hoped Jessie was not the woman Charles Lawson was searching for, prayed it was not so. Rafe appeared so certain that Jessie had never been married, so Lucas knew she must have been a virgin when Rafe pulled her out of the river. It was just as obvious that she was no longer innocent in the ways of a man. Not that Lucas could blame them for anticipating their vows. Keeping his distance from a woman as lovely as Jessie would be a hardship for any man, especially when confronted with her on a daily basis as Rafe had been.

"Hey, Lucas!"

The shout brought Lucas back to reality and he realized he'd reached town without being aware of it. He reined up beside Bill Sweeney, who was closing up his blacksmith shop.

"You're late closing tonight, aren't you, Bill?"

"Yeah," Sweeney replied. "I sure am hungry, too. Thought you might want to join me for supper at the cafe."

"Much obliged," Lucas said as he dismounted. "But I just come from the Sutherland place. Took supper with them."

"I heard about the trouble out there," Sweeney said. "Sure am glad Rafe got there in time. Wouldn't want anything to happen to Jessie and that sweet little girl of his. Seems like some men got more than their share of problems."

Lucas felt his muscles tense. Bill had recently visited Waco. Had he seen that poster of Jessie there? Despite his efforts at control, his voice held an edge as he questioned the smithy. "How's that, Bill?"

"Well, hell, Lucas!" the smithy swore. "A man shouldn't have to lose the woman he loves twice! Losing Gerta in childbirth knocked the stuffing outta Rafe. It'd go mighty hard on him if he lost another woman. And the baby, too."

"Sissy was never in danger. Jessie saw to that."

"Heard about that, too. Folks say she knew he was coming and hid that little girl in the cave."

"Folks always got plenty to say about whatever happens,

Bill." He grinned wryly. "And sometimes they get it right, too. But not this time."

"Figures." Sweeney flashed his smile. "You can give me the straight of it over coffee."

Since Lucas only had an empty house to look forward to, he accepted the invitation with a curt nod. "You go ahead. I'll meet you there after I take care of my horse."

Sweeney went to the cafe while Watson headed for the livery, feeling a sense of satisfaction that he'd put off being alone with his thoughts for a while longer.

Dread settled over Jessie as the strains of "The Wedding March" reached her. The music swelled in volume, soaring out, wrapping around her, and urging her forward toward the man who waited at the altar . . . the man who would soon be her husband.

Her legs felt numb, barely able to hold her weight as she moved reluctantly toward the inevitable, to take the vows that would bind her for the rest of her life. And, although she should be thankful for that fact, for some unknown reason she dreaded the event.

She moved closer, clutching the bridal bouquet in front of her as though using it for a shield. But the flowers could not protect her from what waited, nor could the man who stood at the altar . . .

Rafe! she cried silently, even as she wondered why she did so. There was no reason to be afraid, she told herself. Not when she was marrying the man of her choice.

Arriving at the altar, she stopped beside her groom, and responded to the marriage vows when the need arose. Then it was over and her groom raised the veil that covered her face and she looked up at him. Her mouth opened in a silent scream as she realized the man she'd married was a stranger.

Jessie sat upright, her eyes wide with horror, her heart beating at a frantic pace. But it had only been a dream, she chided herself. Only a nightmare.

Had it really only been a nightmare, though? Or had the dream been a memory from her past?

When Lucas Watson opened his office he went straight to the WANTED posters, sliding Charles Lawson's out of the pile and studying the woman whose face was depicted there. No matter how much he told himself it could be someone else, he realized he didn't believe it. The face looked too much like Jessie's. Surely there were not two such women in this old world.

With a heavy sigh, he crumpled the poster and tossed it in the trash. Then he went through the other posters, found several that were out of date since the wanted men had already been caught, and crumpled those, too. When he'd finished, there were five posters that had been thrown away. He was about to take the trash out and burn it when he heard a commotion outside. He pushed his chair back and went outside to quiet the disturbance. As he strode toward the crowd, he was unaware that Timmy Carter was entering his office.

Timmy Carter was disappointed when he saw the sheriff leave his office. He'd hoped to have a few words with him before he went to school. Sheriff Watson had all the answers to his questions and last night, after he'd gone to bed, he'd thought of another question that only a man like the sheriff could answer.

Knowing the sheriff would return soon, Timmy seated himself in the chair beside the desk. His flickering gaze traveled around the office, looking for something of interest; he saw the wastebasket, already almost full. Since the sheriff depended on him to keep it empty, he picked up the trash and took it outside and dumped it in the trash barrel.

Suddenly the wind gusted, whipping his hair into his eyes and blowing some of the papers out of the barrel. He bent over to pick them up and, noticing one was squashed into a ball, he flattened the paper out across his knee. He'd thought the posters pictured outlaws, but this one had a lady on it. Although she looked familiar, he didn't recognize her. The words printed above the face didn't help because he was only in the first grade and hadn't yet learned his letters, much less how to put them together to make words. But his ma would know what they said. He'd ask her when he went home.

Smoothing the paper again, he folded it carefully, then pushed it deep inside his pocket.

The sheriff was still outside when Timmy replaced the wastebasket. With a reluctant sigh, he left the office and headed across town toward the schoolhouse.

As usual, he was late and drew the teacher's notice immediately. Things went from bad to worse the rest of the day. He couldn't remember his numbers right, used one "M" when he had to print his name, which made the teacher mad, and when he reached for his knife to dig a splinter out of his finger, the teacher caught him in the act and fixed him with a mean glare.

"Timmy Carter!" Her voice, as usual, was hateful. "What are you doing back there?"

He jerked his head upright, trying to hide the knife from her eagle eyes. When he spoke, he was proud that his voice didn't wobble. "I ain't doin' nothin', Miss Jones."

"Is that a knife?"

Timmy looked at the floor, then made himself look at her again. "Yes, ma'am."

"Then come up here!"

Sighing, he shoved himself off his seat and, on legs that wanted to tremble, went to her desk.

She held out her hand and he knew that she expected him to put his knife there, but he gripped it tightly, feeling a knot close his throat.

"Timmy!" she said sharply. "Give me that knife."

He wanted to protest, to tell her the sheriff had given him the knife for his birthday, that it was the best present he'd ever had, but he knew it would do no good. She didn't care about the knife being a gift, not a hateful old meanie like her. She continued to sit there, her mean eyes glaring at him, her hand held out for the knife.

Timmy swallowed around the obstruction clogging his throat. "Aw, please, Miss Jones. The sheriff gave me this knife for my birthday."

"The sheriff should have known better. You're too young to have a knife. And even if you weren't too young, school is not the place for a knife. Now give it to me."

He gave her the knife.

"Now empty your pockets."

"Empty my pockets?" He couldn't understand why she asked that. He had given her the knife, the best thing he'd ever owned, and now she wanted the rest. He thought about the bird's nest in his pocket, and the smooth rock he'd found at the dry wash only this morning. And the big, black marble he'd won fair and square from Joey Robinson. Would the teacher take those, too?

Sighing heavily again, he dug in his pockets and pulled everything out.

"Put everything here, Timmy." She pointed at her desk.

He piled everything on her desk and watched her go through the assortment. She tossed the bird's nest and the rock into the trash, studied the black marble for a moment, then tossed that, too. "What's this?" she asked, picking up the folded paper.

"Nothing," he mumbled.

He'd already lost the important things. The picture didn't matter one way or the other. At least not to him. But the way her eyes widened when she spread it out and stared down at the woman's face, it must have meant something to the teacher. Something nice, he decided, when she smiled real big. Maybe it meant enough that she'd let him keep his stuff. It was sure worth a try.

He tapped a finger on her desk until she looked up at him. "Could I have my stuff back, Miss Jones?" he asked timidly.

"Yes," she said impatiently, turning her attention to the poster again.

Timmy wasted no time scooping his possessions into his palm and shoving them into his pocket again. Before the teacher could reconsider, he was already in his seat. He wondered again why the teacher found the poster so interesting, but having no way to answer that question, he soon forgot it. The rest of the day Timmy worked diligently on his letters, hoping the teacher would forget he existed.

As she seemed to do.

Something was wrong with Jessie. Rafe knew it as surely as he knew himself. She'd been quiet that morning, not her usual self, so much so that Karin had commented about it when the family had gathered for the noon meal.

When Jessie failed to notice the meat platter that had been passed to her, Karin spoke up. "What's the matter, Jessie? Did Victoria say something to upset you?"

"Victoria?" Rafe inquired. "She came to visit?"

"Yes," Karin replied. "And so did Mrs. Walker and Granny Wyatt."

Rafe's brow furrowed and his eyes darkened as they met Jessie's. "Why did they come?"

"They offered to help with the wedding," Jessie mumbled, forking a slice of ham onto her plate before passing the platter on to Danny.

"That was nice of them." Rafe studied Jessie's bent head and watched her push her peas around on her plate with her fork. "What did you tell them, Jessie?"

"I . . . uh . . ." She flicked a quick glance at him, then turned her attention to her food again. "I said I would let them know if there was anything they could do."

"Uh-huh."

She looked at him again, and saw the silver glint in his eyes—hot and angry—then quickly looked away again.

"What's going on, Jessie?"

She didn't pretend to misunderstand him. She caught her lower lip between her teeth, then looked at him again. "Maybe we should discuss this later," she suggested.

"Discuss what?"

"Not now," she said unsteadily.

"There's nothing to discuss, Jessie," Rafe said firmly. "Not now, or any time in the future. It's decided. And nothing anybody has to say is going to change that."

"What's decided?" Danny asked, his gaze flicking between his father and Jessie, the meat he'd just speared with his fork poised near his mouth.

"What's going on, Jessie?" Karin asked, her blue eyes wary. When Jessie remained silent, she turned to her father. "Pa? What are you and Jessie talking about?"

Rafe's eyes never left Jessie. "Nothing, Karin. Nothing for you to worry about. The wedding's going to take place as planned."

"The wedding?" Her face paled, then flushed with angry color. "Why shouldn't it take place, Pa? Is somebody trying to stop you from marrying Jessie?"

"Never mind, Karin."

"Jessie?" Karin appealed. "What is Pa talking about?"

Jessie looked around the table at Rafe and his children. His jaw was grim, his eyes molten steel. Karin, usually so quiet, was tense, her cheeks flushed angrily at the thought that she might lose the woman who'd come to mean so much to her. And Danny, who was struggling to make sense of the quiet argument taking place around him.

Jessie's eyes filled with moisture and she blinked rapidly to stop the tears from overflowing. She couldn't face the thought of losing Rafe, yet knew she must consider that possibility.

Unable to bear the pain that suddenly gnawed at her gut, Jessie shoved back her chair and rushed out the door. Sobs shook her as she ran toward the barn, where she could deal with her pain in secret.

But as she entered the shadowy interior, she felt hands grip her upper arms and spin her around.

Fury swept through Rafe as he stared into Jessie's eyes. He wanted to shake her until her teeth rattled, until every thought of Charles Lawson was gone from her head. All day he'd been consumed with a desperate need to protect their future, wanting to spirit her away to some secret place where nobody could ever find her. It was obvious she had been giving in to her fears, had even been thinking the marriage might not take place. Well, he damn well wasn't going to put up with it.

Jessie stared up at him with tear-washed eyes. "It's no good, Rafe. Don't you see? The woman that man—that Charles Lawson—is searching for must be me. It would be too big a coincidence otherwise. The name is the same. And Lucas said she had my face."

"I know what Lucas said." His voice was grim, his hold tight. "But I don't give a damn, Jessie."

"Rafe . . ."

"Save your breath! We are going to be married. Nothing is going to stop that from happening." He watched her tears spill over and slide down her face and with a rough growl, he yanked her tight against him, holding her close against his heart where she belonged. "It's going to be all right, sweetheart. Everything's going to be fine."

She sobbed against his chest, soaking his shirt thoroughly before slowly relaxing against him. He smoothed her hair, murmuring sweet nothings to her as though she were a hurt child until, finally, with a shudder, she drew back and looked up into his eyes.

"I h-had a d-dream last night."

"And that's what set you off?"

She nodded her head.

"Do you want to talk about it?"

"I was at a wedding." She straightened his collar, unable to meet his gaze. "I was the bride." She felt his body stiffen, but made herself continue. "The groom was a stranger, Rafe." She bit her lower lip to stop it from quivering. "You weren't there. Just me and that s-stranger and a roomful of people I d-didn't know."

"Oh, honey," he chided, lifting her chin, forcing her to meet his gaze. "That doesn't prove a thing. Lucas told you about that WANTED poster and it worried you. The worry carried over into your dreams." He kissed her softly. "That's all it was. Just the worry over what he told us. And it's over nothing. There's not a word of truth in that poster."

"How can you be sure?"

"Because I know you, Jessie. In every sense of the word. I was your first man, love. Don't you remember? No man had ever had you before me. And no man will come after me."

He kissed her deeply then, hungrily, his lips scorching hers, stoking a fire in her lower belly that burned higher and higher until it threatened to consume her. When he lifted his head her knees were so weak she would have fallen if Rafe hadn't been holding her so tightly.

"I think we shouldn't wait two weeks to be married," he said unsteadily, leaning his forehead against hers. "I think we should be married this week."

"I wish we could," she said and sighed heavily. "But the children will be disappointed if they can't participate in the wedding. Karin was planning on being my bridesmaid and we were going to use Sissy for flower girl and . . ."

"I know. Danny was going to carry the ring." He groaned and kissed her again. "Why in the world did I ever agree to this, Jessie? I don't need fancy doings to make me your husband. I just need the legal stuff done with so I can sleep with you in my arms at night."

"Sleep?" she teased, peeping up at him from beneath a fringe of thick lashes. "Is that all you want to do? And here I thought you were dying to make love to me."

"You know damn well I am," he grumbled.

He pressed her lower body against his to make her aware of that fact. But even as her body responded to his, Jessie couldn't keep the fear from intruding again, fear that her past was catching up to her and when it did, she would lose this man who meant so much to her.

Chapter Twenty-One

" . . . And she said you shouldn't't've give it to me, Sheriff. And she made me give it to her."

Timmy Carter's indignant voice intruded on Lucas's thoughts as he completed his report on the latest disturbance. The man who'd created that disturbance—a stranger passing through—was in a cell behind him, sleeping off the booze he'd guzzled at the saloon.

"She shouldn't have done that," Timmy finished plaintively, winding down from his explanation. "Right, Sheriff?"

Wondering what in hell the boy was talking about, Lucas studied him with a raised brow. "I don't think I got all that, son," he said. "Maybe you'd better tell me again."

Disappointment glittered in Timmy's eyes. "You wasn't listening to me?"

Lucas Watson felt like a low-down polecat. He knew how much the boy depended on him, and for a moment he was tempted to lie, to say he'd been listening, but just didn't understand yet. Then he thought better of it. The boy didn't need lies, even to save his feelings.

"No, son," he said. "I purely wasn't paying attention. And I'm mighty sorry for that. But with everything that's been happening around here today my mind got awful tied up. But I'm listening now."

So Timmy started explaining again. He told how the teacher took his knife away and made him empty his pockets out. How she'd thrown away his bird's nest and the smooth stone and the black marble he'd won. "And then she saw that poster and got interested in it and . . ."

"What poster?" Watson growled.

Timmy flinched, shrinking into himself and the sheriff cursed silently. He'd frightened the boy when that had not been his intention. He reached out a hand and gripped the youngster's shoulder gently.

"I didn't mean to scare you, son," he said. "But I need to know what you meant about a poster." His gaze searched the boy's. "Did you take one of the WANTED posters from my desk?"

Timmy looked shocked. His eyes became round with surprise. "No, sir!" he said firmly. "I wouldn't do nothing like that."

Watson breathed a sigh of relief, then put on a wide smile. "I didn't think you would, son," he said gently. "But I thought I oughtta make sure. You know how it is."

"Yeah, Sheriff," Timmy agreed. "And I wouldn't never touch anything on your desk. You gotta believe that." His young face was so earnest, so trusting, that Watson had trouble resisting the urge to pull the boy into his arms. Timmy wanted terribly to be treated like a man and would probably object to such an action. After all, he'd once said that men didn't hug each other.

"I do believe it, pardner," he said gently. "Of course you wouldn't touch anything on my desk."

"But it would be okay if it was in the trash, wouldn't it?" Timmy asked, his eyes wary. "Wouldn't it, Sheriff?"

Lucas felt an ache in his gut. He didn't want to ask, but knew he must know. "Did you take the WANTED poster from the trash, Timmy?"

"Yes, sir," Timmy said, his lower lip quivering. "It was okay, though?" His eyes pleaded with Lucas. "It was just trash, wasn't it?"

Lucas nodded his head, knowing there was nothing else he could do. "Yeah, son. It was just trash."

It was as though a weight had suddenly been lifted off the boy's shoulders. Timmy smiled at him. "Good. 'Cause I was gettin' worried about it. 'Specially since the teacher kept staring and staring at the paper like she was real interested in the words on it . . . or something." He shuffled his feet, stuck his hands in his pockets, and began to edge away from the desk. "I better go home now," he said. "Ma will be waiting for me."

"Yeah," Lucas said gently. "You do that, boy. You go on home now."

Lucas had already seen the empty wastebasket and realized that Timmy had been there to empty it. But surely the poster he had found wasn't the one with Jessie's face on it. Surely not.

But even as he went outside and gathered up the crushed posters and spread them out to look at the faces, he knew in his heart he was wrong. And when every one of them had been spread out before him, only one was missing.

It was the poster of Jessie.

The sun was sinking below the horizon when Johnny Walker showed up at the kitchen door. He leaned against a porch column and turned his attention toward the western sky as though he'd just come to view the sunset from that vantage point.

Karin, who had been setting the table for supper, made a rude noise in her throat, then slapped the last fork down on the table, shoved open the screen door, and glared up at Johnny.

"What are you doing here?" she asked tersely.

His eyes never wavered from the crimson and purple that washed the sky above the horizon. "I come to see Danny," he replied quietly.

"In a pig's eye!" she snapped. "Since when do you come around here to see my brother?"

That got his attention. His gaze left the sunset and fixed on her; she almost flinched from the anger she saw there. "Since you took up with Joe Bob Thompson," he replied grimly. "Now where's he at?"

"Joe Bob Thompson?" She arched a flaxen brow. "How should I know? He doesn't live here."

"I'm not looking for Joe Bob," he growled. "I'm looking for Danny. Now, go get him, Karin!"

She didn't budge an inch. "Don't you be giving me orders, Johnny Walker," she snapped, placing both hands on her hips and rolling up on the balls of her feet as though preparing herself for battle.

Jessie hovered in the background, wondering if she should intervene. A movement through the window caught her attention and she looked closer and spied Rafe and Danny coming across the barnyard. She realized the choice had been taken from her. Rafe would never condone Karin's rudeness to a guest. Jessie reached the door in four quick strides.

"Johnny," she said, gripping Karin's forearm with warning fingers. "How nice to see you."

He mumbled something under his breath and Karin,

ignoring Jessie's silent message, said, "What's that, Johnny? What did you say? Speak up so's a body can hear you."

He lifted a flushed face and glared furiously at Karin. "Told her I was pleased to see her!" he snarled.

"You don't sound too pleased," she said, her lips curling into a smile that didn't reach her eyes.

"Karin," Jessie said warningly. "Your father is coming in for supper."

Karin flushed as she saw her father approaching, with Danny loping along beside him.

"Looks like you're in luck, Johnny," she said tartly. "Here comes Danny . . . along with Pa."

Johnny flattened his lips and threw another hard glare at Karin before turning to watch the two Sutherland males approach. Jessie couldn't help feeling sorry for the young man. He'd really wound up in hot water on that hayride. So hot, in fact, that he might do better to forget about Karin and find himself another girlfriend.

"Hi, Johnny!" Danny called out. "You ready to go?"

"Yeah." Johnny turned to give Karin a triumphant look before striding toward her brother. The two spoke together for a few moments before they drifted apart, Johnny headed toward the barn while Danny followed his father inside the house.

"What was that all about, Danny?" Karin asked, winding her hands together nervously as she watched her brother.

Danny's face reflected his confusion. "What was what about?"

"Johnny," Karin replied impatiently. "What does he want with you?"

"Oh. We're going fishing together." Danny shoved a sweat-dampened curl out of his eyes and turned to Jessie. "Jessie, would you mind if I made us some sandwiches so's we can eat at the river? Pa said I had to ask you."

"Of course I don't mind." Jessie flicked a quick glance

at Karin's rigid stance. Perhaps there was hope for Johnny yet. If he played his cards right. "In fact," she continued, "I'll make the sandwiches myself. And throw in several oatmeal cookies for good measure."

"Thanks, Jessie." Danny grinned. "You're gonna be the best ma a kid ever had." The grin faded as he flicked a quick glance at his father. "Next to Ma, of course."

Jessie smiled at him. "Of course," she agreed softly.

There was an ache somewhere in the region of her heart as she watched Danny leave the room with Karin following close behind. She could hear the murmur of their voices as they spoke together, and when they returned, Danny grabbed the sandwiches Jessie had prepared and joined Johnny, fishing poles in hand.

Rafe, who'd been seated at the table holding his youngest daughter in his lap, relinquished her to Jessie and turned his attention to Karin, who looked as though she'd just lost her best friend.

"What's the matter, Karin?" he asked gently.

Jessie tried not to listen to their conversation as she settled Sissy in her highchair, but without leaving the room, there was no way to avoid hearing the exchange between Rafe and his daughter.

Karin was explaining that she and Johnny had argued on the hayride, but omitted giving a reason for that argument. She ended the explanation with, "And I don't want him coming around here anymore."

"Don't you think you're being unreasonable, Karin? Just because you're at odds with Johnny doesn't mean the whole world should be."

"But I don't want to have to look at him, Pa!"

Rafe could understand her feelings. If he lost Jessie it would be hard to see her on a regular basis, hard to be near her and know they would never be together. But Karin was young, too young to know love, to be aware of how much pain could come from loving the wrong person. At least he hoped so.

"Do you want me to explain to Johnny?"

"Explain what?" she asked in alarm.

"That his presence is painful to you."

"No!" she gasped. "Don't tell him nothing, Pa. Please."

"I won't." He covered her hand with his own. "But something needs to be said or he's likely to keep coming around."

"Can't you just tell him you don't want him to come?"

"What reason would I use?"

"Danny's too young for him."

"He's only a year younger than you. No. That won't do at all. And it's not up to me to stop him from coming, Karin. He's your friend."

"Not any more."

"End of discussion," he growled, dismissing the subject of Johnny Walker. He looked at Jessie and smiled gently. "Supper's getting cold, and I like my food best when it's hot."

Stabbing a slice of roast beef with his fork, Rafe shifted it to his plate, then passed the platter on to Karin. Although Karin had no appetite, she took a small portion, then passed the platter to Jessie.

Karin was aware of the conversation flowing around her as her father talked about the work he'd accomplished that day, encouraged by Jessie's questions. When supper was over, she helped Jessie clear the table. But when the fishermen returned with their catch, Karin quickly left the room.

Johnny stayed for a while, discussing crops with Rafe; then, after a quick glance toward the room occupied by the girls, he sighed heavily and said his goodbyes.

Moments later, Karin left her room and went to Danny's. She seated herself on his bed beside him and made idle talk for a while, hoping her brother would volunteer the information she wanted. The information that she *needed* to set her heart at rest. But when he didn't, she decided to stop beating around the bush.

"What did you two talk about while you were fishing?"

"Nothing important." Danny's attention was on the wooden owl he was carving from a piece of oak he'd found near the river.

"Like what?"

"I dunno." He flicked an amused glance at her. "We mostly sat and fished."

"But when you did talk, what did he say?"

"Said the fish wasn't bitin' very good."

Karin's lips flattened and her blue eyes narrowed. She realized Danny knew what she was about and was determined to keep her from learning Johnny's feelings. "Danny," she said impatiently, "you must have talked about other things. Now tell me what they were."

Danny's fingers stilled and he shot her an aggravated look. "Leave me be, Karin. I'm trying to finish this owl for Jessie."

Putting her hands on her hips, Karin glared at him. "I'm not leaving until you answer my question, Danny. So you might as well do so."

"What do you want me to say? We was fishin', Karin. And fishermen don't talk much when they're fishing."

"Did he mention Elizabeth Rollins?"

"Nope."

"Did he mention me?"

"Wouldn't tell you if he did."

"Why not?" Her tone was as exasperated as her mood.

"Because it wouldn't be right, telling you what Johnny told me."

"Then he did talk about me."

"I ain't gonna say, Karin. So you might just as well shut up."

With her lips tight with anger, Karin rose from his bed and flounced from the room. It would be a cold day in July before she'd forgive her brother for taking Johnny's side against her.

A cold day in July.

Chapter Twenty-Two

Lucas had been meeting the stagecoach for the last three days. But somehow, he sensed this was the day Charles Lawson would come. He watched the stage roll by in a cloud of dust, headed for the livery stable where a fresh horse would be supplied before the journey continued.

"Whoa!" shouted Beaver Jones, the grizzled driver. The wheels had barely stopped rolling before Beaver jumped down and slammed his palm against the coach door. "Everybody out!" he yelled. "End of the line!"

Since the stagecoach would be leaving for Fredricksburg within the hour, there were apparently no passengers going beyond Castle Rock.

As Watson neared the livery the coach door opened, smacking the side of the coach with a loud thud, and a scrawny, middle-aged man wearing a wrinkled brown suit stepped out. The man who followed appeared impatient with the other passenger, as though he had pressing business that needed tending without delay. *He was the one.*

He was a young man, not more than twenty-five, dressed in a gray suit with an embroidered vest. A gray beaver hat sat atop his head; his boots were shiny, as though they were rarely used or had been purchased for the trip.

The newcomer extracted a traveling bag from the boot of the stage, then turned to survey his surroundings. Lucas knew the exact moment when his badge caught the other man's eyes. The stranger tensed, his gaze lifting to meet the sheriff's; then he strode quickly forward, covering the distance between them.

A smile stretched the stranger's lips. "Sheriff! How did you know I'd be on today's stage? Never mind. I'm just glad you're here. Saves me the trouble of looking you up."

He offered his hand, but Lucas ignored the gesture, intent on taking the other man's measure.

"I'm Charles Lawson. But I imagine you already knew that." His brow furrowed and something flickered in his blue eyes. "Or am I being presumptuous in assuming you were here to meet me?"

"You came on a fool's errand, Lawson," Watson growled. He had to try to discourage the other man, even though he was almost certain it would do no good.

Lawson's gaze narrowed. "I came because someone—I suppose it was you—sent me a telegram." He reached inside his coat pocket, extracted a piece of yellow paper, and held it out. "It came three days ago, Sheriff . . ."

He paused questioningly and Lucas supplied his name.

"The telegram came three days ago, Sheriff Watson. Are you saying you didn't send it to me?"

"Yep."

"You did send it?" Lawson's tone was exasperated.

"Nope."

Lawson waved the telegram at Watson. "Read it for yourself, Sheriff. Then tell me why you think I came on a fool's errand."

Lucas took the telegram. There were only six words but that was enough. *Your wife is in Castle Rock.* Although the telegram was unsigned, there was no doubt in his mind who had sent it.

"Somebody's just fooling around," he said gruffly. "The woman you're looking for is not here."

Charles Lawson stiffened and his blue eyes narrowed. "You might be right, Sheriff. But I don't think so. I don't suppose you'd object to me hanging around for a while. Somebody sent me that telegram. If I ask around long enough, that same somebody might come forward."

Lucas sighed heavily. Charles Lawson appeared to be a determined man, maybe as determined to find Jessie as Rafe was to keep her whereabouts a secret. There was bound to be trouble when the two men chanced to meet. Maybe it would be better for Rafe if that meeting took place under the watchful eye of the law.

But Lucas was unwilling to concede yet. "There's no need to question the townsfolk," he growled. "I know the woman in question. But she can't be your wife, nor nobody else's."

"How do you know that?"

"Just know it." Lucas wasn't about to get in a discussion about how he knew Jessie had been a virgin.

"This woman . . . does she have a name?"

"Ever'body's got a name. Some might not remember it, though."

Charles's heart gave a leap of hope. Was the woman Jessica? His Jessica? "Are you saying she has no memory?"

"Guess so."

"I want to see her."

"Reckoned you would."

"Where is she?" Charles asked impatiently. Getting answers from this damned sheriff was harder than getting milk from a stallion.

The sheriff's lips flattened. "I'll take you there."

"No need," Charles said grimly. "Just tell me how to get there."

"Nope. We'll go together." Lucas entered the stable. "Need my mount," he told the liveryman. He nodded toward Charles, who had followed him reluctantly. "He'll need one, too."

Shortly thereafter, Lucas rode out of Castle Rock, followed closely by the man who claimed to be Jessie's husband.

Rafe was in the corral working with the sorrel when he heard the sound of approaching hooves. Recognizing Lucas Watson as the foremost rider, Rafe looped the rope around the top rail, swung the gate open, and waited beside the corral.

Lucas reined up beside Rafe and dismounted.

"What brings you out here today, Lucas?"

From the corner of Rafe's eye he watched the other man dismount. He had blond hair curled beneath a beaver hat; when he smiled, his teeth were a startling slash of white against sun-darkened skin.

The stranger flicked a quick look toward the house, then returned his gaze to Rafe. Laugh lines radiated from the corners of his vivid blue eyes.

"Hello, there." Although the stranger smiled at Rafe, his searching gaze was already making a quick sweep of his surroundings. "Is this the Sutherland farm?"

The short hairs on the nape of Rafe's neck rose. His stance became rigid with dislike—a peculiar reaction, since he was usually an amiable man.

"Who is he, Lucas?" he growled.

Before Lucas could reply, Danny stepped out of the barn, carrying a bridle with a broken strap. "I didn't know you were here, Sheriff." He flicked a quick look at the stranger before turning to his father again. "Do you want me to replace the leather on this bridle, Pa?"

"Yeah."

Although obviously curious about the newcomer, Danny turned back into the barn again.

The stranger had been watching Danny. The moment the boy disappeared from sight, he turned his attention to Rafe again. "I take it that's your son."

"Yeah."

The blue eyes began to twinkle. "You don't talk much, do you?"

Rafe's lips twitched. "Not much. But I don't reckon you rode all the way out here just to ask me that."

"No." The man's expression became serious and he stuck out a hand. "The name's Charles Lawson."

Rafe felt as though he'd been punched in the gut. He remembered the name; in fact, he'd never forget it. When he spoke, his voice was cold. As were his eyes, and he ignored the outstretched hand. "What do you want?"

Lawson's hand dropped. "I think it's apparent you already know why I'm here."

"You've made a mistake."

"Have I?"

As though waiting for that exact moment, Jessie opened the door and stepped out on the back porch. "Rafe!" she hollered. "Do you know where Danny is?"

Rafe cursed silently as Lawson's head swiveled around and he caught sight of Jessie.

"Jessica." Lawson's expression underwent a drastic change, from serious to extreme joy, as he quickly covered the distance separating him from the house.

"Dammit!" Rafe swore.

He wasn't about to let Charles Lawson anywhere near

Jessie. His hands fisted as he turned to intercept the other man, but Lucas stopped him, blocking his way.

"Dammit, Lucas! Get out of my way!"

"Give him a minute, Rafe," Lucas growled.

"Like hell!" Rafe snarled, dodging around the other man.

But it was already too late. Charles Lawson had reached Jessie. His hands were around her waist, lifting her high in the air, then lowering her again as he whirled her around and around. He laughed then, joyfully, triumphantly, as though he'd just discovered a hidden treasure.

Jessie struggled against his hold, her expression a curious blend of fear and surprise. Fear won out.

"Let me go!" she cried.

It seemed forever before Rafe reached them. He gripped Lawson's upper arm and yanked him away from Jessie. "Let her go!" he snarled.

The expression on Lawson's face was one of pure shock. "Jessica? Darling, what's wrong?"

Rafe snatched Jessie from the other man and tucked her close at his side. His fists ached to smash Lawson's nose, to see it crumple beneath the blow.

"Easy, Rafe," Lucas growled. "Don't do anything foolish."

"Rafe!" Jessie's voice trembled, as did her knees. "Who is he?"

Lawson's expression became one of anguish. "Jessica? Don't you know me?"

"No!" She curved herself against Rafe's side, seeking the refuge of his arms. "Who is he, Rafe?" she asked again, even though she had become certain of the stranger's identity. "What does he want with me?"

"Jessica," Lawson pleaded. "Don't look like that, darling. I'm your husband."

Cold fear slammed through Jessie and she could feel

the blood sweeping from her face. She clutched the front of Rafe's shirt and buried her head against his chest, refusing to look at the other man. "Go away! Please, go away!"

"Jessica, darling." Lawson held out a beseeching hand and there was real anguish in his eyes. "Have you forgotten me so easily?"

She clung tightly to Rafe. "It's not true, Rafe! You said it was a mistake, that I couldn't have been married to anyone."

"No. It's not true." Rafe's eyes were molten steel and his voice grated harshly as he held her against him. "I don't know what your game is, Lawson. But you're not married to Jessie."

"I have proof of our marriage."

Lawson reached into a breast pocket and removed a tintype. He held it toward Jessie, but she ignored him. However, Rafe took it from him and studied it closely. The woman who resembled Jessie was wearing a wedding gown. He crumpled the tintype in his hand and tossed it aside.

"That proves nothing." Rafe narrowed his eyes and fixed Lawson with a flinty look. It met a blue stare as unyielding as marble. The air vibrated with tension as the two men appraised each other in silence.

It was Lawson who finally broke that silence. "The hell you say! It's a picture of Jessica and me just after we were married."

"Jessie's never been married."

"Dammit, man! That's Jessica in that tintype! Any fool can see that!"

"No." Rafe was unyielding. "It's somebody else, somebody that looks like her."

"Then who is she?" Lawson challenged. "Where does she come from? Tell me that if you can."

"You don't know how close you're coming to being dead, Lawson," Rafe growled. "It would be in your best interest to leave now, while I've still got a mind to let you go."

Lawson looked at Jessie, huddled in Rafe's arms; then he said, "I'll go now. But you haven't heard the last of this. Jessica is my wife and I won't leave town without her."

"Then prepare yourself for a long stay," Rafe snarled.

Moments later, he watched the two men ride out.

That night, Lucas returned to offer his apologies.

He followed Rafe into the parlor, where Jessie sat with her mending.

"It wasn't me that sent that telegram, Rafe." Lucas's expression was grim. "I thought I'd destroyed the poster, but somehow, Timmy Carter got hold of it and took it to school."

"Then Corabelle sent the telegram," Rafe said harshly. "I never knew a woman could hold so much spite."

Jessie's fingers worked the needle through the seams of Rafe's shirt where the stitches had come loose and tried to ignore their conversation. But she couldn't ignore her thoughts so easily. She didn't remember the man who claimed to be her husband, yet he seemed sincere when he'd spoken of his love for her. How could she have forgotten him, though, if he really was her husband? And why would he lie about a thing like that?

"It doesn't matter who sent the telegram," she said softly. "What really matters is whether or not he's telling the truth. If he's my husband, then do I really have any choice . . . ?"

"Stop it, Jessie," Rafe said roughly. "You know you couldn't have been married."

"The marriage might not have been consummated, Rafe," she said gently.

"Then it never was a real marriage," he said. "It can be set aside."

She put down her mending and met his eyes. "I have to talk to him, Rafe. You must see that."

"No, Jessie. I don't want you anywhere near him."

Jessie turned to Lucas. "Talk to him, Lucas," she pleaded. "Make him see I need to know about myself . . . about my past."

"She's right, Rafe."

"Dammit!" Rafe swore. "He'll do something . . . or say something that will make her go with him. No! I won't have it. I won't let him anywhere near her."

"He can't make her go if she doesn't want to, Rafe," Lucas said grimly. "You know I wouldn't let him force her to go anywhere."

Rafe felt as though he was drowning and the lifeline he'd been thrown was about to be yanked away. He didn't want to relent, yet the expression on Jessie's face told him she was determined.

"All right," he muttered. "But if she has to see him, then she'll have me along, too. I won't let him near her alone."

"Do you want him to come here?" Watson asked.

"No. We'll come there. Do you know where he's staying?"

"At the boardinghouse."

"Then tell him we'll be there at ten tomorrow morning."

After the sheriff left, Rafe and Jessie sought privacy in the barn. She melted against him, opening her mouth to his demanding kiss.

Rafe's heart ached as he probed the sweet warmth beyond Jessie's lips. He forced himself not to think, not to consider the consequences of their meeting on the morrow with the man who claimed to be her husband.

Instead, he concentrated on the womanly scent of her as he plundered her mouth with a possessive tenderness.

Scooping her into his arms, he carried her to the pile of hay that was still covered by a blanket and gently placed her there. Then, after removing their clothing, he fastened his lips on hers again and covered her body with his own. They made love with a fierce passion enhanced by the bittersweetness of an uncertain future. Then they lay together, locked in each other's arms, until the rooster announced the birth of a new day.

Charles Lawson stood at the window of his second-story bedroom and watched the rising sun paint the sky with a crimson blaze. Under normal circumstances he would have enjoyed the sight, but not today. The sunrise was a reminder that his appointment with Jessica and the man who'd saved her life was only a few hours away.

If only he could have seen her alone.

He didn't blame Rafe Sutherland for loving her, nor for wanting to keep her by his side. Jessica was a rare treasure; Charles had known that since the day he'd laid eyes on her. But she was his!

When she'd disappeared, everyone thought her dead, and he had wanted to die, too. Yet he didn't have the courage to take his own life. He had gone on, day by day, simply existing . . . until he received the telegram. Only then did he start living again. He had kept the telegram to himself—his uncle would be angry, but he would deal with that when the time came—knowing he might need time to convince her to return with him. And now, with her amnesia, he would have the time he needed.

Charles's lips tightened as he thought of Rafe Sutherland

again. He had to use all his wits this morning, must convince her. Sutherland would fight to keep her, but Charles would fight equally hard. He had to fight. There was too much at stake. He must take her home with him, back to the ranch where she belonged.

Nothing else would do.

Several hours later, Charles led Jessica and Rafe Sutherland into the parlor of the boardinghouse.

Despite Charles's best efforts to separate them, Sutherland had taken charge of the meeting and seated himself beside Jessica on the settee.

Jessie fought nausea as she watched Charles Lawson seat himself in the chair closest to her. At Rafe's prompting, he began his explanation of how she came to be alone.

"You disappeared shortly after we married, Jessica," he said gently. "Nobody knew what happened to you, but we were afraid you had been abducted and possibly murdered."

"Why would you think that?" Rafe asked sharply.

"What else were we to think?" Charles asked reasonably. "We had arrived at the ranch and I had gone to the barn to unhook the carriage while Jessica went to our room upstairs. What was to be our room," he amended. "But when I went upstairs she was gone. And her horse was gone from the corral." He looked away from the two of them as though unable to bear the sight. "We were so happy, looking forward to our future together . . . and now . . ."

Rafe ignored the words, asking another question instead. "Do you know of any reason she would be frightened to stay there . . . at the ranch you mentioned?"

"There was no reason. She'd lived there all her life."

"She was born on the ranch?"

"Yes." Charles laughed harshly. "I've known Jessica

since she was fourteen years old. That was the year we met. When her mother married my uncle.''

"And her mother lives on the ranch?"

"No. Charlotte died six months ago."

Jessie felt the pain of her mother's death, as though it was a fresh one. But it wasn't, she reminded herself, since she couldn't remember it happening. "How did she die?" she asked in a calm voice, watching the hands resting on her lap tremble.

"An accident," he replied softly. "Her carriage turned over. She died instantly."

The anguish deepened. She leaned back on the settee, helpless to combat a sudden, whirling sensation. "Do I have any brothers or sisters?"

"You had a brother. He died, too."

"Another accident?" Rafe asked grimly, his tone bordering on accusation.

"An accidental shooting."

"Seems to me there's been an awful lot of accidents in her family."

"All real accidents, I assure you. Each one was thoroughly investigated."

"And her grandparents?"

"They passed away before she was born."

"Where is my home?" Jessie asked.

"Just outside Waco," he replied. "The ranch is well known. Large, by any standards."

"You said Jessie was born on the ranch. That she'd lived there all her life. Since her relatives are gone, does that mean she owns the ranch?"

"Well . . . uh, no, it doesn't. Her stepfather, my uncle, owns it now. It came to him through Jessica's mother."

"I see. So nobody benefits by her death?"

"No! Absolutely not."

Rafe's hand tightened around Jessie's. "What about Jessie's father?" he asked. "How did he die?"

"I really don't know. That happened before I met the family. I think it was before my uncle met them, too."

"I see." Rafe studied the other man intently. "Have you ever met a scarfaced man, one who has a scar across here?" He slashed his finger across his jaw.

"Uh . . . no. I don't think so. Why?"

"He tried to kill Jessie."

That got a reaction. Charles Lawson's face blanched. "Oh, God, no! He said . . ."

"I thought you said you didn't know him."

"I don't. But I heard folks talk about a man like that."

"So he comes from the Waco area, does he? It might be a good idea to give the sheriff that information."

"Does he have something to do with Jessica's disappearance?" Lawson asked.

"We think so."

"Jessica," Lawson asked softly. "Are you coming home with me, darling?"

"No. She's not," Rafe said. "Jessie and I are engaged to be married."

"She already has a husband," Lawson said quietly. "It isn't legal to have two. And I refuse to release her."

"She doesn't have to live with you."

"No. But I don't have to give her a divorce, either. And she can't marry you without one."

"The marriage was never consummated," Rafe said bluntly. "She's more my wife than yours."

"She's . . ." Charles Lawson's face paled and his vivid blue eyes held anguish when he looked at Jessie.

"Stop it!" Jessie grated. "Both of you stop it! I'm not some bone you two can fight over. I have feelings!"

"Jessie, love," Rafe said gently. "Let me take care of this."

"No! This is my life!" Tears filled her eyes and rolled down her cheeks. "God, I have to get out of here! I have to leave."

She hurried out the door and Rafe threw a look at Charles. "Now look what you've done," he snapped. Then he hurried after Jessie, bent on getting her back to the farm before she fell completely apart.

Chapter Twenty-Three

Darkness covered the land and, with Sissy asleep in bed, the rest of the Sutherland family gathered in the parlor.

Karin appeared nervous as she seated herself on the settee near Jessie's rocker. It was obvious she knew something was happening that would affect the whole family's future, yet she had no way of determining just how much since neither Danny nor Karin had been told about Charles Lawson.

Picking up her basket of mending, Jessie seated herself in the rocking chair and began to thread her needle so she could mend Rafe's shirt.

Rafe's gaze flicked between his two oldest children. He dreaded having to tell them about the man who claimed to be Jessie's husband, yet knew he must. There were only a few days left before the wedding day, and Karin was already asking questions, wondering why Jessie had stopped working on her wedding dress.

Clearing his throat to gain their attention, he said, "I

guess the two of you have been wondering what's going on around here."

Danny was seated by the hearth, working on the carving he meant to give Jessie. At Rafe's words, he looked up. "Has something been happening?"

"Oh, you goose!" Karin said. "You never pay attention to what's going on in your own family."

"Something's going on?"

"As a matter of fact, yes," Rafe replied. "We've found out where Jessie belongs."

Karin's eyes widened. "What do you mean, Pa?"

"Just what I said, Karin."

"Well"—her voice was indignant—"we already knew where she belonged. She belongs here with us. Doesn't she?"

"Yes, but . . ."

She interrupted her father. "Does this have something to do with that man Sheriff Watson brought out here?"

Her voice had become high-pitched with anxiety, as though she already knew what her father had to tell them, and it broke Jessie's heart.

"Yes," Rafe said gruffly. "He claims he's Jessie's husband."

"No! He can't be!" Karin jerked to her feet, her blue eyes flashing with anger. "Jessie is going to marry *you*, Pa. She's going to be our mother."

Rafe's expression hardened, became grim. "I don't like this any better than you do, Karin." He knew how his daughter felt. Hadn't he reacted in the same way when he'd heard the news? Even now, after seeing the tintype of Jessie and Charles decked out in their wedding finery, he didn't want to accept that fact. But, no matter how hard his heart rebelled against accepting another man for her husband, he was afraid it must be true.

"Well, do something then," Karin cried. "Jessie can't leave us. She promised she'd be our mother."

Jessie thought her heart would break. She had promised, but then, she'd apparently made other promises first.

Danny was watching them silently, his hands frozen in motion. Only his eyes seemed alive and they flicked between Jessie and his father. And there was something about them, a look that she'd never seen there—a longing when he looked at Jessie that told her he'd been struck dumb by the news.

"I wish I could do something," Rafe said grimly. "But the fact is, he's her husband. The wedding won't take place on Sunday."

"So you're leaving, Jessie? Just like that?"

"No, she's not leaving!" Rafe said.

Silence filled the room, and in that silence a knock sounded on the front door. Everyone seemed to be frozen, their faces turned, staring at the door.

Jessie felt certain she knew who was there, and that she couldn't leave this family yet. Not tonight. Oh, God, why was this happening?

Her movements were slow as she set aside her mending and crossed to the door. Turning the doorknob, she pulled the door open and stared up at the tall figure who leaned against the porch rail.

"Johnny." Her voice showed her surprise.

"I come to see Danny," Johnny said gruffly, looking beyond Jessie into the parlor where Karin stood poised, as though for flight.

Uttering a wild cry, Karin swept past Johnny and ran out into the night, headed for the barn where she could be alone with her pain.

Tears filled Jessie's eyes and she saw Johnny looking after Karin, his expression one of extreme longing mingling with worry.

"What's the matter with Karin?" he asked, his attention focused intently on her.

"She's hurting, Johnny," Jessie said softly. "Go to her. She needs you."

As though he'd suddenly been freed from heavy chains, Johnny took off at a run, headed for the corral and Karin, all pretense that he'd been visiting her brother apparently forgotten.

"You don't want to leave us, do you, Jessie?" Danny had finally found his voice.

"She's not going anywhere," Rafe said roughly, his gaze on Jessie. "We're just having to postpone the wedding until this is all straightened out."

"She can do that?" Danny asked. "She can marry us when she's already married to somebody else?"

"The marriage can be annulled, Danny."

"Annulled?" Danny questioned.

"That means to set aside."

"I didn't know that," the boy said thoughtfully. "I thought when you got married it was for life . . . unless somebody died."

Jessie's heart surged with pain as she silently admitted the truth of Danny's words. A truth that she'd already known, yet had refused to acknowledge. The boy was right. A marriage was for life, not just until one partner decided he wanted out. If she disregarded that truth for her own reasons, what kind of message would they be sending to the children?

"It usually is, son," Rafe said gruffly. "But in Jessie's case . . . well, she doesn't remember being married, so . . ."

"No, Rafe," Jessie said around the knot lodged in her throat. "Danny's right. Marriage is forever. Nothing changes that."

"You don't know what you're saying!" he snarled, pulling her into his arms. "You don't know him, Jessie. He's a stranger to you."

Her lower lip quivered as she fought for control. "He's my husband, Rafe. Nothing can change that."

She breathed in the scent of him, a combination of leather and hay blending with a purely male scent that was his alone. She knew she should push herself away from him but she couldn't deny herself when they had so little time left together.

After hearing Danny's words, she realized there was really no choice. No matter how much she had come to love Rafe, no matter how much she wanted to mother his children, she had sworn before God to love another man, to cherish and obey him for the rest of her life. No matter that it was going to feel like her heart was being ripped out of her body when she left the man she loved and his children who had become so dear to her, she had to find the strength to do exactly that.

She lifted her head and met his gaze and saw such terrible longing there that she almost cried out. She wanted to wrap her arms around him, tell him she would never leave, do anything to take away his intense pain.

Burying her head deeper against his shoulder, she fought against the tears. She couldn't break down, she told herself, couldn't allow him to know how leaving him would tear out her heart. But despite her efforts at control, the tears came. Shudders shook her small frame as sobs wracked her body.

Rafe's arms tightened around her and he held her against him, muttering loving words as he stroked her back helplessly. The tide of emotion threatened to consume him as well.

He was vaguely aware of his son leaving them alone before he sank down on the settee with Jessie in his arms. No matter what happened, he couldn't give her up, his heart cried. But somehow, he knew that this time the choice wasn't his alone.

Jessie had decided. And even though she was in his arms, crying her heart out because of that decision, her honor would make her abide by that same decision, would make her adhere to her wedding vows.

Johnny found Karin in the barn, leaning against the nearest stall, sobbing so hard that her frail body shook. The sounds ripped through him, creating a hard knot of pain somewhere near his heart.

"Karin," he said huskily, sliding his arms around her waist.

Although he'd expected her to resist, she turned in his arms and put her head against his chest.

"What is it, Karin?" he asked gruffly. "What's the matter."

As though his voice had broken a dam and released a heavy flood, she sobbed harder, sliding her arms around his neck and clinging tightly to him.

Johnny didn't know what to do. His eyes burned as he held back his own tears, swearing silently that whoever had done this to her, whoever had caused her so much pain, would have to answer to him.

"Sweetheart," he whispered. "Don't . . ."

But she continued to sob, shudders shaking her slender body as she clung to him, crying all the while as though her heart was breaking.

Johnny continued to hold her, his heart aching for the girl he held in his arms, the girl he'd known since early childhood. When her sobs finally ceased, she told him what had happened and he realized there was no way he could make things right for her.

And he felt as though he'd failed her.

* * *

Charles pushed open the door to Dr. Jacob Lassiter's office. He needed some information before going to the Sutherland farm.

After introducing himself, Charles apprised the doctor of his reasons for coming. "I understand you've been attending my wife, Jessica."

"That is correct." Lassiter's voice was less than welcoming.

"Is this memory loss she's suffering permanent?"

"It's hard to say," Jacob said. "Her memory has been gone for some time. There is a chance, of course, that she may remember her past one day, but there's as good a chance that it will always be lost." He studied Charles with hard, cold eyes. "Am I right in assuming Jessie has no memory of you?"

"Yes, that's right. But if you're doubting the validity of our marriage, then let me assure you I have proof." He reached inside his coat pocket and pulled out the tintype of Jessica and himself in their wedding garments.

Jacob Lassiter remained unmoved. "I heard about the picture. I'm wondering why you chose to bring that instead of your marriage license."

Charles shrugged. "Because the license had no picture on it. The tintype did." He turned to go, but paused at the door and looked back. "I'm wondering why you should question our marriage. After all, you're only her doctor."

"No. I'm her doctor, but I'm also a man who loves her." Jacob Lassiter's expression was hard, uncompromising. "And I damn well won't allow anyone to hurt her without paying a price," he added, an unmistakable warning in his voice. "Not anyone. Even a husband."

Charles nodded abruptly. "Hurting Jessica is the last thing I would do. But your warning is duly noted."

He was thoughtful as he left the doctor's office. It appeared Jessica had made a place for herself in this town. Everyone spoke kindly of her . . . except the schoolteacher, who obviously had eyes for Rafe Sutherland.

The Sutherland children were a problem that Charles had not foreseen. It was more than obvious that Jessica loved them as they must love her. But, given time, they could have children of their own and the dream that Charles had made real would come true. He and Jessica would have a happy life. He would see to that.

Since the day he'd met her, he'd wanted nothing more than to love her and be loved by her. Granted, she didn't love him now. But she would . . . in time.

All he had to do was wait, be patient. And love would eventually come.

Chapter Twenty-Four

Rafe felt cold as death as he readied the horse and carriage that would carry Jessie away from him. He railed at fate, and at Jessie's stubborn determination. Allowing her to leave was tearing him apart, but he was unable to convince her to stay. Each time he tried, it brought on another bout of tears that made his heart break in two, but did nothing to sway her decision.

How was he supposed to live without her? How was he supposed to get through each day—each long, lonely night—knowing she was out there somewhere, wanting him as he wanted her, yet living with another man, tasting another man's kisses, allowing him to love her in the most intimate way?

Rafe bent over at the waist, pressing his fists against his heart, wanting to tear that aching organ right out of his chest to stop the terrible pain that threatened to rip him asunder.

Finally, he straightened, a cold light entering his gray

eyes. He had a job to do and he would do it. She insisted on honoring her vows and he refused to plead with her uselessly, something that would do nothing to change her mind and would only make things harder for all of them.

When he stopped the team beside the porch, she was waiting. She bent and kissed Sissy lovingly, then turned to embrace Karin. But the girl moved swiftly back, tears rolling down her cheeks unchecked.

Jessie turned away, then climbed into the carriage; when they rode away, she never looked back.

The ride to town was silent, neither of them able to speak lest their words bring on another bout of weeping. Jessie was conscious, though, of Rafe's stiff body only a foot away, of the tension of his grip on the reins. And she knew the sorrow he was feeling because she felt that way herself.

She wanted to cry out, to tell him to stop, to turn around and take her back, but knew she could not. She had duty to hold her to her course, honor to keep her there.

Jessie tried to stop her thoughts of her time with them, but they refused to obey. She remembered clearly the way he'd looked that night when she first awoke, the sight of him with his unshaven jaws and tender smile. She'd known then what kind of man he was. And from that moment on, her feelings for him had grown.

How would she survive without him? How would he raise his children alone? Would he raise them alone or would he find himself another wife, another mother for them?

Her thoughts were in turmoil as they rode into Castle Rock. The town bustled with activity. Wagons rattled by with a jingle of harnesses and the thud of shod hooves as the townsfolk engaged in their usual activities.

Rafe pulled up at the livery stable and helped Jessie down. When he met her eyes, his were hot, turbulent with emotion.

"Rafe . . ." Jessie curled her fingers around his upper arm. She didn't know what to say now that the time had come for them to part. So she just looked at him, hoping he'd see the love that she felt for him, the anguish that tore at her very soul.

"Don't do this, Jessie," he said harshly. "If you go with Lawson . . . if you do this to us, then it will be the end of what we had together. You can never come back."

Tears filled her eyes and she blinked them away. She couldn't allow herself to break down where everyone could see. *Oh, God,* she cried silently. *Give me the strength to leave him!*

"I mean it, Jessie," Rafe's expression was uncompromising. "Don't expect me to be waiting if it doesn't work out."

He hated himself for saying that, yet he was fighting for her in the only way he knew how.

"I w-won't," she said unsteadily.

"You're not going to change your mind, are you? You're really going to go through with it?"

"Rafe, please understand why I have to do this. Please."

"I understand, Jessie." Pain gnawed at Rafe's gut. It would have been easier to lose her to death. At least then, the choice would not have been hers. But how was he going to live knowing she was living with another man, lying in his arms, having his children? Oh, God, how could he stand knowing that she'd chosen another man over him?

He had to get away from her, had to keep a grip on his emotions until he could leave town, could find a place to be alone.

Rafe's gaze swept over her one last time, burning her image into his memory. Then, before he realized what he was doing, he reached out and gripped her upper arms tightly, pulling her hard against his body. His mouth closed over hers in a hard kiss that would have to last him a lifetime. Then he put her away from him and walked away, his long strides carrying him swiftly to the feed store.

Jessie fought against tears as she watched him leave. She touched her mouth with trembling fingers, tempted to follow him, to beg him to take her with him, yet knew she could not. Slowly, on unsteady legs, she headed toward the boardinghouse where Charles was staying.

Each step she took carried her farther away from Rafe. She wanted to turn around, to run back to him, bury her head against his shoulder, yet she could not. Instead, she forced herself to go on.

She was vaguely aware of conversation as she passed the stores. Voices rose and fell but Jessie paid them no mind. Her thoughts were totally absorbed with the man she'd left behind. Rafe. The man she loved.

The three-storied boardinghouse was painted pale blue and edged with white around the windows, porch columns, and balconies. Jessie mounted the steps and opened the door to a dim foyer. Straight ahead, a narrow stairway led to the second floor. To her left was the open door of the parlor where Mrs. Newsom, the landlady, sat piecing quilt tops. She was an energetic, wiry woman with the open friendliness of one who never met a stranger.

As Jessie closed the front door, the woman set aside her piecework and rose to her feet. "Jessie. How nice to see you again. Do you have time to join me for tea?"

Jessie wanted to accept, to have a reason to delay her meeting with Charles, but she was afraid if she did she would change her mind, run back to Rafe, and beg him to take her home with him. And she couldn't. Not when she'd vowed to love and cherish another man for the rest of her life.

"Not right now," she replied. "I need to talk to Charles."

"I understand, my dear." The woman's expression was one of sadness. "You go ahead and speak to your husband. I imagine he's about done with his visitor."

"Charles has a visitor?"

"Yes. His uncle. I forget his name." She laughed huskily. "You know my memory these days. That's the part I hate most about growing old."

Wondering about the man who'd come to see her husband, Jessie climbed the stairs to the second floor. The hall carpeting covered the sound of her footsteps along the hallway. As she neared Charles's room she could hear muffled male voices.

Jessie wondered, momentarily, if she should descend the stairway again and join his landlady in the parlor, then decided she would not. She had to tell Charles her decision immediately. Had to let him know she was willing to accompany him home if he was willing to allow her time before they consummated their marriage.

Fisting her hand, she knocked gently. The voices became louder as the door, which apparently hadn't closed enough to latch, swung open a crack.

"No. I won't have it, Uncle Zeke." Charles's voice was raised in anger. "I would never have agreed to the marriage if I hadn't believed Jessie would come to love me in time."

In time? She hadn't loved Charles when they were married as he claimed?

"Love!" the man called Zeke spat. "There's no such emotion, Charles! It's just a word used by sentimental fools. It has nothing to do with us."

"You're wrong, Uncle Zeke. I love Jessie. I always have."

"You're a fool, Charles. You're not in love with the girl. You just want to bed her, and you knew marriage was the only way you'd ever have her that way."

"You're wrong," Charles said again.

"You listen to me, boy, and you listen good. The time

for choices is past. There's too much at stake here. Too many things have happened since I agreed to a marriage between the two of you." His voice was hard with anger. "We have to get rid of her now."

"Get rid of her? What are you saying, Uncle Zeke?" Charles sounded distraught. "What really happened to Jessie on our wedding day? You didn't really mean to murder her, did you?"

Jessie's heart thumped like a hammer as the salty taste of fear swept through her.

"I did what I had to do, boy. And I wouldn't hesitate to do it again."

"But she doesn't remember that day."

"Her memory might come back, and I won't take that chance. Not when she heard me talking to Jeb. She found out the ranch belonged to her, knew everything! I wouldn't have known she'd heard us if I hadn't seen her on the stairs. She locked her door against us and climbed out the window. She managed to reach the stable without us noticing. She'd have got clean away if I hadn't seen her riding away and hollered to Jeb to go after her and kill the bitch."

Kill the bitch!

Jessie heard a deafening rush of blood through her ears and her head began to pound. *Kill the bitch . . .* those three words cut through the fog and mist covering her memory like a knife, leaving her shocked. She had a sudden image of a middle-aged man standing in a doorway, his face mottled with rage, yelling out those words. *Kill the bitch!*

Her skin prickled with cold, her heart hammered beneath her ribcage as emotions flooded through her. Memory swirled around her like dry leaves in a windstorm.

She saw herself dressing for her wedding, knowing Charles was waiting at the church in town. Felt her fear of the future, yet knew there was nothing else she could do because her stepfather, Zeke Carson, had told her he would no longer support her, that she'd have to marry his nephew or find herself with no means, at all. Her mother had recently passed away and she'd known that Charles loved her. And so she'd agreed to the wedding.

Jessie remembered having left her pearls in the safe in the study and went downstairs to fetch them. Finding the study door open, she overheard Zeke Carson talking to Jeb, the scarfaced man who'd come to the Sutherland home. That conversation had told her Zeke had been lying, that her mother had not owned the ranch as Carson had thought. The ranch had been left to Jessie in trust until she reached the age of twenty-one—only six months away—or until she was married, which meant Carson would lose everything unless he found a way to control her property. So he had devised the plan to marry her off to Charles.

And Charles had known of his plans!

"Dammit!" The raised voice brought her back to reality. "You will do as I say, Charles!"

"No!" Charles cried. "I'll have no part in it!"

There was a muffled thud, like a fist connecting with flesh, then Zeke said, "Don't you sass me, boy!"

"I'm not a boy, Uncle Zeke. I haven't been for a long time."

"You damn sure ain't a man, neither! If your pa was alive he'd be ashamed of you for going against your kin."

"I won't do it," Charles said again.

"Then I'll find somebody who will."

"Be reasonable, Uncle Zeke. You can't hide something like that. Her mother died under mysterious circumstances. If Jessica dies the same way, the sheriff will be suspicious. He might start digging and find enough dirt to hang you."

"I won't be caught. She don't have no kin to wonder

about the way she died. And without somebody pressing for answers, the sheriff will be easy enough to handle.''

''Rafe won't let you get away with it.''

''Rafe? Are you talking about that hick farmer she's been living with?''

''Yes. His name is Rafe Sutherland, and he would never allow her death to go unavenged. He'd have plenty of questions and would never rest until they were answered.''

''There'd be no reason to suspect me.''

''There's Jeb.''

''Jeb? He's dead. He can't tell nobody nothing.''

''Rafe has already been digging into Jeb's past. He knows Jeb came from the Waco area and it wouldn't take him long to discover he worked for you.''

''Sutherland won't be a problem.''

As footsteps approached the door, Jessie staggered back. With her hand pressed against her stomach, Jessie stumbled toward the stairs. She had to get away, had to keep them from learning her memory had returned. At least until she found Rafe.

The sound of squeaking hinges sent her scurrying behind the stairwell where a closet took up most of the space. She opened the door and slid inside, waiting in the darkness until she was certain her stepfather had left. Then she opened the door again . . . and found herself face-to-face with Charles.

The look on her face told its own story.

''You heard.'' His voice was flat, emotionless, his expression that of a man who had lost everything dear to him. He held out a hand and she backed away.

''Don't you dare touch me!''

''Jessica,'' he pleaded. ''I love you. Please believe that.''

''I would never have believed you capable of such perfidy, Charles. You conspired with my stepfather to have me murdered.''

"No, Jessie. I knew about the ranch, but I never intended you harm. I wouldn't have agreed to anything like that. I swear it, darling. I would have found the courage to kill him myself before allowing him to hurt you."

"You lied to me."

"No. I love you, darling. We love each other. I didn't know . . ."

Revulsion swept across her face. "I thought we were friends. I believed in you and you betrayed me."

"No, love."

"No matter what happened in the past, today you were conspiring with him to murder me."

"No, Jessica. Oh, God, no. Don't you see? That's the reason I told him about Rafe Sutherland and what he'd learned about Jeb. I thought he would understand that murdering you wouldn't profit him, that Rafe would see him hang for the deed. Oh, God, Jessie. Please believe me. I knew nothing of what went on the day of our wedding. I was waiting at the church for you. We loved each other. We . . ."

"Don't lie to me, Charles. I remember everything." Her voice vibrated with anger. "Everything!"

Her lips thinned as she held his gaze; his face paled, his blue eyes flickering with a deep sadness. He reached out, grasping her forearm. "Come to my room so we can talk this out, love."

Although she shook his hand loose, she followed him into his room. She was unwilling for Mrs. Newsom to overhear their conversation.

When the door was closed firmly behind them, he turned to her. When he spoke, his voice was filled with deep regret.

"I hoped you'd never remember, Jessica," he said softly. "I knew it was the only chance I had." He raked a hand through his golden curls and reached toward her again. As before, she avoided his touch.

"How could you have betrayed me so, Charles?"

"I had no idea what he planned. I swear it, Jessica. I would never have agreed had I known. And he knew that. Damn him! He knew how much I loved you. That's the reason he never told me."

"And you think that makes it all right?" she asked. "Just because he didn't let you in on all of his plans? Did you really think forcing me into a loveless marriage was honorable?"

"No. Not honorable. But I thought . . . in time . . . that you'd come to love me as I loved you."

His voice was rough, as though he was in the grip of some strong emotion. There was such pain in his eyes that she didn't doubt his sincerity. But she would never forgive him for his part in what happened to her.

"I don't need that kind of love," she said bitterly. "It's too self-serving. You gave no thought to my needs."

"Don't say that."

"Why not? It's true. You came here and took me away from the family I loved. The man I love . . ." She choked up, unable to go on as she remembered the look on Rafe's face when he'd walked away from her.

"Oh, God, Jessica." Charles voice was desperate. "I hoped you didn't really love him, that it was gratitude you felt."

"You're a fool, Charles."

"Yes," he said sadly. "I suppose I am." He looked away from her. "I'm a fool. A weak fool. But I've loved you since the day we met. You were fourteen and I was sixteen. You had a mother who loved you dearly. And a brother who thought you hung the stars. I was just a boy without family except for an uncle who knew nothing about love. I only wanted one thing from you, Jessica. In all these years I've only wanted your love."

She looked at him with sorrow. "I did love you, Charles. From the day we met you were like a brother to me. And I trusted you to love me in the same way."

His head dipped low and he crammed his hands in his pocket. "I wanted more," he said softly. "So much more." He strode to the window and looked out on the street below.

"I could never give you more."

"I see that now." He swung back to face her again. "Have I lost even that now, Jessica. Do you hate me?"

Her hands clenched into fists. "How could I feel anything else for the man who ruined my life? We can't go back to where we were before." She remembered Rafe walking away from her.

A muscle worked in Charles's jaw. "No. We can't go back. We can only go forward." He looked out the window again. "And somehow, I have to find a way to live with what I've done. To forgive myself for the part I played in ruining your life."

Jessie looked at his tall frame, at the man she'd once loved as a brother. He wanted forgiveness, but how could she forgive him? Her life was a mess. She had walked out on Rafe, on his children, in the name of honor. He would never forgive her. He had made that clear enough before he'd left her standing on the boardwalk. Now her life was a shambles and the man who stood before her had done his part in making it that way.

Charles couldn't bear the look she gave him, couldn't bear the heat of his stuffy room. He tugged open the window and a hot breeze tumbled inside, ruffling the curtains. The sounds from below—hooves pounding against packed dirt, rolling wagon wheels, jingling harnesses—billowed through the room as he stared down into the street. His gaze stopped on a man who had just stepped off the boardwalk. It was the man who'd ruined his life. His uncle.

"Rafe! Rafe Sutherland!"

The voice came from a distance, barely discernible to Charles's ears. He leaned out the window, his flickering gaze finding the man who had just thrown a sack of feed into a buckboard outside the livery stable. It was Rafe Sutherland.

"Rafe!" the voice came again. "Tucker said tell you not to forget your harness!"

Sutherland nodded abruptly, then strode into the livery stable. Charles was turning away from the window when, out of the corner of his eye, he saw his uncle change directions. Zeke's hand was on his pistol as he entered the alley beside the feed store.

It was then he remembered Zeke Carson's words. *Sutherland won't be a problem.*

Charles cursed silently. Uncle Zeke was planning to arrange an accident for Rafe, to get him out of the way.

Charles knew he had to stop his uncle. But even as the thought occurred, he realized all he had to do was wait. To do nothing, to let it happen—and Rafe Sutherland would be dead. Jessica would surely turn to him for support if she had nobody else.

All he had to do was wait.

He looked at Jessica, who watched him with deep sorrow.

"Dammit!" he cursed, realizing he couldn't stand there and do nothing. He swung quickly around, striding across the room to the door.

She frowned heavily. "What is it, Charles? What did you see?"

"Stay in here!" he ordered. "Don't leave this room. Do you hear me, Jessica? Do not leave this room!"

"You can't order me around."

He glared at her and his blue eyes were cold, hard. "Goddammit, Jessica! I'm only trying to protect you! Lock the door and don't open it until I get back!"

As he strode through the door and swung it shut behind him, Jessie hurried to the window and looked down into the street below. A horse and rider rode by, followed by a horse and carriage. Nothing to cause alarm. Her gaze shifted to the cafe across the street where three old men sat on a bench.

Knowing there must have been something more there when Charles had looked down on the street, Jessie's gaze swept farther and she saw him entering the alley beside the feed store. Her gaze flickered back and forth to the street, then the alley, then farther down where Rafe's team and wagon waited near the livery stable.

Where was Rafe? And why had Charles insisted she stay in his room with the door locked? Why did he want her out of sight? Surely he didn't mean to harm Rafe. No matter what he had done, he would never do that.

Her gaze swept the street again, the storefronts, the sidewalks, taking in everything Charles might have seen below. From her vantage point on the second floor, she could see the back of the livery stable and as she watched, a man came into view. He was stooped over, as though trying to avoid detection.

Was Rafe in the livery stable?

A chill slithered over her like a spider's legs, spreading icy fear wherever they touched. The man was moving in a suspicious manner, and his attention was definitely focused on the stable.

She studied the man closer. There was something familiar about him; the upper shoulders, covered by the gray suit was all she could see, but . . .

Oh, God, no! It was her stepfather, Zeke Carson! But what would he want with Rafe?

Sutherland won't be a problem. The words her stepfather had spoken flashed through her memory and fear became a hard knot in her belly.

"He's going to murder Rafe!"

Gathering up her long skirts, Jessie hurried across the room, through the door, and down the stairs. The front door slammed behind her as she left the boardinghouse and sprinted down the boardwalk toward the livery stable.

One thought was in her mind. She had to reach Rafe, had to warn him before Carson entered the stable and caught him unaware.

Oh, God, she had to reach him, had to stop a madman from ending his life. Jessie had no other thought in her head, only that she had to stop her stepfather from shooting Rafe.

She stumbled forward, pushing past people, unaware of the shouts and the crowd that had suddenly appeared out of nowhere.

There was but one single thought in her mind. She had to get to Rafe before her stepfather gunned him down.

Chapter Twenty-Five

The pungent scent of hay mingled with leather and horses assailed her nostrils as Jessie entered the livery.

Her gaze probed the shadowy confines within, barely lighted by the wide-open doors. Somewhere, she knew, there must be a back door, and it was through that door that danger would come.

"Rafe," she called quietly, urgently, hoping to warn him without alerting the man who'd come to threaten him. "Rafe, where are you?"

The sound of boots thudding against hard dirt jerked her head around—Rafe was approaching, a harness in his hand.

"Rafe! You have to get out of here!"

Realizing the urgency of her warning from the sound of her voice, his strides quickened.

"Jessie?"

She heard the hope in his voice and could have cried

out with joy. Despite his words to the contrary, Rafe would never turn away from her.

"You have to get out of here," she repeated. "My stepfather is . . ."

"Well, well, Jessica," a hated voice that she remembered so well mocked from the back of the livery stable. "Have you suddenly regained your memory? How terribly inconvenient."

She whirled around. "You might as well leave while you can," she said, managing to instill some bravery in her voice. "You have nothing to gain by his death. Nothing at all."

"That's what you think, is it? Well, you're wrong, my sweet. I have everything to gain by his death. And by yours."

"What's going on here?" Rafe asked, stepping in front of Jessie to shield her from the other man. "Who are you?"

"I'm Jessica's stepfather. And I stand to inherit the ranch after she's gone."

Rafe's glance flickered to Charles, who stood behind Jessica's stepfather. "Is this what it's all about then?" he asked. "You wanted her dead all the time. You bastard!"

There was so much feeling behind the word that Charles actually flinched as though he'd been shot.

"No," he denied. "I told the truth. I love her."

"She doesn't need your kind of love," Rafe snarled.

While he talked, his eyes were searching the shadowy livery, looking for something to use as a weapon. His flickering gaze stopped on several horseshoes hanging from a nail fastened to a post a short distance away, then returned to the man pointing the pistol at them.

"So you'd kill for her ranch."

"Damn right I would. I'd do whatever it takes to make it mine."

Gripping Jessie from behind him, Rafe urged her toward the post, slowly, to keep her stepfather from knowing his intention.

He knew horseshoes would not stop bullets, but perhaps they would do enough damage to allow her to flee. But he had to keep them talking.

He looked at Charles. "Was the wedding a lie, too?"

"We were going to marry," Charles said defensively. "I was already at the church when she rode away on that horse. I had no idea what they had planned."

"Shut up, Charles," his uncle snarled.

"What difference does it make?" Rafe asked. "You've made no secret of your plans to murder us. So why not admit the truth?"

"You're right," Zeke said. "There's no reason not to. Well, truth be known, I married her mother for the ranch. And when she died, I thought it was mine."

"Was my brother's death really an accident?" Jessie asked.

Her stepfather smiled, and it was purely evil. "He wasn't as manageable as you, Jessie. He stood to inherit before you." He waved the gun. "So you see, I really had no choice except to rid myself of him."

"Are you such a weakling, Charles, that you'll allow him to murder Jessie right before your eyes?" Rafe asked harshly.

"He'll do anything I tell him," Jessie's stepfather said.

"No, dammit!" Charles said. "I told you I won't stand by and allow you to hurt her!"

"Shut up, Charles!" his uncle snarled. "And if you don't have the courage to watch me kill them, then get out of here while I do it."

Timmy Carter had taken the back alley on his way to school that morning, hoping he might find something good to add to his collection—like he'd done yesterday when he'd found the cigar. It had only been smoked halfway down so he'd been able to trade it to Corky Duncan for a blue-colored stone he'd found in the river.

As he passed the open door of the livery he heard a man talking about killing somebody and darted quick to one side and peeked inside. Although he couldn't see very much in the shadows, the light shining through the door at the other end had been enough to glint against the steel barrel of a pistol that one man had pointed at another.

Easing away from the livery, he waited until he was far enough away so they wouldn't hear him, then ran toward the sheriff's office for help. He was breathless when he shoved open the door.

"Howdy, pardner."

The sheriff greeted him just like he always did when Timmy came to see him, but the boy knew this time was different. This time they really were partners, for without his help, a man might be murdered. Heck, a whole bunch of men might die without them working together. And he'd tell the sheriff so just as soon as he got his breath back.

Lucas Watson frowned as he realized the boy was breathing so hard he couldn't speak.

"What's wrong, Timmy?" he asked. "Why were you running?"

"Cause there's a man . . . a man with a gun . . . in the livery stable."

"Is there now? And what's so scary about that? You've seen guns before. Lots of men carry them."

"Yeah. But this one's going to shoot somebody with his."

"Are you sure about that?"

Timmy nodded. "I heard him say so, Sheriff. And I saw the gun. It was pointed at Mr. Sutherland—and there was a lady there, too. I saw her. She was standing behind Mr. Sutherland, like he was kinda hiding her from the other man. But I saw her good enough.''

''Dammit!'' Lucas was almost certain he knew what was happening. Things had come to a boil and Rafe and Charles Lawson were bent on killing each other and somehow Jessie had wound up in the middle of things.

He ran out the door and raced down the boardwalk, weaving his way between passersby, knocking against those he could not avoid. His boots pounded loudly against the boards; he realized the sound might alarm whoever had the gun and cause him to fire. He leapt off the boardwalk into the street, barely escaping being run over by a carriage, trying desperately to reach the livery before Rafe either murdered, or was murdered himself. Either way would bring pain for his family.

Jacob Lassiter had been on the point of entering the cafe when he saw Lucas running toward the other end of town. Fearing his services would be needed, he forgot about feeding his face and hurried after the sheriff, managing to reach the stables only moments after the lawman.

Rafe was near the post now, and he knew he had to make his move.

''Jessie,'' he whispered, reaching behind him to squeeze her hand. ''I'm going to try to distract him. When I say go, I want you to dodge behind those bales of hay stacked over yonder. And stay there.''

He felt her squeeze his hand and knew she'd heard him and understood. Charles was still arguing with his uncle but the man had never taken his eyes off Rafe. All Rafe needed, though, was a few moments. Just long enough to allow Jessie to reach cover. The sound of the gunshots should bring help. If he was lucky, her stepfather wouldn't have time to shoot her as well.

"Now, Jessie," he said softly. Then, raising his voice, he yelled, "Go!"

She moved with him, he going for the horseshoes, she dashing toward the stack of hay. He heard the sound of a shot and felt a burning pain in his chest; then he snatched the horseshoes off the nail and threw one toward the man with the pistol.

"No!" Charles shouted, struggling with his uncle for the gun.

His uncle flung him aside, then shot at Rafe again. The force of the bullet flung him backwards, but the horseshoe he'd thrown struck the man on his upper body. Not hard enough though, to deflect another bullet. Rafe didn't feel the slug entering his body, only felt a sense of floating. His head was whirling, blackness was closing around him, and then he knew no more.

"Rafe!" Jessie screamed as she watched him fall.

Forgetting her own circumstances, she made a wild dash toward the man she loved, the man who lay so still on the floor.

"Jessica!" Charles cried. "Look out!"

But Jessie had no thought for her own safety, didn't see the gun barrel rise and point at her, didn't see Charles, her childhood friend, fling himself in front of the gun and take the bullet himself. She only saw the man she loved, crumpled against the haystrewn floor, blood seeping from the chest wounds the bullets had inflicted.

Another shot rang out and she waited for the impact of the bullet that never came. And then hands were lifting her away from Rafe, caring hands that sought to soothe, to calm her fears.

"No, no!" she cried, struggling against the man who held her. "I need to see him!"

"Let Jacob examine him, Jessie," Lucas said gently.

With her heart hammering inside her chest, Jessie watched the doctor bend over Rafe. "I don't feel a pulse," he said grimly.

And then Jessie knew no more.

Chapter Twenty-Six

Jessie didn't know how long she'd been unconscious, but when she regained her senses, she was stretched out on the floor with Lucas kneeling beside her.

Her nostrils twitched, assailed by the stench of burnt gunpowder that almost covered the familiar scent of hay. And beyond those odors, she perceived another one . . . the coppery smell of blood.

Blood. Rafe's blood.

Oh, God, Rafe had been shot! Killed!

She pushed herself to a sitting position, her gaze darting frantically around the stable that was empty now save for Lucas and herself.

"Where is he, Lucas?" she asked huskily. "Where is Rafe?"

"They took him to the doctor's house."

Her heart leapt with hope. The doctor's house? Not the undertakers? She swallowed around the obstruction that blocked her throat. "To Jacob's house . . . Does that mean he's not . . . not . . .'' She found herself unable to verbalize the word.

"No." He squeezed her hand gently. "Rafe is not dead, Jessie. At least not yet. Jacob finally found a pulse."

Joy streaked through Jessie, and she felt as though a heavy weight had suddenly been lifted off her shoulders. She covered her face with her palms and her shoulders shook with silent sobs. She hadn't lost Rafe. There was still a chance.

"Jessie . . ." Lucas's voice was hesitant. "Rafe was alive when they carried him out of here, but you have to realize he's not out of the woods yet. His wounds are mighty serious and . . ."

"I have to see him," she interrupted. "Now."

Bracing her palms on the floor, she tried to push herself upright, but her knees wouldn't cooperate. They refused to lock together.

"Settle down, Jessie," Lucas commanded. "You're still too shaky. Just give it a little more time."

"I can't, Lucas. I don't know how much time Rafe has left. I have to be there. Don't you see?" Her gaze fell on a horseshoe nearby. Rafe had thrown it at Zeke Carson. She turned to look at Lucas. "What about my stepfather?"

"Your what?"

"My stepfather. He's the one who shot Rafe."

Lucas's lips flattened and when he spoke his voice was as cold as his eyes. "He won't be troubling anybody no more, Jessie."

"He's dead?"

"Yeah."

"And Charles?"

"Dead, too." Jacob was silent for a long moment, then said grudgingly, "Charles Lawson took the bullet meant for you, Jessie."

Jessie tried to find forgiveness in her heart for Charles,

but at the moment there was none. He had lied to them, had made them believe she was his wife. And because he had lied, had not told them the truth, they were not prepared when her stepfather came. It might have been Zeke Carson who had fired the shots into Rafe's body, but if Charles had stood up to his uncle, had refused to do his bidding, then none of this would have occurred.

"Help me, Lucas," she commanded, curling her fingers around his arm and gripping tightly. "I need to go to Rafe."

"All right, Jessie."

Lucas pulled her upright and held her there with an arm around her waist. Then, together, they made their way to Jacob's house near the edge of town where he had set aside two rooms for his business.

The door was opened by his housekeeper, a middle-aged woman whose hair was streaked with gray. "Hello, Lucas," she said, stepping back to allow them entry. "I kinda expected you'd be around sooner or later."

"Howdy, Sarah," he greeted. "I don't think you've met Jessie."

"No. But I've heard about her." Sarah smiled at Jessie. "I don't suppose there's anybody in this county that hasn't heard about the woman who lost her memory. Nor the fact that she was planning to marry Rafe." Her faded blue eyes darkened with sympathy. "I am so sorry, my dear. So sorry about what happened."

Fear clutched at Jessie, squeezing her heart with a mighty grip. "He's not . . ."

"Oh, no!" Sarah interrupted. "At least not yet. But it doesn't look good."

"I need to see him."

"I know." Sarah's faded blue eyes were full of compassion. "But the doctor is still working on him, my dear. We can't disturb him just yet. There were so many bullets in him . . . too many holes. And he . . . Rafe lost a lot of blood.''

Bullets meant for me, Jessie silently told herself.

She swallowed around a tightness in her throat. ''I need to stay close by him.''

''I know.'' Sarah beckoned them into the parlor. ''Just find a comfortable seat in here, love, and I'll bring you a nice cup of tea.''

Tea! Tea wouldn't heal Jessie's pain. But neither would railing at the woman. She slumped down in an overstuffed chair to wait.

''Jessie . . .'' Lucas said hesitantly. ''Did Charles tell you anything about himself, about his family? I need to let someone know of his death.''

''He didn't have to tell me anything, Lucas. I remember everything now.''

His brow arched. ''You do? Since when?''

''Since I overheard him talking to my stepfather. Something he said triggered my memory. Charles was completely alone except for his uncle . . . and me.''

''I see. Do you want me to make the funeral arrangements?''

''Yes. Please.'' She had no interest in her stepfather. Nor in Charles, at the moment. Perhaps later she could forgive him for his part in what happened. But not yet. Not while Rafe lay dying. *Oh, dear Lord, please don't let him die!*

Somewhere in the back of her mind she was aware of Lucas leaving the room. But her thoughts were turned inward, to Rafe, and the short time they'd had together. Too short.

If only she had followed her heart instead of her mind, Rafe would have been safe at home when Zeke Carson arrived in town.

If only.

Oh, God, why had she believed Charles's lies?

The sound of heavy footsteps outside the doorway jerked her out of the past and into the present. She rose quickly as Jacob Lassiter entered the room. Her gaze met his and she saw the compassion in his eyes.

Her hands fisted at her sides and she licked lips that had suddenly gone dry. "He's still alive, Jacob," she said hoarsely. "Please tell me that Rafe is still alive."

"He is, Jessie," he said gruffly. "For now. But he's in a bad way."

Although his voice wasn't the least bit encouraging, Jessie couldn't keep her hope at bay. Rafe was alive when she'd thought him dead. Not gone yet, still breathing, and where there was life, there had to be hope.

"I want to see him."

"I'm not so sure that's a good idea . . ."

"I want to see him!" she snapped.

He nodded abruptly. "All right. But just for a few minutes."

Jessie followed Jacob down the hall to a room he'd set aside for such emergencies. Her gaze spanned the distance to the bed and tears blurred her vision as she saw the man lying there. So still and quiet.

Blinking the tears away, she hurried forward, her eyes glued to Rafe. He was so pale, every drop of color gone from his face. And there was a bandage on his left shoulder where blood was seeping through.

She picked up his cold hand and held it against her cheek. "Rafe," she whispered. "I'm here, darling. I'm right beside you."

A hand gripped her shoulder and she looked up to see Jacob beside her. Jessie reached out and covered his hand with her own.

"He's so cold," she whispered.

"He lost a lot of blood."

"How bad is it, Jacob?"

"You might as well know he likely won't pull through. I'm surprised he's still with us."

"He's strong," Jessie said fiercely. "He works hard. Always has. And he keeps himself fit. He'll make it. He's just got to make it."

"Jessie," Jacob said compassionately. "I know you love him, dear. But please don't get your hopes up. It will only make it harder for you when he goes."

"He's going to live, Jacob," Jessie said fiercely. "He has to live."

A long silence followed her words. Then Jacob cleared his throat. "You've been through quite an ordeal yourself, Jessie. It would be better if you leave now. Go home and get some rest. I'll take care of him for you. I'll do everything possible to save him. And . . ."

"No," she said fiercely, clutching Rafe's hand tighter, holding it against her breast. "I'm staying right here, Jacob. I want to be here until . . ." Her voice trailed away. She couldn't finish the sentence, couldn't verbalize that she wanted to stay with Rafe until he died. It was foolish, she knew, but maybe, if she didn't speak the words aloud, then perhaps it wouldn't really happen.

"What are you doing for him?" she asked.

"Nothing now," he replied. "I dug out the bullets . . . three of them. One bullet was in his hip, another lodged precariously close to his heart. The other one was high on his shoulder. But he lost so much blood, Jessie, that his survival is chancy, at best."

"But that's the only problem now?" Jessie asked. "The loss of blood?"

"Not the only problem," he replied. "If it was, then I might think there was a chance. But working around the heart is a tricky thing. Too many things to go wrong. And the shock itself is sometimes too much for a body to sustain." He sighed heavily. "In cases like this I feel so helpless. I probably should have just left the bullet in his chest instead of digging it out."

"Would it have made his chance of recovery any better?"

"No. The slug was placed where, even if he recovered, it would eventually have worked its way into the heart muscle. At best, I would only have bought him a little more time."

Jessie's grip tightened around Rafe's hand and the tears that she'd been holding back spilled over to rain down her face. "Rafe," she sobbed, bending over the bed. "Please wake up. Please, Rafe. I don't want to lose you. I *can't* lose you. If you die, darling, then I want to die, too."

"Don't say things like that!" Jacob snapped. "You don't mean it, Jessie."

"Yes, I do!" she cried. "I mean every word of it. I don't want to live without him. Oh, God! I can't live without Rafe! Rafe, don't leave me alone!"

She was unaware of Jacob's grip on her upper arm until he tried to drag her away. "Jessie," he said gently. "This is doing neither of you any good. I must insist that you leave now. You're not helping Rafe by upsetting yourself this way."

"No!" Jessie cried wildly, jerking away from him. "You can't make me leave him."

"Come on, Jessie," Jacob said harshly. He pried her fingers loose from Rafe's hand. His grip tightened even more as he dragged her away from the bed where Rafe lay so still.

Jessie's legs crumpled beneath her. Sweeping her into his arms, Jacob carried her back into the parlor and stretched her out on the settee. "I have some powders that will calm you, Jessie," he said gruffly. "And they will help you sleep."

"I don't want your powders," she whispered, turning her face away from him.

"You should take them, though," he encouraged. He sat beside her. "Have you thought about the children at all, Jessie?"

She turned to look at him then.

"The children need to know about their father." Jacob studied her pale, distraught features. "Go back to the farm. You can't do anything for Rafe here, but you could help his children. He would expect that, you know."

The children. She had completely forgotten them. But she couldn't leave yet. She wiped her eyes and met Jacob's with an even look. "I won't leave Rafe," Jessie said huskily. "If you won't let me stay with him here then I want him moved to a room in the hotel."

"Be reasonable, Jessie," Jacob said. "He's in no condition to be moved anywhere."

"You believe he won't last the night, so what difference does it make?"

He gave her a long, silent look.

"I won't leave him," she said again.

"You aren't doing him any good by becoming hysterical."

"I'm not hysterical," she replied. "I need to be near him, Jacob. I need to be there, holding his hand, when the end comes. I won't let him leave this life without me beside him."

In the face of her determination, Jacob gave in. He realized he would have felt the same way had it been her lying in that bed, so he understood her feelings all too well. "All right," he said gruffly. "I'll move a chair in there where you can rest. But you must remain perfectly quiet."

"Thank you, Jacob," she said quietly. "I will. Would you ask Lucas to send someone out to stay with the children?"

"Yes, of course," he said gently. "I'm sure Granny Wyatt will be glad to go."

Returning to Rafe's room, Jessie seated herself in the overstuffed chair that Jacob had placed beside the bed. She twined her fingers through Rafe's, flinching inwardly at the feel of his cold flesh against hers. His fingers were limp and flaccid as though he were only a shell. She refused to accept that fact, though, refused to acknowledge that his mind and spirit had already departed this world.

"Rafe?" she whispered. "Can you hear me, darling? I love you, Rafe. I think I have since the moment I woke up ... after you pulled me out of that river, almost drowned. You breathed life into me then, and in some cultures, that means you are responsible for me. You can't leave me, darling. Do you hear me?" She bent closer and cupped his face between her palms. "I love you, Rafe. I don't know what I'll do if I lose you, darling."

She kissed him softly on his cool lips and waited for a response. There was none. No sign of life, except for the barely perceptible rising and falling of his chest.

"Wake up, Rafe. Look at me." Tears flooded her eyes again, making his face blur. "I need you, darling. I love you. And the children need you." Oh, God, the children! What would they do without their father?

"You need to wake up, Rafe. For the children. You can't leave them alone."

Hours passed, and Jessie continued to sit beside the bed, talking to Rafe. There was no sign of movement. She could have been talking to herself for all the good it was doing, and yet she couldn't stop. Dared not. The pain in her heart had become so fierce it caused a choking sensation in her throat and, no matter how hard she tried to deny the fact, she had become certain in those hours that Rafe would not survive, that he was completely lost to her.

Suddenly she could stand it no more. She had to get

out! Needed to scream, to let loose the pain that overwhelmed her.

Sliding back the chair, she hurried out into the night and released her anguish into the dark.

Jacob found her there, leaning against a porch rail, her shoulders shaking with sobs. He pulled her into his arms and held her tightly against him until she stopped crying, then followed her back into the room where Rafe lay.

Resuming her seat at Rafe's bedside, Jessie fixed her gaze on his pale face while Jacob examined him again.

"There's been no change, Jessie," he said quietly. "And there's no sense you staying here beside him."

"I won't leave here, Jacob."

"I know that. But I have a spare bedroom. You could use that and get some sleep."

"No." Her gaze remained fixed on the man who meant so much to her. "I want to stay here beside him. But you go on to bed, Jacob."

"All right. But call me if you need me."

He left her alone then, and Jessie continued her vigil, continued to watch for some sign of life in a body that remained motionless.

It was barely dawn when Jacob entered the room again. He glanced at her pale face and studied her rigid expression; then he frowned at her. "Did you get any rest at all?"

"There will be time to rest later," she said.

He checked on his patient, then turned back to Jessie. She looked up at him hopefully. "Is he any better?"

He shook his head. "No." He sighed. "I suppose we ought to send for the children."

"Yes."

"You need to get out, Jessie. To breathe the fresh air. Why don't you have some breakfast, then walk with me to the sheriff's office? We'll have Lucas send someone for the two older children. For Karin and Danny."

"What do I tell them, Jacob?" She rubbed her red-rimmed eyes. "Do I tell them the truth, that their father is dying?"

"You'll think of something, Jessie." He took her arm and raised her to her feet. "But right now, let's get some food into you, or else you won't have the strength to face what is sure to come."

"Just the thought of food makes me nauseous, Jacob." Even as she said the words, Jessie knew she must try to eat. Rafe was dying and the children needed her. She was the closest thing to a parent they had now. And she couldn't let them down.

Jessie looked back at Rafe then, her heart in her eyes. God, how she loved him! She had placed his hands on his stomach and as she turned away she saw a flicker of movement.

She turned back quickly, her eyes widening with disbelief. Again, she saw movement on his stomach. Was it only his breathing, or had he actually moved a finger?

"Jacob?" she whispered. "I saw him move."

He frowned at her. "Are you sure?"

"I think so." She watched closely, saw the movement again. "There! Did you see that? His finger twitched."

Yes. Jacob had seen it himself. But he knew that sometimes a body twitched involuntarily, even after death. He took Jessie's forearm again, but she jerked it away and dashed toward the bed again.

"Rafe! Rafe, wake up!" she cried.

"Jessie," Jacob said gruffly. "Come away. Rafe can't hear you. He's beyond hearing anything."

"No! He moved, I tell you!" She leaned over the man in the bed and slapped his face gently. "Rafe! Come on! Wake up, damn you! Wake up!"

Rafe groaned softly and his eyelids fluttered, then

opened to a mere slit. "Are . . . you trying . . . to beat me to . . . death?" he asked weakly.

"Well, I'll be damned!" Jacob swore, coming swiftly to the bedside and taking Rafe's wrist between thumb and forefinger.

Jessie watched anxiously as Jacob examined his patient. Then he looked up at her. "His pulse is strong and regular. Beats me how it happened, but I believe the old boy's going to live after all, Jessie."

"Oh, God," she cried softly. "Thank you! Thank you for giving him back to me." She scattered kisses over Rafe's dear face until he laughed softly and protested.

"You're going to . . . drown me with tears."

She drew back then and covered his mouth with hers in a long, sweet kiss. "Do you know how much I love you, Rafe Sutherland?" she asked softly.

He smiled at her and joy was in his eyes. "No. But you can spend the rest of your life convincing me."

"I will," she promised softly. "Oh, darling. I will do exactly that. For the rest of our lives."

ROMANCE FROM JANELLE TAYLOR

ANYTHING FOR LOVE   (0-8217-4992-7, $5.99)

DESTINY MINE   (0-8217-5185-9, $5.99)

CHASE THE WIND   (0-8217-4740-1, $5.99)

MIDNIGHT SECRETS   (0-8217-5280-4, $5.99)

MOONBEAMS AND MAGIC   (0-8217-0184-4, $5.99)

SWEET SAVAGE HEART   (0-8217-5276-6, $5.99)

ROMANCE FROM FERN MICHAELS

DEAR EMILY   (0-8217-4952-8, $5.99)

WISH LIST   (0-8217-5228-6, $6.99)

AND IN HARDCOVER:

VEGAS RICH   (1-57566-057-1, $25.00)